D0269264

Pel among the pueblos

Spring, Evariste Clovis Désiré Pel decided, was a good time. Burgundy was looking its best, and even a Chief Inspector of the Brigade Criminelle of the Police Justiciaire of the Republic of France could feel well-disposed towards the world.

But his mood was short lived. Apart from a series of muggings in Dole, a bank robbery in Auxerre and a hit-and-run in St Rémy, there was one incident that Sunday morning which interested Pel more than any. Two ageing crooks had died in a double shooting: Serrano Navarro, of Mexican parentage, with a degree in art at the Sorbonne and an interest in fraud, theft and possibly drugs; and Paul Desgeorges, his bulky bodyguard. The chief suspect, Marc Donck, known as 'the Bookworm', can't be found. Nor can Jacqueline Hervé, Navarro's attractive secretary.

The investigation grinds to a frustrating halt until a summons to the Chief's office reveals that Donck has been found and arrested – in Mexico. Someone has to fly there and bring him back to face a murder charge.

To Pel anywhere beyond the bounds of his native province is outer darkness, but Mexico – ten thousand kilometres away from his beloved Burgundy and Geneviève, his new wife!

A spell among the pueblos springs some surprises for the lugubrious flic, but a shoot-out under a moonless night sky back home brings Pel his final reward.

By the same author

Death set to music
Pel and the faceless corpse
Pel under pressure
Pel is puzzled
Pel and the staghound
Pel and the bombers
Pel and the predators
Pel and the pirates
Pel and the prowler
Pel and the Paris mob

PEL AMONG THE PUEBLOS

Mark Hebden

Constable London

First published in Great Britain 1987
by Constable and Company Limited
10 Orange Street London WC2H 7EG

ISBN 0 09 657330 6
Set in Linotron Palatino 10 pt by
Rowland Phototypesetting Limited
Bury St Edmunds, Suffolk
Printed in Great Britain by
St Edmundsbury Press Limited
Bury St Edmunds Suffolk

British Library CIP data
Hebden, Mark
Pel among the Pueblos
Rn: John Harris I. Title
823'.914[F] PR6058.A6886

ISBN 0 09 467330 6

Though Burgundians might decide they have recognized it – and certainly many of its street names are the same – in fact, the city in these pages is intended to be fictitious.

1

Spring, Evariste Clovis Désiré Pel decided, was a good time. It was a period when even an ageing chief inspector of the Brigade Criminelle of the Police Justiciaire of the Republic of France could feel well disposed towards the world. Especially when he was married to a woman who seemed not only able and willing to put up with his peculiarities but even to love him for them. When Pel had married the Widow Faivre-Perret he had gone into it with the gravest misgivings. He had never doubted his own feelings about her but he had often worried over hers about him. Not that he didn't think she had a faithful heart; it was just that he personally had always considered Evariste Clovis Désiré Pel a bit of a pain in the neck and had half-expected her to go off the boil as soon as she'd really got to know him.

After two years, however, his wife was still there, still pandering to his eccentricities – strong feelings, was what Pel called them – still making sure he was well fed and properly dressed instead of looking like a ragpicker's mate as he had before his marriage; even still keeping in order his former housekeeper, Madame Routy, whom she had most gallantly taken on with Pel. On her, even, she had wrought what was nothing less than a miracle. From being a bad-tempered old curmudgeon who did nothing but watch television and could cook nothing but casseroles – which Pel had always been delighted to walk out on at the last moment so she would have to eat them herself – she had become a paragon of virtue, complete with white overall, splendid dishes and television restricted to off-duty hours.

Pel had often wondered how his wife had done it. A whip? Or thumbscrews? Perhaps even the rack? Because as soon as she vanished to Paris on one of her occasional business trips and Pel was alone for a day or two, the old mutinous, television-watching casserole-cooking Madame Routy re-emerged, as forceful as if she'd never been tamed. With Madame at home, however, she was never bad-tempered – except with Pel, who was always happy to respond in kind, because living in peace with Madame Routy was utterly beyond him. Since Madame Routy had also found living in peace with Pel very much the same, they had both silently agreed to carry on their vendetta, but had obligingly left out Madame Pel who, since it seemed to keep them happy and gave them something to do, was quite willing to accept the feud in her usual relaxed manner.

He breathed deeply and was just about to light a cigarette when he remembered it was time to decide to stop smoking. Pel decided to stop smoking about three times a week, though nothing ever came of it. Not even all the warnings he read managed to help him succeed and, in any case, he was usually half-hearted about it and liked to make great play of the announcements of the cigarette manufacturers that their cigarettes could give satisfaction without causing danger. Unlike Gentle Jesus, however, though they were mild they could still hardly be called meek.

He decided to give it one more try and, instead of lighting up, drew a deep breath, filling his lungs with good fresh air. It wasn't half as satisfying as cigarette smoke, but he frowned and gritted his teeth. It was far too beautiful a morning to start dying of cancer, and Burgundy was looking its best.

From Leu where he lived, Pel felt he could see it all, the Burgundy of the vines, the Burgundy of the forests, the Burgundy of the pastures and the rich meadows that nurtured the splendid Charollais. Wine, wood and beef, the three things that made Burgundians the men they were, the things that made Pel the man he was – or might have been, if he could only have given up tobacco.

He looked about him. The sky – a good Burgundian sky – was blue. The grass – good Burgundian grass – was the bright green of the new year. The air – good Burgundian air – had about it the bouquet of good Burgundian wine. No wonder the province had always been a power in the land.

The hour was late for Pel. He didn't rest easily in bed but this Sunday morning he had taken his time rising because he had promised to take Madame Pel to see an aunt of hers at St-Seine l'Abbaye. Madame Pel's relations, he had long since discovered, were a race apart. They were all elderly and all seemed to suffer from bad hearts, asthma, gangrene, senility, congenital leprosy, or just plain fading away. Throughout Pel's courtship, they had spent their time dropping like flies so that it had been only with the greatest difficulty that he had ever managed to see the Widow Faivre-Perret at all. He had often wondered, in fact, how he had managed to get her to the altar because she was always being called away at the most inopportune moments to attend a sick-bed, a funeral, or the reading of a will.

Nowadays he did his best to avoid the relations, but they were too numerous to ignore completely and, since they all appeared to be wealthy and since Madame Pel seemed to be the only member of the younger generation in the family, she was due to inherit all their money. To Pel – who, however, never considered himself grasping, just careful of the future – that made a big difference so that he conceded an occasional grudging visit, if only to make an inspection and decide how much they were worth and how much longer they'd got before their fortunes found their way into Madame Pel's bank. Madame pretended to be shocked at his attitude but, in fact, she too occasionally found the demands on her a little wearing, and was able to weather them by extracting in her quiet way a little comedy from the situation through Pel's black humour on the subject.

However, with spring in the air, it was good to be alive and Pel was unable to resist a small dance. Nothing much, because Pel was no dancer. Just a few steps round the edge of the garden.

'Have you hurt your foot?'

At the words, Pel stopped dead, one leg in the air. Staring about him, he found himself looking into the bright black eyes of a small boy who was crouched by a hole in the hedge which separated the Pel property from the house next door. He wore too-tight, too-brief shorts, ankle socks and solid shoes, and his bare legs were marked with enough cuts, scratches and grazes to suggest he had had an argument with a tiger. His crew cut could at best only be called casual.

Slowly Pel lowered his leg, his face pink. The wind ruffled his sparse hair and he brushed it down hurriedly.

'No,' he said. 'I haven't.'

'I thought you were limping.'

'No,' Pel said. 'I wasn't. I have a stone in my shoe.'

The small boy gestured behind him. 'I've come to live next door,' he pointed out.

'Oh!' Pel remembered he had seen furniture vans and a lot of activity a few days before.

'I'm Yves Pasquier. Who're you?'

'I'm Pel.'

'Pel what?'

'Just Pel. That's my name.'

'My father's an architect. You're a policeman, aren't you? My father doesn't think much of policemen.'

Pel decided at once that he wouldn't like Yves Pasquier's father. 'Perhaps he doesn't know many,' he said stiffly.

'He's heard of you, though,' Yves Pasquier conceded. 'He's seen your name in the paper. He says you're all right.'

'I'm obliged, I'm sure.'

'I'm going to be a policeman when I grow up.'

Pel managed a smile. It could hardly have been called a full-throated one because he didn't smile often and was out of practice. But he approved of small boys who wanted to be policemen. It meant there would always be recruits for the fight against crime. To Pel the fight against crime was a crusade. He had already enrolled Madame Routy's nephew, Didier Darras, who had grown up so fast he made Pel feel positively senile. He was now in uniform as a police cadet and Pel was pulling strings like a puppet operator to get him a job in his office in the place of the cadet who normally worked there but had finally gone on to the streets as a fully fledged cop.

He was just wondering what to say next when a young woman appeared at the other side of the hedge. She was pretty and, since Pel liked pretty young women, he managed a death's head grin at her.

'I'm his mother,' she said. 'I'm Marguerite Pasquier.'

They shook hands solemnly. 'Pel, Madame.' Pel wasn't giving anything more away. With the names he possessed, he'd have had her rolling on the ground shaking with laughter. To Pel his names were a sensitive point, so much so his wife had long since realized it was better simply to address him by his surname alone.

They exchanged courtesies, then the small boy was dragged

indoors for his breakfast. As he headed towards his own breakfast, Pel felt uplifted. Small boys who wanted to join the police and pretty young women who were their mothers were a solace to cynical policemen and he decided he had a good replacement now that Didier Darras had grown up, because Madame Routy, Didier's aunt, could never by the widest stretch of imagination be called pretty.

When he appeared in the kitchen, his wife was at the table pouring coffee. 'I see you've met Madame Pasquier,' she said.

'Yes.'

'She's very pretty.'

'Is she?' Pel had his head down, occupied with trying to spread jam on his croissant with a teaspoon.

'Didn't you notice?'

Pel shrugged. It wasn't very convincing. His wife smiled her small secret amused smile. She knew her Pel by this time, with all his little pecularities, all his doubts and all his strengths. She had been taking a big risk, she realized now, when she had married him, but it seemed to work. A bell rang and Madame Routy appeared. 'Telephone,' she announced.

Pel knew she was addressing him because she never addressed his wife in that manner. Madame Routy thought Madame Pel was a gift from Heaven, even if she regarded Pel as something the cat might have dragged in.

It was Darcy, Pel's second in command. 'Trouble, *patron*,' he said.

'What sort of trouble? Terrorists running rampant through the streets? A visit by the President? Brigitte Bardot about to marry one of us?'

Darcy chuckled. 'A shooting, *patron*,' he said. 'Two guys. One called Navarro. Serrano Navarro.'

'I know that name.'

'Quite likely, *patron*. He has a record. We haven't identified the other yet.'

'When did all this take place? Last night?'

'No, *patron*. About an hour ago.'

Pel's eyebrows danced. 'An hour ago? What happened to the man who killed them? Has he been stopped?'

'He got away, *patron*. Quick take-off. He was seen –'

'He was?'

'– but not identified. I've informed the Chief and all departments. Pomereu of Traffic's setting up road-blocks and Nadauld of Uniformed Branch's getting his boys out. But we're not going to catch him. Not now. He had a car and he could be a hundred kilometres away by this time. And, on a Sunday morning, with nobody about, I dare bet nobody saw him going.'

'So how do we know about him?'

'The housekeeper saw him leave.'

'I'll be down shortly.' Pel paused. 'Tell me, Daniel,' he said, 'why is it murder enquiries always start just as I'm about to sit down to breakfast?'

Darcy laughed. 'I'll try to fix it differently, *patron*,' he said. 'I'll arrange for them to start just as you're about to sit down to lunch.'

'It would at least give me a chance to wake up. I'm never keen on starting work before the streets are aired. Where is it?'

'Sorgeay-le-Petit. Big house as you enter the village. The boys are already there so you'll spot the cars. Local cop was called. Lagé took the call and fixed everything. Photography, Forensic, Doc Minet. They're all on their way.'

'Together, no doubt with the Press.'

'So far, we've had no enquiries, so perhaps they haven't yet heard.'

'Perhaps not,' Pel said. 'But they will soon.'

When Pel arrived at Sorgeay-le-Petit, Darcy was waiting for him. The house was on the edge of the village, large, pretentious and expensive-looking. Police cars jammed the drive and the road outside was full of interested onlookers, men, women, children and dogs.

'Are they bringing him out?' an old man asked Pel as he climbed out of his car.

Reflecting that there'd be a crowd even if the murder had been committeed in the middle of the Sahara, Pel shrugged him off and turned to Darcy who was holding out a packet of Gauloises.

Pel eyed it warily. 'I'd decided to stop.'

'Leave it till tomorrow, *patron*.'

Pel frowned, but he weakly agreed to leave the decision for a later date. According to the experts, the best way to stop smoking was to avoid tension, but the Great Lord God of Stresses and

Strains had long since adjudged that tension was something no policeman could avoid. He took the cigarette.

'In here, *patron*,' Darcy said, holding out his lighter. 'We've got the second guy's name now – Paul Desgeorges. It seems he was bodyguard to Navarro.'

Pel frowned. 'Wasn't this Navarro once involved in some gang business?'

'That's right, *patron*,' Darcy said. 'With our old friend, Maurice Tagliatti. But he was beginning to get on a bit – sixty-four last birthday. I understand he'd retired.'

'It looks like it,' Pel said dryly. 'For good.'

Darcy grinned. 'From the gangs, I mean. He hadn't been involved with them for some time.'

Pel sniffed. 'It looks as though he might have renewed their acquaintance. What do we know about him?'

'Known as Serro le Cerveaux – Serro the Brain. He took a degree in art at the Sorbonne. Not a very good one, but a degree nevertheless. He was an educated crook.'

'Of which there are far too many these days.'

Darcy agreed. 'His line was books. He was believed to be involved in the theft of that Maillol manuscript at Reims seven years ago. He was never pinned down and the police never found the manuscript. He knows his way round art. Maurice Tagliatti has consulted him on things and it's believed he was on the fringe of the theft of the Medusa's head from the Paris Opera House. He was involved in a few other things, too, of course, which weren't art, but that was his chief line.'

'And the other type?'

'Paul Desgeorges. Also getting on a bit. Fifty-nine and growing fat. He'd worked for Tagliatti but seems to have given up when Navarro did. Once a wrestler and a bouncer, and for a time one of Tagliatti's strong-arm boys. It seems Navarro kept him on his payroll as a bodyguard.'

Pel gave a small chilly smile. 'Obviously not the most skilful,' he said, 'since they're both dead.'

Darcy grinned. 'Well, I did warn you they were both getting a bit past it, *patron*. But Navarro had made his pile. We know that from the way he lived. Look at the house.' Darcy gestured at the building before them. 'There are two cars in the garage. Big ones. He wasn't scratching for money. How he got his dough we don't know – dishonestly, I expect – but for the last year or two he seems to have been living off his capital. He hasn't been suspected of being involved in anything.'

'It looks very much as if he was, though.'

Darcy shrugged and led the way into the house. In the library there were signs of a struggle. Serrano Navarro, a heavy harsh-featured man with his haircut *en brosse*, lay on his back near the fireplace, a bullet wound in his chest. Desgeorges lay towards the back of the room, near an overturned armchair. There was a wound in his shoulder and another under the chin. He was fat enough for his body to look as if it had spread – even oozed – sideways. Navarro was wearing blood-soaked pyjamas and a dressing-gown and was unshaven. Desgeorges was also unshaven but he wore a turtle-necked sweater and trousers, though the slippers he wore seemed to indicate he had thrown the clothes on in a hurry. Blood had saturated his sweater and his face was covered with crimson from the wound in the head.

'We haven't touched anything until Photography's finished,' Darcy said. 'The old saying: "Hands in pocket, eyes open, mouth shut, until the pictures have been made."'

Doc Minet, the police surgeon, who was bending over Navarro, looked up as Pel appeared. 'Straight through the heart,' he said. 'He died instantly.' He gestured at Desgeorges. 'The wound to that one's shoulder was inflicted first. The second bullet caught him under the chin, went up through the brain and removed the top of his head. That one was instantaneous, too.'

'For once, we don't have to ask you to guess when it happened. We know.' Pel glanced at his watch. 'One and a half hours ago. What happened, Daniel?'

Darcy glanced at his notes. 'It seems a man appeared at the door asking for Navarro. The housekeeper, who was in the kitchen, says Desgeorges, who'd just appeared, answered the door. She heard him say it was too early, but the guy seemed to be insisting. There was some talk at the door, she says, then Desgeorges went to talk to Navarro. He must have been told to show the guy in because he led him in here. They were talking for a long time, then the housekeeper, who was upstairs by this time, heard angry voices, then shouts, and finally a shot, followed by three more shots. She has a telephone in her room so she called the police from there. Soon afterwards she heard the visitor's car drive away.'

'Have we talked to her?'

'Yes, *patron*. She saw the car arrive. The guy didn't see her but he must have guessed someone else was in the house and bolted.'

'Have we found the car?'

'No, but we will.'

Pel stared at the bodies. 'Why, Daniel?' he asked. 'What was the reason? Robbery?'

'According to the housekeeper, nothing's missing.'

'Nothing?'

'No. Safe's untouched. Silver's still in place.' Darcy gestured. 'Valuable small painting there on the wall. Twenty thousand francs in notes in the drawer of the desk.' Darcy's hand moved again. 'The only thing that was wrong is that that chair was overturned, and there's what looks like a bullet hole in the panelling.'

Leguyader, of the Forensic Laboratory, had men crawling about the floor examining the carpet. He looked up expectantly as Pel appeared at his side because Leguyader liked to think that without his department the police couldn't function. His chief delight was to solve a case purely by forensics or, if that failed, to be able to produce no evidence at all so that the police were at a total loss. Pel had ignored him as long as possible because there was not much love between them, but in the end he had to include him. Leguyader swung round, full of his own importance.

'Well,' Pel said, giving nothing away in the manner of friendship, 'I expect you're itching to tell me. What happened?'

'It looks to me,' Leguyader said, 'as if the intruder, whoever he was, was talking to Navarro when they suddenly – and very fiercely – quarrelled. He shot Navarro before the bodyguard, Desgeorges, who was at the back of the room, could intervene. Then, as Desgeorges charged forward, the intruder stopped him with a bullet through the shoulder and, as he staggered away, shot him again.'

'He must have had his head back,' Doc Minet said. 'Probably yelling with pain. And this time the bullet entered his head below the jaw and went upwards through the brain.'

'Did Navarro or the bodyguard get a shot off?'

Darcy indicated a small automatic half under the desk near Navarro. '6.35,' he said. 'Not used.' He gestured towards an open drawer. 'I think Navarro snatched it from there but was shot before he could fire. Fingerprints will tell us whose it was.'

'And Desgeorges?'

Darcy indicated a heavier weapon on the floor near the body-guard. 'This must have been what Desgeorges had in his hand.' He pointed to the panelling behind Navarro and Pel saw a small splintered hole. 'There's a bullet in there somewhere,' he said. 'We'll have it out eventually. The gun's been fired. You can smell it.'

Pel stared at the weapon. 'But that's not the murder weapon?' he asked.

Leguyader gave a superior smile. 'No,' he said. He half-lifted the overturned chair; underneath it was another gun, a Luger. 'This is.'

Pel glanced at Darcy. Finding the murder weapon seemed an incredible stroke of luck. In most murder cases the police ended up searching rivers, canals, streams, waste ground and rubbish dumps for it. 'You sure?'

'Not yet,' Leguyader said. 'But I think so.'

'Why?'

'Because the wounds on the bodies look as if they were made by a weapon of this calibre.'

Pel glanced at Doc Minet who smiled and gave a reluctant nod, as if he didn't wish to agree with the obnoxious Leguyader but had no option but to do so.

'I'll be certain,' he said, 'when I've examined the bodies. There's one bullet somewhere in Navarro's chest and another one among the bones in Desgeorges' shoulder. There's also one in the panelling and one in the ceiling. When we've dug them all out and Ballistics have had a chance to look at them, we'll know for certain.'

Pel glanced at Darcy. It was rarely they had a piece of good fortune like this because criminals knew enough from watching television that guns gave the game away and that it was better to remove them.

'So why did he leave it behind?'

'In my view,' Leguyader said, 'whoever did it was in here talking to Navarro with Desgeorges looking on, as a good bodyguard would. There was a sudden quarrel. Navarro went for the gun in the drawer but was shot before he could use it. As he fell, Desgeorges charged forward but as he fired he was halted with the bullet in the shoulder. However, he's a big heavy man and the bullet didn't stop him dead. He cannoned into the man with the gun and was shot a second time as they struggled. As he stumbled, he must have knocked the gun from the murderer's hand, then he fell against the chair and knocked it over on to the gun which had skated across the floor. Scrambling to his feet, the murderer looked for it, couldn't find it and decided it was safer to bolt. He guessed someone had heard the shots and telephoned for the police.'

Darcy indicated the telephone on Navarro's desk. 'When you lift the receiver anywhere else in the house, that one gives a loud click. Whoever did it realized what was happening and came to the conclusion it was wisest to vanish.'

'Exactly,' Leguyader said.

'Fingerprints?'

Prélat, of Fingerprints, who was working near the desk, looked up. 'All over the place, *patron*.'

'Whose?'

Prélat indicated Navarro. 'Some are his.' His hand moved to Desgeorges. 'A few are his. There are also others.'

'Members of the staff?'

'The housekeeper says not. She says this room had been cleaned and polished the previous day so there couldn't be many of them. Some belong to a woman.'

'Do we know who?'

'One or two are the housekeeper's. One or two seem to belong to a Jacqueline Hervé, who it appears, worked for Navarro as his secretary-typist.'

Pel's eyebrows twitched. 'What was he doing? Writing a manual on crime?'

Darcy smiled, and gestured at a pile of papers on the desk. 'Seems to be a manual on artefacts and paintings. Desirable objects. Their value and present location. Probably he was proposing to send a copy to every crook in France. It would be a very useful addition to their bookshelves, by the look of it. He could have made a fortune.'

'Where is this Jacqueline Hervé now?'

'She seems to have sunk without trace, *patron*. We've made a few enquiries. I gather from the housekeeper she was rather more than just a secretary-typist. She was also Navarro's adviser in some ways because she'd been in antiques. She was also his girl-friend. There are clothes which must have belonged to her in the main bedroom where he has his things. She seems to have eaten with him, slept with him and spent all her time with him. He gave her some property – a cottage, the housekeeper thinks, though she doesn't know where – and a few items of jewellery.' He held up a photograph of a woman – attractive, sophisticated and clever-looking, with a small button mouth that somehow contrived to look mean and marred the good looks with a calculating expression. 'This is her. I found it in the bedroom. The housekeeper said she heard her on Friday telling Navarro she had to go to Paris to visit her sister who was ill. She had her own car and set off later in the day. That's probably where she is.'

'Find her, Daniel,' Pel said. 'Get the picture reproduced in case we need it. She might just have returned and been taken away because she saw what happened. Now let's have the housekeeper in.'

The housekeeper was a small stout woman with a brown skin, jetty hair, dark terrified eyes and an incipient moustache. Her name was Conchita Esposito.

'French?'

'No, your honour. Mexican.'

'You have a work permit?'

'Oh, yes, your honour. *Señor* Navarro arranged it. I'm from the village of his parents. I knew them well.'

'Is he Mexican?'

'No, your honour. His papa is. Not his mamma. She is French. He does not like French ladies to work for him. He thinks they are not honest. He arranges for me to come.'

'Did you see the man who came here?'

'Yes, your honour. Not well, but a little.'

'Could you describe him?'

She could and Pel turned to Darcy. 'Arrange to get a description, Daniel. Get the photofit boys on the job. Then let's have it distributed. To all departments. All forces.' He turned back to the woman. 'Was he alone?'

She shrugged. 'I think I see someone in the car. But not clearly because he does not bring it in the drive, so I don't know for sure.'

'What sort of car was it?'

'I don' know cars, your honour. Jus' a black car. He leave it in the road.'

'This person in the car. Can you describe him?'

The housekeeper moved her head from side to side. 'No. I don' see. Too far away. Jus' a shape. But is not big. Small. Slight.'

'Tell us what happened.'

She told them in halting French. She had seen the car arrive and the man walk up the drive. She had continued with preparing breakfast in the kitchen, then, while waiting for Navarro to appear, had gone to attend to her bedroom. The visitor was still talking with Navarro in the library. Desgeorges was with them. Suddenly she heard angry voices and almost immediately a shot, and went to use the telephone she had in her room to call the police. As she picked up the instrument she heard three more shots. She dialled the police and as she was doing so she heard feet running down the drive, and then heard the car, which was still waiting, drive off in a hurry.

'This man who came. Tall? Small? Fat? Thin?'

'Small, your honour. But strong-looking.'

'How was he dressed?'

'In a suit, your honour. White shirt. Very white. Very clean. Very neat.'

She had little else to tell them but at least they had a witness who could identify the visitor when they found him.

'Get her down to headquarters,' Pel said. 'Let her see some mug shots. She'll probably find our friend among them somewhere.' He looked about him, satisfied. 'It seems a straightforward case, Daniel. I don't think you need me. I've got to take my wife to St-Seine. I promised. An elderly aunt who can't find anyone else to leave her money to. We'll discuss it tomorrow, by which time you'll probably have picked up both the car and the driver. There'll be a conference in my office. Let's have everybody involved there.'

As he turned away, Judge Brisard arrived. Judge Brisard was the *juge d'instruction* who had been placed in charge of the case and had the right to be present at the scene of the crime. He even had the right to direct the police in their investigations, though

Pel preferred to ignore him and go his own way, something that often troubled Pel's boss, the Chief, because there were constant shrill complaints from Judge Brisard that he was being totally left out in the cold. Sometimes, even, the Chief wished that Pel and Judge Brisard could both be taken out to sea from the Gironde and dropped overboard with concrete weights attached to their feet, because they had been especially created, he felt, by the Almighty for the personality clash of all time. Doubtless, he had often thought, God had arranged it all as a joke.

Brisard was a tall, youngish man with a behind and hips like a woman. He had a big line in marital fidelity with photographs of his wife and children on his desk in his office in the Palais de Justice but, quite by chance, Pel had discovered he had a woman – the widow of a policeman – in Beaune so it didn't carry a lot of weight with him. Pel would always, in fact, have preferred Judge Polverari, who was small, stout, had a ready wit, and like Pel, detested Judge Brisard and enjoyed trading sarcastic comments on him. But there was no getting away from the fact that this time it was Brisard and, despite his mannerisms, he was still a judge so that Pel had to give him what details had already been unearthed.

'Anyone in mind, as the suspect?' Brisard asked.

'We've only just arrived,' Pel snapped.

Brisard's dislike showed like a recalcitrant underslip. A moue of annoyance puckered his mouth until it looked, Pel thought, like a cat's backside.

'Anyone acting suspiciously, I meant,' Brisard explained. 'It doesn't pay to let the grass grow under your feet, you know.'

Not for him, anyway, Brisard thought, or Pel's independent soul would lead him to spirit away the very things he needed to see to form an opinion. The enmity between them was an old one and both were still looking for the opening that would result in the fatal wound. Pel had long been hoping that Brisard, caught in his girl-friend's bed when he ought to have been busy on a case, might be drummed out of the judiciary. Preferably with all the other judges, barristers and solicitors drawn up in a hollow square to watch his buttons being cut off.

Brisard's hope was that Pel would commit an appalling *faux pas* and be carted off in disgrace to Number 72, Rue d'Auxonne, by which charming name the local gaol was known. After that, he felt there might be other more distant gaols. It was a pity, in fact, that Devil's Island was no longer operating, or he might manage to arrange for Pel, like Dreyfus, to spend the rest of his days there.

They sparred together for a while then Pel headed for his car. 'Keep an eye on it Daniel,' he said. 'Let me know what develops. You have Lagé. Who else do you want?'

Darcy grinned. 'I'll pick them when I've discovered what we're into,' he said.

2

When Pel and his wife arrived home that evening, Yves Pasquier was sitting on the grass by the front gate. With him was a small black dog, so shaggy it was difficult to tell which end was front. Only the fact that one end moved rapidly from right to left indicated that it was the other end that bit.

'This is Gyp,' Yves Pasquier observed as Madame Pel disappeared into the house. 'Her real name's Gypsy. She's been done.'

'Done?'

'Spayed. You know – so she can't have pups.' The boy sighed. 'I wouldn't have minded pups,' he said.

As Pel turned to follow his wife, he found Yves Pasquier was still with him.

'Do you know anything that will dissolve chewing-gum?' the boy asked.

'You have problems with chewing-gum?'

'*Maman* doesn't like me having chewing-gum. So when I come home from school I have to get rid of it. The other day she caught me before I was ready so I had to stuff it in my pocket. It's got a bit mixed up with some string and some marbles.'

'It's a serious problem,' Pel agreed. 'Now, if you'll excuse me, I ought to go in.'

'That's all right. I'll come with you.'

Pel's eyebrows lifted but he didn't object. For a man who had never had much patience with his fellow men – not even with himself at times – he got on remarkably well with small boys. In a way, it was one of the burdens he had to bear that Didier Darras, whose friendship he had cherished for so long, was now wearing a police cadet's uniform and was worrying because his girl-friend, who had been devoted to him ever since she had first hit him over the head with her doll, had begun to notice that other police cadets were interesting, too.

He held the door open and the boy entered. Madame Routy placed a piece of cake she had baked in front of him. He nodded, took a bite and mumbled thanks through his mouthful.

'You been solving a crime?' he asked.

'Here and there,' Pel said.

'Caught any criminals?'

'Not today. But there's plenty of time.'

Leaving the boy stuffing cake into his face, Pel went to the telephone and rang the Hôtel de Police. Darcy had nothing new to report but he seemed very optimistic. 'Leguyader's theory about the shooting seems to be correct,' he said. 'And Prélat says he has some good prints. We've still got the housekeeper down here going through the mug shots and she's picked out a few interesting ones.'

Returning to the kitchen, Pel found Yves Pasquier pushing the last mouthful of cake away. He uttered a muffled 'Thank you', swallowed enough to make speaking possible and announced that he had to be going.

Madame was in the salon watching the news on television.

'The youngest of our new neighbours,' Pel said. 'He ate a slice of cake.'

'He does that almost every day.'

'Do we send a bill to his parents?'

'I think Madame Routy enjoys him coming.'

'Good God!' That Madame Routy could possible enjoy anything beyond television – with the possible exception of Pel's whisky when he wasn't looking – had never occurred to him.

'What has Daniel to say?' Madame asked.

'He seems very happy with the way things are going. We seem to know exactly what happened for a change. All we have to find out is *why* it happened. If we get that we ought to know who did it. That's the way it usually goes.'

This one was going to be different, though.

By the time the conference in Pel's office started, the Hôtel de Police was a hive of activity. In Pel's own office, Claudie Darel –

for the moment unassisted by a cadet because the last incumbent had disappeared on to the streets and had not yet been replaced – was putting all the papers ready. Sergeant Bardolle was shouting into the telephone, big and bulky, his iron voice shuddering the windows. As he crouched at his desk, Sergeant Misset came in, full of false bounce because he was really a sad individual with a failing marriage and no interest in his job.

'Dry up,' Bardolle said. 'I'm talking to Marseilles.'

'Why don't you use the telephone then?' Misset asked.

Bardolle glared and Pel frowned. He didn't like Misset but always – always – just as Pel was about to send him off for some stupidity or laziness back to Uniformed Branch to direct the traffic round the Porte Guillaume, he managed to produce a rabbit from the hat and save himself.

De Troquereau had his head down with Nosjean, both young, slim and good-looking, De Troq' a baron with a baron's tastes, Nosjean looking like the young Napoleon. They were often together, good friends despite both being engaged in pursuing Claudie Darel. There was also Lagé, plump, slow-moving and heading for retirement; Aimedieu, looking like a mischievous choirboy; Brochard and Debray, pale-haired and pale-eyed and so alike they were known as the Heavenly Twins; and finally Lacocq and Morell, only recently brought in from Uniformed Branch and used chiefly as errand boys.

Eventually, Darcy appeared, handsome and immaculate, looking like a film star from the days when film stars looked like film stars and not like corner boys in jeans and windcheaters. He was in a newly pressed suit with a white collar that seemed to saw at his ears, and his teeth – those magnificent teeth that captivated every woman who ever saw them – shone as if they'd just been gone over with scouring powder. He spoke a few words to Nosjean, the senior sergeant, picked up a pile of papers and swept everyone who was involved into Pel's office.

The report from Ballistics showed that the gun found under the overturned chair was without doubt the murder weapon. Three shots had been fired from it, and all three had been found. One was in Navarro's chest, one in Desgeorges' shoulder, and one in the ceiling, almost lost among the plaster medallion in the centre. Judging by the angle, this one had first passed through Desgeorges' head.

'And the gun was covered with dabs,' Darcy said.

Prélat, of Fingerprints, looked up. 'There were some good ones,' he said. 'We're checking them now.'

'We had the Mexican woman here for a long time last night,' Darcy went on. 'She picked out several faces, most of which she later discarded. Three, she insisted, could have been the man she saw: Marc Donck, known as the Bookworm. Like Navarro, he's a brain that went wrong. Picked up for burglary when he was a student and been at it ever since. Jean-Pierre Lefêvre, known to be keen on breaking and entering. And Pierre Rebluchet. Known as Pierrot-le-Pourri. We sent him down for the châteaux art thefts but I gather he's now out. There was one other, but he's still inside so we can forget him.'

'Let's check them, Daniel.'

Darcy also reported that a black Citroën had been found abandoned in the next village, Sorgeay-le-Grand, and enquiries had shown it to have been stolen in the city the previous morning.

'We think it might be the one that was used to visit Navarro,' Darcy said. 'Prélat's boys are going over it now for fingerprints.'

Photofit descriptions of the man Señora Esposito believed she had seen had also been worked out. 'We'll get them prettied up and sent out to all stations,' Darcy said. 'And we'll also get out descriptions for television and the newspapers.' Darcy frowned. 'One very odd thing, *patron*. We found that Navarro had turned to reading history.'

'History? I thought he was interested chiefly in artefacts.'

'Well now he seems to be interested in history. There were several books on his desk dealing with the French intervention in Mexico in 1861.'

Pel was no historian and required some enlightenment.

'I had a talk with De Troq',' Darcy said. 'He knows about it. In fact, he appears to have an ancestor who was there with the French Army. Napoleon III attempted to put an Austrian archduke on the throne there.'

'I didn't know Mexico had a throne.'

'It did once. Napoleon tried to revive it.'

'In the name of God, why?'

'Lots of reasons, *patron*. I'll need to do a bit of reading. But it seems Napoleon thought it might be a good idea to use his archduke as a means of collecting some bad debts. Something of the sort. It didn't work. The Mexicans shot the archduke.'

'Oh, charming! What has this to do with us?'

'Navarro had a Mexican father, you'll remember. When he died, his mother brought him to France and he grew up here. He also had a Mexican housekeeper.'

'Is it significant? I have a French housekeeper. Other people have Portuguese or Italian.'

Darcy refused to be put off. 'It's worth checking,' he said. 'There might be a connection.'

Because he didn't know much about his country's history and still less about Mexico's, Pel passed over it hurriedly, deciding to leave it to Darcy to find out more, and began to go through the day's list. The army of criminals who appeared to be trying to undermine the Republic of France had been busy. There had been a series of muggings in Dole, a bank robbery in Auxerre, a hit and run in St Rémy, a rape case, and a few break-ins here and there about the city – nothing much, considering.

'There's also,' Darcy said, 'a very nice thank you from Lyons for picking up that counterfeiter, Jean-Paul Leroy, with his stock of phoney notes and can they have the dud money back some time?'

'What is it?'

'Mostly 50- and 100-franc notes. It's not important but they'd like to have it. Perhaps they're going to have it framed.'

'No hurry,' Pel said. 'They have what they need to convict him and, with a double murder, we've plenty to occupy us.'

'Finally –' Darcy cleared his throat, faintly embarrassed '– there's a new rash of alarms from the supermarket at Talant.'

Pel sighed. The supermarket at Talant was one of their *bêtes noires*. It seemed to have intruders the way most people had mice.

'Find anyone?'

'No. But there've been three false alarms in the last three weeks. Every time the manager's been turned out but nothing's been stolen, and there were no indications of any breaking in.'

'It sounds as if they need a new alarm system,' Pel growled. 'Better get someone to go round and tell the manager what we think of him.'

Darcy nodded and skated a sheet of paper across the desk. 'We've also had a request from local insurance companies to keep an eye on the car-park at Métaux de Dijon. There's been a rash of stolen cars.'

Pel frowned. Métaux de Dijon was one of the biggest consortiums in the area and with room for eight or nine hundred cars, the car-park was big enough to present a problem.

'What is it? Teenagers taking joy-rides?'

'It seems to be more than that. A lot of cars have disappeared in the last three years. It's the sort of thing Nosjean's good at. I'll give it to him. He's only got about fifty-four other things going at the moment. He's practically free.'

While they were talking, one of Prélat's men appeared and quietly handed him an envelope. As the door closed again, Prélat opened the sheet of paper, stared at it and looked at Pel.

'Reports on the fingerprints at Navarro's home, *patron*,' he said. 'Several sets: Navarro's. The housekeepers'. Desgeorges'. The secretary, Jacqueline Hervé's. And one other. We found three or four good prints and they've been identified as belonging to Marc Donck. Donck's prints are also on the gun.'

'That seems to wind it up,' Pel said. 'Find out where Donck is, Daniel.'

'They're still working on the abandoned Citroën,' Prélat continued. 'If Donck's fingerprints are on that, we've got him.'

Pel sniffed. 'We've got nobody,' he warned. 'Not until we have him behind bars. All the same, it's a good start.'

By afternoon, they had Prélat's report on the abandoned Citroën. It was short and to the point.

'Somebody had made an attempt to wipe it clean, *patron*,' he said. 'Somebody who knew what he was doing. But he missed one. Just one. It was Marc Donck's.'

'Do we need to look much further, *patron*?' Darcy asked. 'We have Donck's prints at Navarro's house, on the gun and now on an abandoned stolen car, believed to be the one used at Sorgeay. We also have his description by the Mexican woman and the photofit picture, which could also be Donck.'

'Have we found out where he is?'

'Not yet. But we will.'

Just as Pel was preparing to go home, Darcy appeared again,

this time in a hurry. '*Patron*,' he said, 'I've just discovered an interesting point. I was checking on Navarro.'

'Was he involved in anything?'

'Nothing we can find. But his sister married a type called Martin – Henri Martin, who was a professor of history at the university until he packed it up to make a living by writing. I've looked him up.'

'And?'

'His wife was Henrietta Navarro. Married her fifteen years ago.'

Pel shrugged. 'So? It's not unknown for honest people to have dishonest relatives or in-laws. Or for dishonest people to have honest relatives and in-laws. What about the secretary, Jacqueline Hervé?'

'Seems to have vanished, *patron*. I've had Brochard and Morell on it. They've contacted all her friends and relations. No sign of her. Last in touch with her parents in Auxerre three months back. She doesn't seem to have been one for the family much and only contacted them occasionally and rarely visited them.'

'What about the sister in Paris she's supposed to have visited?'

'We found her address from the parents. She's not heard from Jacqueline Hervé for two years and certainly hasn't seen her.'

'So her story to Navarro was a false one?'

Darcy nodded. 'That's the way it looks, Patron.'

Pel was deep in thought. Why would Jacqueline Hérve disappear as she had? And why should she lie to Navarro? It was always possible she'd quarrelled with him or walked out on her job, but the Mexican woman had reported hearing no angry exchanges involving her, and on the last occasion she'd seen her with Navarro they had seemed on good terms. In addition, while the excuse of visiting her sister in Paris seemed to indicate that, although she may have been deluding him in some way, it also indicated she was still on speaking terms. So why had she disappeared? Had she been fiddling Navarro's money? Had she a spare boy-friend somewhere?'

They had to find her because she was probably the key to the whole thing. Pel felt faintly frustrated. They had a double murder and they even had a suspect, whose fingerprints had been found at the scene of the crime, on the murder weapon, and on the car they believed he had used in his get-away. Yet, somehow, there was something wrong, because they had no inkling of why the crime had been committed and the only person who was likely to know anything about it had disappeared.

The puzzle was compounded the next day when Darcy came back from the university. He was frowning and obviously a little out of his depth. As he entered Pel's office he lit a cigarette. Pel had just resisted lighting one and Darcy's action melted all his resolve. With a sigh he lit one himself.

'This is a funny one, *patron*,' Darcy said. 'I've been doing a little checking on Martin. He *did* marry Navarro's sister, Henrietta Navarro, known as Riri. They had the usual business in the Maire's office then went to the Church of St Dizier for the marriage to be blessed. The priest who conducted the ceremony – it was in March 1971 – is dead now but it's all there in the register, as it is in the Maire's office records. The best man was Serrano Navarro. I've checked Henrietta Navarro's address at the time and it turns out to be the same as the address Serrano Navarro gave when he was picked up on suspicion of handling that Medusa's head that disappeared in Paris. That isn't coincidence, *patron*. That's fact.'

Pel frowned. 'What are you suggesting Daniel? That she worked with Navarro?'

'Oh, God, no, *patron*! In fact, I don't really know what I am suggesting. But I haven't finished yet. Listen a bit longer. I asked at the university about Martin. He's known there all right. He was a highly respected member of the faculty there until five years ago.'

'*Was?*'

'Yes, *patron*, *was*. He was asked for his resignation.'

'Surely to God *he* isn't a criminal?'

'Let's put it this way, *patron*. I'll tell you all I know. Henri Martin was educated at the Sorbonne, specializing in European history. But later, apparently like other historians, his interest was caught by other parts of the world and he went on to the French colonies. He wrote a book on the subject, *La France et ses Colonies*. It did very well and made him money, which, apparently, is quite a feat these days with non-fiction. He then turned his attention to France's intervention in Italy in the middle of the last century when the place was just a collection of small states struggling to become a nation.'

Darcy held up his finger. 'Another book, *patron*. On the Italian Risorgimento. It involved a study of Garibaldi. He then went on to a historical biography of Marshal Bazaine. It's not hard to understand why. Bazaine was involved in Algeria and in Italy so it's normal enough that his interest should move on to Bazaine. But, about then, someone accused him of stealing whole chunks of the book he'd written on the Risorgimento and the university authorities began to look askance at him.'

'How did you get on to this?'

'Angélique Courtois.'

'Angélique Courtois?' It was hard to keep track of Darcy's girl-friends because he had girl-friends like most people had dandruff.

'The one who works at the university.'

'You're seeing her again?'

'I've never stopped seeing her.'

'What about Odette Héon, and the one with red hair?'

Darcy grinned. 'Oh, I never give any of them up. I have a stable of them. Like a racehorse owner.'

'Don't they ever learn about the others?'

'Sometimes.'

'Why don't they shoot you?' Pel gestured. 'Go on.'

Darcy glanced at his notebook. 'By this time, Martin was heading the history department, but it seems that his book on the Risorgimento was nothing but a rewrite of a book by a type called André Mallet, and included no original research. I'm a bit out of my depth but this is what I'm told. It seems plagiarism's hard to prove, though, and nothing came of Mallet's annoyance. But the university had been alerted and, when documents disappeared, they began to look again at Martin. Again nothing was proved but then they learned of other documents that had been missed – at the Bibliothèque Historique in Paris and from the Library of the University of Naples, where Martin had been doing research. Again nothing could be proved but the libraries had their suspicions. Gradually, Martin was eased out.'

Pel was listening intently now.

'It didn't worry Martin,' Darcy went on. 'He'd become well known by this time and was regarded as a good popular writer of history. His books sold well, he did work for television. They made a big series two years ago on the French North African colonies with his book as a basis and he was employed as adviser. The thing that's interesting, though, is that at this moment he appears to be engaged on a history of the French intervention in Mexico.'

'Him, too?'

'Yes, *patron*. What you might call a coincidence, isn't it? I went to see his wife. She agreed that Navarro was her brother, but she apparently isn't in touch with him and hasn't been for years. I'd say she was honest even if her brother's dishonest and her husband belongs on the shady side of straight.'

'Go on.'

'I asked her what her husband was working on and she told me, as the man at the university I saw did, that he was working on a big book on the French intervention in Mexico in 1861. Apparently it was rather a shady business managed by a few dubious politicians and financiers who foisted the idea off on to Napoleon III and the Empress Eugénie, his wife. Because of that, historians have tended to avoid writing about it; it's not a piece of French history we can be very proud of.'

'Did you see Martin?'

'No, *patron*.'

'Why not?'

'He seems to have disappeared.'

'Martin, too? Could it be with Jacqueline Hervé?'

'I tried that on her. He has a way with women and likes them too much, it seems. But she doesn't think he's ever heard of Jacqueline Hervé. But she did think he might have seen Navarro. Navarro was part Mexican, as we know, and apparently Martin had been to ask him the whereabouts of certain documents he was after. So he might just have met Jacqueline Hervé.'

'Had she any idea why he'd disappeared?'

'None, *patron*. Apparently the marriage's pretty fragile and he often disappears to do research – when he isn't chasing girls. She grew tired of it and she seems to live her own life with her own friends and associates. She's an analytical chemist and she met Martin when she was a lecturer at the university. But now she works for Produits Pharmaceutiques Bourguignons. There are no children.'

'So there's nothing very odd about him disappearing and her not knowing where he is?'

'Well, not exactly, *patron,*' Darcy agreed. 'except that she says his passport isn't in his desk where he normally keeps it.'

'So he's abroad then. Did she know where?'

'No, *patron,* she didn't. But she thought it might be Mexico.'

3

When Darcy appeared the next day, he was in a frustrated mood. He had been trying to find Jacqueline Hervé but she seemed to have had no friends save the dead Navarro, and he had been unable to find the property Navarro was reputed to have given her.

'I've tried the estate agents, *patron*,' he said. 'I thought she might be there. But none of them knows anything about it. I've also tried the lawyers. I got nowhere. So it's either registered under a different name, or else Navarro just handed her the deeds which he'd had changed to her name by some lawyer somewhere outside this area.'

'Or else,' Pel suggested, 'it's just a rumour and he didn't give her any property.'

'Or that,' Darcy agreed.

'What about Donck? Have you heard anything of him?'

'Still looking, *patron*. I've heard he was seen in St-André de Nidon. I've got enquiries going there. We'll turn him up.'

Nosjean followed Darcy into Pel's office. He was carrying a thick folder of paper, which turned out to be the reports on the cars stolen from the car-park at Métaux de Dijon.

He looked puzzled. 'I think we've got a funny one here, *patron*,' he said. 'You remember the rash of stolen cars from the car-park at Métaux de Dijon? Well, it seems that the insurance companies were the first to notice it. They have a get-together occasionally when they sink their business differences and chat generally about what's happening in insurance, and it seems they're a bit worried about the number of times they're having to pay out for stolen cars. What's odd, they say, is that none of them have ever been reported found. They're blaming us.'

Pel frowned. 'Have you checked the list of stolen cars?'

'Yes. What they say seems to be correct. We have no record of them. And what makes it odd is that cars stolen from other places such as Radiocommunication, the hospital, Lait Bourguignon – all big places employing a large number of people with large car-parks from which cars are obviously stolen from time to time – occasionally later turn up. In the last three years 57 cars have been reported stolen from Métaux de Dijon and not one's been turned up. In the same period, of the 17 taken from Radiocommunication 10 were later found – taken away by kids or someone whose own car wasn't running for some reason or other and helped himself. At the hospital 12 cars disappeared, of which 9 were recovered. It's odd that more were taken from Métaux de Dijon than anywhere else and that none of them were recovered. I got the figures from the insurance people.'

'Do Métaux de Dijon have supervision on their car-park?'

'They have a man keeps an eye on it, but not full time, and they don't admit responsibility. It's just a wide area of asphalt and they maintain that the cars left in it are the employees' responsibility, not theirs.'

'Did Métaux de Dijon learn of these thefts? Were any reported to them by their employees?'

'No. They didn't expect them to be reported to them but they thought someone might have made a complaint. But when they checked they found no one did.'

'That's odd, isn't it? With that number. Didn't the men's union report it and ask for supervision? It would be unlike them to miss an opportunity like that. No strikes? No sit-ins? No demonstrations? After all, demonstrations have become an international disease. I'd have expected a protest march down the Rue de la Liberté on a Saturday.'

Nosjean smiled. 'Nothing like that, *patron*. Inspector Pomereau, of Traffic, went to see the union officials, but they said nobody had complained to them. They'd heard about the stolen cars but in every case the owner had preferred not to make a complaint.'

Pel sniffed. Pel's sniff had a great ability to convey his thoughts. This one conveyed grave doubt. 'What are your thoughts?' he asked.

'I have a suspicion someone somewhere's working a racket.'

After expressing his suspicions, Nosjean's first move was to contact one of the city motor-insurance firms – Assurances Mutuelles, near the Porte Guillaume. He chose that particular one because he happened to have his eye on one of the girls who worked there. She looked like Charlotte Rampling and any girl who looked like Charlotte Rampling always immediately caught Nosjean's eye and he'd spotted her while making enquiries about a set of stolen porcelain. Sometimes he struck up an acquaintance with a girl who looked like Catherine Deneuve or Sophia Loren – once even one who looked like the young Brigitte Bardot – but it was always the ones who looked like Charlotte Rampling who kept his interest the longest.

She exchanged a few warm words with him and took him in to see the manager, a stout man called Jean Aubineau with a mandarin moustache and dark spectacles which made him look like a gangster from an American film on television. He explained that the question of the missing cars had first arisen quite casually at the meeting of insurance operators a week or two before.

'Groupe Druot mentioned it first,' he said. 'Then Gau Assurances mentioned that they'd had some, too. All from the car-park at Métaux de Dijon. So had we. When we got talking about it, it seemed everybody had and that seemed odd enough for us to contact the Hôtel de Police. We felt perhaps they weren't doing their job.'

'Is it new, this rash of thefts?'

'At Métaux de Dijon? Yes and no. But the number's increased. In the last three years there were 57. The three years before there were only 31. The three years before that only 24.'

'So is all crime,' Nosjean pointed out. 'What about in the past? Were they reported then?'

Aubineau frowned and glanced at a notepad. 'They seem to have been. Why would they *stop* reporting them?'

Nosjean shrugged. 'Do you always pay out on a stolen car?'

'If it's insured for theft, of course. Most of them are, but sometimes they're recovered after they've reported them stolen, so then we don't pay out. But as you can see, there've been more than ever lately. And –' Aubineau gave a frustrated gesture' – none have been found.'

'What do the company say?'

'What you'd expect. It's not their responsibility. That's normal enough. It's the same with other firms. They agreed to put a watch on when we mentioned it to them but with 900 cars, it's very difficult. It seems the cars disappeared without being noticed. Nobody saw any cars leaving the car-park with unidentified drivers.'

'The owners all claimed insurance?'

'Yes. They were all insured for all the usual. Damage, theft and so on. One or two fairly recently, which seems suspicious.'

'And all were paid out?'

'Yes. *We* certainly did, and when this thing came up we got our heads together and found that all claims had been paid out by other insurance firms.'

'What sort of cars were they on the whole? New? Old? Expensive?'

Aubineau shrugged. 'Like most factory-workers' cars. Not new. But most of them seem to go in for good-quality cars, because a lot of them are mechanics or fitters or engineers and they service them themselves and they know a good car when they see one. If not, they have mates who'll do the job cheaply in their spare time.'

'Value?'

Aubineau shrugged. 'Around 35,000 to 40,000 francs. That sort of figure. Their cars are in good shape on the whole but, often they're not new. Some even are old.'

'What about the cars reported stolen?'

Aubineau grinned. 'Just past second-best. They'd been bought second-hand mostly, as I say, and the owners had had them two or three years. In several cases they were thinking of changing them. Value depreciated to around 25,000 francs. Perhaps a bit more. About that.'

'What about new cars with a value of around 50,000 to 60,000 francs or more? How many of those disappeared?'

Aubineau seemed surprised at the question then he frowned. 'Since you mention it,' he said, 'none.'

'But there were some new cars in the car-park, surely?'

'There must have been.'

'Then that's odd, isn't it? Why steal an old car when there were new ones to be taken?'

Aubineau shrugged. 'Perhaps the new ones are harder to get into.'

'Are you in constant touch with other motor-insurance companies?'

'Most of the time. One of us is always claiming against another. You know how it is. A man's in collision with another car and claims insurance. So does the other driver. So we get our head together to decide if one of us can claim against the other. Where it's a case of admitted or clear responsibility, that insurance company pays up. It saves time.'

'So could you contact all these colleagues of yours in the business and ask them to let you know next time they have a claim for a stolen car from Métaux de Dijon? So I can look into it.'

'Sure.'

'In the meantime –' Nosjean touched his nose '– keep it under your hat.'

Nosjean was frowning when he went to visit Inspector Pomereu of Traffic. Pomereu had had a man watching the car-park at Métaux de Dijon for some time now in the hope of catching some persistent thief, but he hadn't seen anything untoward.

'Mostly the cars seem to have disappeared during the night shift,' Pomereu explained.

'That makes sense,' Nosjean said. 'When it's dark a man could walk into a big car-park like that and help himself, couldn't he?'

'Not if he's working there, he couldn't. He'd be missed from his bench. And no matter what shift he's on, at this time of the year it's hardly dark except in the very middle of the night.'

'Would some man who couldn't start his car take a workmate's car to get home?'

'Well, he might, but I'd have thought he'd arrange for it to be found later, and my man didn't spot anything.'

'Are the cars checked as they leave?'

'When the gates are opened the whole shift stream out. Several hundred cars. It's impossible.'

'Perhaps they ought to be, all the same.'

Pomereu gave a small chilly smile. He wasn't a man given to much humour. 'I suggested that to Métaux de Dijon. The reply I was given was, "Try to hold up the home-going crowd at the end of a shift and there'd be a riot."'

'Even when cars are being stolen?'
'That's what they say.'
'Is your man discreet?'
'We brought him in from Callou-sur-Ille, so he's not known.'
Pomereu's second in command produced the list of stolen cars which Traffic carefully kept up to date. The number reported stolen from Métaux de Dijon seemed very small.
'Is this all?' Nosjean asked.
'All that have been reported. I expect there were more but we can't do much if they're not mentioned to us.'
'If my car were stolen,' Nosjean said slowly, 'the first thing I'd want is to have the guy in court so fast he'd be breathless, and I'd report it straight away to the police. Why didn't these types?'
Pomereu joined in. 'As a matter of interest,' he said, 'I've heard they're having a similar problem at Nantes. At the metalworks there. Compagnie Française de Produits Métallurgiques. It's another big outfit like Métaux de Dijon. Could it be a gang working the country?'
'It might well be,' Nosjean agreed. 'And it might be bigger than we think. I'll warn other forces to take a look at their lists of stolen cars and where they were stolen from. Let me know if you get any more from Métaux de Dijon.'

They seemed to have lost Marc Donck, and Jacqueline Hervé had become the subject of a nation-wide search. As the days passed they were coming to the conclusion that Donck had bolted with his mysterious companion straight for Paris and had boarded the first aircraft out of France. No sign of him had been turned up, and Jacqueline Hervé was the greater worry because she might have been abducted or even murdered, and police throughout the country were on the look-out for her. Her picture had been televised and sent to all police stations but nothing had been heard.
'It's not unknown for people to disappear,' Pel admitted. 'I read recently of a type who walked out on his wife and stayed away for seventeen years, then simply returned and took up where he left off.'
'And she let him?' Darcy's eyebrows rose.
'As far as I can make out.' Pel frowned. 'There could be a

thousand and one reasons why she's disappeared, of course. If she was Navarro's sidekick as well as his mistress, she's probably none too honest herself. She probably helped herself to property of his – jewellery, valuables, bonds, that sort of thing – and took the opportunity to bolt.'

'She didn't take the money in the drawer in the room where he was shot, *patron*. And there was a lot.'

Pel admitted the fact, but there were reasons why she might not have, probably some of them none too easy to explain. After all, she hadn't been in Paris where she had said she was going to be. So where was she? Had she, despite what the housekeeper said, been in the house all the time? Had she heard the shots and rushed in to see what had happened, seen Navarro dead and been too scared to go any further? But that seemed to suggest something very odd. Because if she *were* in the house, why had she taken the trouble to announce she was going to Paris?

'And,' Darcy asked, 'why didn't she raise the alarm?'

As the days passed, it began to look as though Pel's estimate of Jacqueline Hervé was right and she'd bolted with valuables of Navarro's. She was probably whooping it up at that moment in Miami or the Seychelles, probably merely St-Trop'. Unless, of course – and the more he thought about it, the bigger seemed the possibility – she had disappeared with Marc Donck. The coincidence was very marked. They had both disappeared at the same time and nothing had been heard since of either. It was something they had to bear in mind, especially since it grew more and more to seem as if Marc Donck had made it safely out of the country, so that he would now become just one more statistic, one more digit under 'Unsolved Crimes'. It was pointless losing sleep over it. There were plenty of other things to lose sleep over. The usual muggings. A couple of break-ins. A fraud case in Lyons, where the Lyons police had demanded their help and which was complicated enough to have occupied Pel for some time.

Then one day Darcy burst in. 'We've found Donck's hide-out, *patron*,' he said. 'He has a flat in St-André de Nidon. I sent Brochard and Morell over there at once in the hope he might be there. They haven't rung in, so I think we ought to go, too. It'll probably give us some clue to where he is.'

Marc Donck's flat was above a butcher's shop and Brochard

and Morell were waiting in a car outside when they arrived armed with a search-warrant signed by Judge Brisard.

'He's not here, *patron,*' Brochard said. 'According to the butcher there, he hasn't seen him for around a month.'

'Since he knocked off Navarro,' Darcy pointed out. 'All right, let's get inside.'

'The butcher has a key, *patron,*' Brochard said. 'It's actually *his* flat.'

The flat told them very little. Clothes still hung in the wardrobes. There was food in the cupboards and even a bottle of sour milk in the refrigerator, which seemed to indicate that Donck had left in a hurry. They searched all the usual places, all the drawers and cupboards and under the mattresses. As they worked, Pel poked his nose into the bedroom. Items of women's clothing hung in the wardrobe, and there was a night-dress under the pillow.

'He obviously had a lady friend,' he said. 'Do we know who she was?'

Brochard shrugged. 'The butcher says he'd seen a woman but he didn't know her.'

'What was she like?'

'Tall and fair,' he said.

'Is that all?'

'He didn't look very hard, *patron*. He says it was none of his business.'

'It might be a good idea to find who she is and pick her up. She could probably tell us where Donck's got to.'

They examined the pillows, turned back the carpets and checked for loose floor-boards that might conceal a hiding place for something what would give a clue to where Donck was. Finally they checked the curtains and took out every book Donck possessed. The shelves indicated his interests and they were by no means those of an ordinary thief. There were novels, histories, dramas, discourses of various kinds – the reflection of the mind of an intelligent educated man.

'No wonder they called him the Bookworm,' Darcy said. He fished out one of the volumes and began to study it. Then he frowned and held it up. 'Notice this, *patron*?' he said. '*L'Intervention Française au Mexique, 1861* – Charles Blanchot. The French Intervention in Mexico, 1861. Published 1911. It seems Donck was *also* interested in French diplomacy over there.'

It was puzzling. Nothing appeared to have been stolen from Navarro's home and they had found nothing in Donck's flat which could be traced to Navarro – nothing, in fact, to connect the man they suspected of murder and his victim, save for a book which showed they had a mutual interest in the French intervention in a foreign country over a century before, an interest they seemed to share with the victim's brother-in-law, an ex-professor of history with a reputation for somewhat shady dealings connected with research.

As they worked, Brochard, who had been going through every scrap of paper in an over-full waste-bin from under the sink, appeared. He wasn't looking very happy because the waste-bin hadn't been emptied for some time and the weather was warm so that it had a very ripe smell attached to it. He had its contents on a newspaper in the kitchen and had been pawing through them with great distaste.

'I've found this, *patron*,' he said. 'I heard you talking and I thought it might be interesting.'

It was a request for a travel visa for Mexico. It appeared to have been made out wrongly and thrown away. On the back was a faint imprint of the office stamp of the Grandcamp Travel Agency near the Porte Guillaume and the date on it was five weeks earlier.

It was beginning to look without doubt as if they had lost their quarry. They now knew with certainty who had killed Navarro and Desgeorges, but it seemed the murderer had eluded them by acquiring a visa and disappearing across the Atlantic. Where he was now they had no idea.

'Think he's working with Professor Martin?' Darcy asked.

'I doubt it,' Pel said. 'But it could certainly be that he's interested in the same thing.'

'Why? The intervention in Mexico was 120 years ago. Martin might be interested but I wouldn't have thought Donck was.'

'Unless Martin had discovered something of value and Donck wants to get his mitts on it.'

'So where does Navarro fit into it?'

'There is a connection. Martin's interested in Mexico in 1861 or thereabouts. Perhaps his interest isn't entirely honest. If what his wife says is true, then perhaps he turned for information to her brother, Serrano Navarro, a man like her with a Mexican background, and Donck stole the information Navarro possessed, which he'd passed on to Martin.'

'What's Martin after, then, *patron*? Something valuable? Something he's picked up in his research but wasn't sure about, so that he went to Navarro for help and told him about it? And that started Navarro studying the period, too, because it occurred to him that, if he was quick, he might get to whatever it was Martin wanted before Martin did? Then Donck appears on the scene, having also found out about this mysterious something, visited Navarro and tried to get the information from him? It ended up with him shooting Navarro and, when Desgeorges tried to intervene, him, too.'

'It seems to link up,' Pel admitted. 'But it doesn't seem to make a lot of sense.'

'And how,' Darcy asked, 'did Donck get to know about this thing that was interesting Navarro? – whatever it was. They've never worked together. I went through their records. There's no evidence of collaboration in anything at any time. The only thing they had in common is that both are university graduates.'

'And both dishonest.'

Darcy shrugged. 'That, too.'

Pel frowned. He already had suspicions that would answer some of their questions. 'Let's have Prélat's boys give the place the once-over,' he said. 'You never know. We might find Martin's dabs here. Or that Mexican housekeeper's. Perhaps even Brigitte Bardot's.'

What they got didn't surprise him much.

Darcy was just wondering again what had happened to Jacqueline Hervé when Prélat arrived.

'A lot of dabs,' he said. 'Mostly Donck's. But a few in the bedroom that we also found at Navarro's place.'

Pel's eyebrows rose. 'Jacqueline Hervé's?'

'The very same.'

Pel looked at Darcy. 'No wonder Donck became interested in what Navarro was after. *She* told him. She was playing fast and loose with Navarro.'

'Donck's a good-looking type,' Darcy agreed. 'And he's nearer her age, too. And she'd have known what Navarro was up to if she shared his bed. Somehow, she got to know Donck and decided he was a better bet. And, after the shooting, Donck, now clearly in possession of whatever it was Navarro had learned, disappears with her, in the hope of getting to it first. She took the night off, not to visit her sister but to contact Donck. She was the passenger in the car.'

'Donck's probably already in Mexico, picking up whatever it is he's after, and planning to get into the United States before Martin discovers he's ahead of him. Was there *nothing* missing from Navarro's home?'

'Nothing we can pin down, *patron*. I had the housekeeper go round the place.'

Pel frowned. 'Could it be something other than valuables? This thing seems to hang on some information Donck acquired, which he obtained from Navarro, who got it originally from Martin, who got it from his research for the book he was doing. Any papers?'

'No, *patron*. There's nothing missing. Not even any sign of disorder. Navarro's notes for his book on valuables hadn't even been disturbed.'

'Perhaps there was talk of collaboration – you-need-me-and-I-need-you stuff – and the information was produced but not handed over. There've been cases before when information's been produced and then there's been a quarrel and a shooting, so that whoever did the shooting disappeared with the information without having to disturb anything.'

Darcy admitted the fact. 'Which means,' he said, 'that, instead of just Donck being involved, there might be Donck *and* Martin – both looking for the same thing.' He frowned. 'This, *patron*,' he ended, 'is a funny one.'

Pel agreed. 'Normally,' he said, 'we know how it was done, where it was done, when it was done, why it was done. We know the victim and the reason, but we don't know the murderer. That's something we work out from the other facts. This time we know who did it, when it was done and how it was done, but we don't know *why* it was done. It turns the whole process upside down. Let's ask Paris if they've got anything on Donck. He used to operate up there as part of Pépé le Cornet's gang.'

'How about asking Pépé himself?'

Pel gave a small dry smile. 'You could try,' he said.

4

A few enquiries to the personnel manager at Métaux de Dijon revealed nothing very odd to Nosjean. Nobody had noticed anyone away from his bench in the middle of the night shift for any longer than it took to use the lavatory.

'What about during the break?' Nosjean asked. 'There is one, surely?'

'Oh, yes, there's a break.' The personnel manager smiled. 'There has to be. The union sees to that.' The personnel manager was young and bright-eyed and looked as though he knew every trick in the industrial book.

'But nobody disappeared?'

'None reported. The foremen watch for that sort of thing all the time. The unions are rigid about us behaving ourselves, so we're rigid about their members doing the same. It works.'

'*Could* someone disappear for a while during a break?'

'Not long enough to steal a car.'

It made sense and Nosjean was busily working his way that evening through the list of stolen cars when Aubineau rang to say another car had been reported stolen from the car-park, this time a Peugeot 304, number 73 AK 37, coloured red, two previous owners, value about 33,000 francs.

'He's not one of ours,' Aubineau said. 'He's with Assurances Générales. They passed it on to me because I asked them to, as you said.'

'Got the owner's name and address?'

'Yes. François Orain, 1, Rue des Acacias.'

'I'll see him.'

Before leaving the Hôtel de Police, Nosjean called in on Traffic. They had had no complaint from François Orain.

That seemed odd in itself and Nosjean was at 1, Rue des

Acacias early next morning when the night-shift workers were due home. As he waited he saw a car draw up and a man in overalls climb out. As he headed for the house the car drew away. Nosjean was at the gate as the man was putting his key in the lock. He was young and dressed in a track suit and windcheater and carried the overalls he wore at work over his arm because of the heat.

'You François Orain?' Nosjean asked.

The man turned. 'Yes.'

Nosjean showed his identity card with its tricolour strip. 'Police,' he said.

He was studying Orain's face. Did he see a small flash of alarm cross his features? It might have been nothing but Nosjean was a keen and alert policeman who had jumped swiftly to senior sergeant through diligence and astuteness.

'What's wrong?' Orain said.

It seemed a strange question considering he had just had his car stolen. Nosjean would have expected the question to be 'Have you found it?'

'You've just had your car stolen, I believe,' he said.

'Oh!' Orain seemed surprised. 'Yes.'

'May I come in?'

'Sure.'

While Orain's wife prepared a meal and coped with four young children, Orain led Nosjean into the garden. Nosjean noticed as he passed through the house that it seemed well looked-after and as if Orain earned good money.

Orain produced a bottle. '*Coup de blanc?*' he asked.

'Your car,' Nosjean began, as they sat on white-painted chairs in the tiny garden with their glasses. 'Peugeot 304, wasn't it? Colour red. Number 73 AK 37. Three years old.'

'That's right.'

'Good condition?'

Orain shrugged. 'It wasn't new but I looked after it. I'm a fitter so I know something about engines.'

'You've claimed on your insurance, of course?'

'Well, yes.'

'But you haven't reported it yet to the police?'

Orain seemed a little confused for a moment. 'Well, no. I hadn't had time. I was going to.'

'You should always report things like this to the police first,' Nosjean chided. 'Immediately, in fact, then we can get a message out to the patrol cars who could very well spot it passing as it got away. When a report comes in at once, they've been known to pick up stolen cars within an hour of them disappearing.'

Orain looked sheepish. 'I just didn't think. I was going to, of course.'

'When did it disappear?'

'During the night of the 15th. I was on night shift. When I came to leave it wasn't there.'

'Did you report it at work?'

'I didn't think.'

'Not to your union official?'

'No.'

'It would help. There've been a lot of cars disappear from Métaux de Dijon lately.'

'I just didn't think.'

Orain seemed not to think a great deal.

'What are you going to do about transport?'

'Well, there's a bus out to the factory, but it's slow. I expect I'll get a regular lift until I can pick up a cheap second-hand car to tide me over. Then perhaps later, when I've time to look around, I'll buy a better one.'

'Attached to your car, were you?'

Orain gave a small smile. 'As much as you can be to a second-hand car. Perhaps if it were new, it would be different.'

'Have you *never* had a new car?'

'I've never been able to afford one.'

On his way back to the Hôtel de Police, Nosjean had to pass the supermarket at Talant. It was still early but there was a police patrol car outside and Bardolle was there with Misset, who was looking bored behind the dark glasses he wore. It seemed there had been another alarm and Bardolle was looking furious. Alongside him was the manager, red-faced and unhappy, who had been called from his breakfast to investigate.

'Another,' Bardolle snarled as Nosjean drew his car to a stop by the group. 'Last night. There was no wind, no rain, not even a breeze. It was calm and still, and yet the alarm goes off.

I think a lorry passed, or an old man sneezed on the way to the bar.'

'Anything stolen?'

'Nothing.'

A small limping figure appeared from behind Bardolle. Nosjean recognized it as Edouard Fousse, known to the police as L'Estropié – the Limper. He had a twisted leg which was the result of falling off a wall when he was attempting to enter a factory on the industrial estate to the south of the city, and he was very familiar to the members of Pel's squad because he had a history of fraud and theft, though curiously never concerning anything of much value. He'd had a background of violence in his youth but he hadn't been involved in anything of that sort since his injury, and instead had gone in for dandyism. Now he wore well-pressed pink trousers and a pale-green sweater. In his ear was a gold ear-ring and round his wrists a gold chain. Another gold chain hung round his neck.

'An old guy on his way to work last night,' he said with a grin. 'That's what did it. He broke wind and the alarm went off. Special high note, perhaps. You've heard of Le Pétomane, that type on the stage in the last century who could fart the "Marseillaise".' He looked at Bardolle. 'Or perhaps it was you, stamping round with those great feet of yours.'

'Push off!' Bardolle turned furiously and the little man slipped away, grinning, with a hop, skip and jump on his lame leg.

'No joy?' Nosjean asked.

Bardolle scowled. 'Nothing,' he growled. 'Nothing stolen. No door forced. Nothing. It's that shitty alarm. It goes off if you look at it.' He stared at L'Estropié's grinning little figure. 'You know,' he said bitterly, 'he might well be right. Perhaps someone *did* fart.'

When Nosjean returned to the Hôtel de Police, he made a point of checking with Pomereu's man about the disappearance of Orain's Peugeot.

'I saw nothing,' the cop said. 'I was there all the time, prowling around. No cars went out of that car-park during the night shift.'

'So what happened to Orain's car? Taken up by a whirlwind, was it?'

'That place has five exits and cars pour out three abreast at the end of a shift. That's when it must have gone.' The policeman frowned. 'But nothing left during working time.'

'Didn't fall asleep for an hour or so, did you?'

The policeman was indignant. 'No, I didn't! Though I wouldn't have minded. I'll be glad when I'm off this job. I don't like that car-park. I'd rather be back on my own beat in Callou-sur-Ille.'

Nosjean was puzzled. If no car was taken out during the night shift, then Orain's Peugeot *must* have left with the flood of other cars at the end of the shift. Nosjean was beginning to grow very suspicious. There was something about all these stolen cars, he decided, that decidedly smelled of fish.

As he sat at his desk, Aimedieu was smoking a cigarette at the desk next to him. He was discussing with Lagé his latest job.

'Five-hundred-franc notes,' he said. 'Banque Français Agriculture at Cloing reports them regularly. They wondered at first if they were counterfeit.'

He was about to disappear to Cloing to make enquiries but he was a little puzzled because he wasn't certain what he was enquiring about.

'They *aren't* counterfeit,' he said. 'The bank says so. So what am I asking about?'

He had a strong suspicion, in fact, that he was on a wild goose chase. The bank had apologized for causing the police unnecessary work, so what was the fuss for?

'It's just,' he said, 'that, up there, incomes are small, so 500-franc notes are pretty rare.'

'Perhaps someone's come up on the lottery,' Nosjean said.

When Bardolle appeared, he was still in a bad temper and requested an opportunity to talk to Pel. Not long before he had been a uniformed policeman in Mongy to the north of the city but his sharpness during the case of a drowned girl had brought him into the city and plain-clothes work. He was astute and keen but there was still something of the country cop about him and he looked a little like a frustrated bull.

When Pel called him in, he entered slowly and carefully. He

was so big and so wide, he was always terrified he'd take with him Pel's coat-stand – four hooks for inspectors and above; most people hung their coats on a row of hat-pegs on the wall. He also sat carefully, because the spare chair didn't look very strong, and he was very careful not to rest his hand on Pel's desk. Bardolle's fists were as big as coal grabs and weighed about as much, and he was afraid the desk might collapse.

'Talant supermarket,' Pel said. 'You've been having trouble there?'

'I've warned them it's time they got a decent alarm system,' Bardolle said.

'I think it is,' Pel agreed. 'Have you checked it?'

'Yes, *patron*. There seems to be nothing wrong with it. But it goes off for no reason at all. One night the wind blew and it went off. Another night it was the rain. One night they said it was because the army had passed a convoy of military vehicles within thirty metres of the place.'

'Do you believe it?'

Bardolle blinked. He looked like a thirsty cart-horse looking for a drinking trough. 'I don't know what to think, *patron*,' he admitted. 'I've never heard of an alarm that goes off because of the wind. But this one seems to. That little bastard, Edouard Fousse, said it was because I'd been walking round the place and disturbed the wiring.' Bardolle was sensitive about his size. 'My weight, *patron*,' he explained. 'The cheeky con. He's always there ready for a good laugh when we turn up and find nothing wrong.'

'Who's been working with you?'

'Misset.'

Pel frowned. He didn't trust Misset. He was the one flaw in Pel's team. Once handsome but now fading as the beer he drank caused his features to thicken, he was always on the point of leaving his wife but never failed to plead family life as an excuse for getting out of work.

'Are you watching the place at night?'

'Yes, *patron*. When I'm not on something else.'

Pel nodded sympathetically. Most of his team were handling half-a-dozen cases at once, like jugglers juggling with half-a-dozen chamber-pots, so that they had to keep their eyes on all of them at once. Crime had reached such proportions a man with only five or six cases on his hands was considered to be taking it easy.

'What about the alarms?' he asked. 'Are they always during the night?'

'Or the early morning, *patron*.'

'Who was on when they occurred?'

'Me, the first time, *patron*. The other three, Misset.'

Pel sniffed. It could have been that Misset had been having a drag at a cigarette round the corner, or been snatching a quick one in a nearby bar, perhaps even in a dark alley-way with a girl he'd picked up.

'Try someone else,' he suggested. 'Do you work all right with Brochard?'

Bardolle frowned. Brochard considered himself a funny man and he was too often funny about Bardolle's size for Bardolle to be enthusiastic. But he was supposed to be able to handle such situations and he nodded.

'Brochard's all right, *patron*,' he conceded.

'Right. You've got Brochard. Keep an eye on the place.' Pel paused. 'And, while you're at it, are you keeping an eye on Edouard Fousse, too?'

'It's not him, *patron*,' Bardolle said. 'At least he never seems to be there when we arrive.'

'He's got a record. For theft.'

Bardolle frowned. 'Well, he isn't stealing anything from the supermarket,' he said, 'because nothing's missing. After the second go, I got the manager to make a particularly fierce check. He didn't want to because I made him make a note of everything that was available on the shelves at night when they closed and that meant he had to keep the staff late and pay them overtime. But he did it. Nothing was gone.'

'Anything in there worth stealing?'

'Plenty, *patron*. But nothing special. Food, obviously, but they'd have to steal so much they wouldn't be able to carry it. There's a chemist's shop but it doesn't carry much beyond aspirin and perfume.'

'Tranquillizers?'

'Yes, *patron*. But none missing.'

'Nothing of real value?'

'No, *patron*. There's a jewellery shop of a sort, too. But most of what they sell's junk. Not really worth stealing. It's not a hypermarket with motor bikes and things like that. They'd have to steal a hell of a lot to make it worth the effort.'

'What about money?'

'None missing, *patron*. None at all. Very little kept on the premises. Manager drops it at the bank after closing time. Collects all the takings, counts them, watched by one of the security men with a pistol, then takes the money to the bank. Then he runs the security man back to his car and goes home. I've warned him I think it's dangerous and someone some day's going to learn his routine and hold him up.'

'Quite right. Very sensible. Right, what about people? Anybody found near the premises?'

'Nobody. One here and there. Nobody more than once.' Bardolle frowned. 'Except that cheeky con, L'Estropié. He always turns up to laugh at us.'

5

The Chief's conference to discuss the cases they were handling didn't take long.

The Chief, Pel's boss, was a big man with a red face who loved his food. He had been a champion boxer in his youth and sometimes when Pel was being difficult he felt it would be nice to slip back into old habits and take a swing at him.

He liked to know what was going on in his diocese and he usually had a lot of pots on the boil and, though Pel was his chief cook and bottle-washer, the Chief could never have called him the easiest man in the world to work with. Though Pel was bright, the Chief didn't consider him one of God's most inspired creations. In fact, sometimes he felt He ought to apologize for not doing a better job on him. Well aware of all Pel's failings, his inability to stop smoking, his uncertainty in his private life, his inability to make friends, his constant bickering with Judge Brisard, the Chief, however, also knew that in his professional life, though he was prickly, awkward and arrogant, in his own way he was brilliant. Pel would have agreed with him. It wasn't that he thought he was better at his job than other people, just that other people weren't as good as he was.

The Chief studied him warily, a slight figure – only just big enough to scrape into the force – his spectacles on the end of his nose as he studied the file in his hand, and he realized that, despite all Pel's faults, he was glad he had him.

'Let's have the details again,' he said.

Pel opened the file and laid a notebook alongside it on the polished table top between them.

'Serrano Navarro,' he said. 'Aged sixty-seven and well known to the police. Long and distinguished record.' Sarcastically, Pel pushed across the table a sheet of paper containing the late Serrano Navarro's life history as far as the police were concerned. It contained every kind of criminality save violence and sex. Navarro hd been brought up before the magistrates for the first time at the age of twenty and had been appearing in court on and off ever since. Despite his failures, however, he appeared to have prospered because he had ended his life in a large house in the country with a housekeeper to look after him and a bodyguard to keep away his enemies, and of late, it seemed, had eschewed all his old wicked ways and concentrated solely on fraud and theft and, possibly, drugs.

'Reason?' the Chief asked. 'Why was he shot?'

'The only inference we can draw,' Pel said, 'is that somehow he was involved with something in Mexico.'

'That's a reason for shooting him?'

'With Navarro it might well be. He liked to say he'd retired, but that didn't mean he didn't keep his eyes open for anything that might benefit him, and he'd recently been in touch with Professor Henri Martin.'

There was a pause and Pel went on to explain. 'Martin's a professor of history with several well-known books behind him. But –' he paused '– he has a reputation for twisting evidence to suit his ideas and –' he paused again '– of stealing documents for his work.'

'So Professor Martin's also not completely honest?'

'That seems to be the view of his colleagues who doubtless know him better than we do.'

The Chief waved them on and Darcy took up the story.

'Professor Martin's an expert on late nineteenth-century France,' he said. He'd done the required reading by this time and was showing off a little. 'He's produced work on the Panama Scandal, the sale of honours uproar, and a few more. He disappeared at the beginning of April, though he's probably just doing research abroad. One other thing –' here Darcy gave thanks for having picked an intelligent girl-friend, because her remarks had led him to make a few enquiries in the right place '– Navarro has a Mexican background and is known to have been visiting libraries recently, investigating the intervention by France under Napoleon III in Mexico in 1861, when an attempt was made to impose on the Mexican people a puppet emperor, the Archduke Maximilian, brother of the Austrian Emperor, Franz Josef.'

'Why in the name of God would Navarro become involved in that?' The Chief was as bewildered as everyone else had been.

Pel shrugged. 'He's Martin's brother-in-law,' he pointed out. 'And it started about the time Martin disappeared.'

'What about the girl, Jacqueline Hervé, and Marc Donck?' The Chief was anxious to get to the nitty-gritty.

Pel explained: How Donck came into the picture because Jacqueline Hervé, who was Navarro's mistress, got involved with him, too, and passed on what Navarro was up to – whatever it was; how Donck called on Navarro, quarrelled with him and shot him, unhappily for him leaving behind his gun and a lot of fingerprints.

'A warning was sent to all ports and airports,' he said. 'But it seems they didn't stop to pick up luggage and got out of the country before the alarm was raised. Reports seem to indicate they went first to Spain and picked up another flight from there to somewhere further afield.'

'So –' the Chief doggedly returned to the nub of the matter '– why did Donck kill Navarro?'

'That,' Pel said in his most pontifical manner, 'is something we shall doubtless find out when we pick him up.'

'If he's disappeared abroad, you might *not* pick him up.'

'That seems more than likely.'

They discussed the various angles of the case for some time. There were a lot of curious aspects to it and the Chief wanted to know the answers. Why, for instance, was Navarro suddenly interested in a French Army campaign in Mexico over 100 years earlier? Had Martin engaged him – because he was part-Mexican and his brother-in-law – to do some research for him?

'That's the way it seems.' Pel pushed his spectacles up on his forehead among the thinning hair that lay across it like strands of wet seaweed on a seashore. 'It looks as though Martin discovered something worth investigating and asked Navarro to check on the background. But Navarro was no fool and he probably also spotted what lay behind Martin's interest, so that in the end both of them were after the same thing.'

'What?'

'It has to be something of considerable value.'

'So what was it?'

'Treasure?' Nosjean suggested. 'Wasn't Mexico the place where the Spanish found their gold in the sixteenth and seventeenth centuries? Weren't their galleons raided by privateers?'

'That gold came from Peru.' De Troq's words came quietly but with the confidence of a man of education. 'West coast of America, anyway. I think it was brought across the isthmus of Panama. The mule trains were often attacked there.'

'What then? What were they after?'

'Inca treasures? Aztec treasures? Mayan treasures?' De Troq' seemed sure of his facts. 'Valuable artefacts? Mexico's full of old burial grounds.'

'It doesn't sound like Martin's line of country,' Darcy said. 'Everything he did was directed towards the last century.'

'And why was Navarro reading up the French intervention?'

'A lot of French money was sent to Mexico at that time and a lot disappeared that was never accounted for. Some of it was funds supplied to the French Army there and a lot disappeared into private pockets. Could Martin have learned where some of it was hidden?'

'It would help if we knew where Martin was at this moment.'

Nosjean looked up. 'Could he be in Mexico?' he asked.

The rest of the day was quiet but somehow Pel had an uneasy feeling that something was brewing and it came as no surprise when he, Darcy, Nosjean and De Troq' were summoned to the Chief's office just before they were due to knock off for the day. He was even more suspicious when the Chief produced a bottle of wine and handed glasses round. Offers of wine were always ominous.

As they sat down, the Chief leaned back in his chair.

'Marc Donck,' he said.

'Ah!' Pel sat upright, expecting to glean information that had come via the experts in Paris. Paris felt they knew everything. They felt they knew how the people of Burgundy behaved and thought and acted, as they felt they knew the people of Seine et Loire, Champagne, Lorraine, Charente Maritime and everywhere else in France. The fact that they didn't was by the way. Only Paris was unaware that they didn't know a damn thing about the rest of France.

'He's been found,' the Chief said.

'What!' This time Pel's uprightness was entirely honest and spontaneous and not performed to please the Chief.

'He's been arrested.'

'Good. We can pick him up then. Where is he?'

The Chief smiled maliciously. Occasionally he liked to startle Pel. 'At the moment he's in a place called the Penitenciaría del Estado.'

Pel looked puzzled. 'The what?'

The Chief repeated the words.

'Where's that?'

The Chief grinned. He was enjoying Pel's bewilderment. 'It's in Mexico. It's a sort of open prison, near Mexico City. He seems to have been involved in a car crash. We have all the details. He was found unconscious but, after they pulled him out, the Mexican police found something that made them suspicious and, after doing a bit of investigating, they stuck him in the penitentiary to await developments.'

'What was it? What we're looking for?'

'At this moment I don't know.'

'Well, it's nice to know he's out of circulation.'

'It's not quite as simple as that,' the Chief said. 'He's wanted in France for a double murder and murder takes precedence over everything else.'

'Do we have a deportation agreement?'

'Whether we have or not, it's been fixed by Paris. He can, and should, be extradited.' The Chief frowned. 'On the other hand, I sometimes wonder if the performance is worth it. It would be much better for France if we left him where he is.'

Pel agreed whole-heartedly. Though as a policeman he felt it was always his duty to apprehend criminals and see them brought to justice, he didn't believe in duplicating effort or wasting money.

The Chief gestured. 'How much better it would be if we could simply send our evidence to Mexico with a request to the Mexicans to have him shot. Think of the time it would save.'

Again Pel entirely agreed.

'However,' the Chief said, 'having brought Paris into it, we can't now ignore it. They have the Minister on their neck because he has the Chamber of Deputies on *his* neck and some idiot representing some half-baked area in the Alpes Maritime will doubtless ask why Donck hasn't been brought home to face trial.' Like most policemen, the Chief didn't have much time for politicians of any creed or colour.

'*Alors*,' he said. 'There you are. He has to be brought back.'

'I'm glad to hear it.' Despite everything, Pel still remained a great believer in a good strong Nemesis pursuing criminals to their doom.

The Chief seemed to be enjoying himself. 'It's going to be a nuisance going to Mexico to bring him back,' he said.

Pel shrugged. 'I suppose so,' he agreed. 'Who's organizing it? Paris?'

'No. Us.'

For the first time, Pel began to be suspicious. 'That means sending someone to bring him home,' he said.

'That's right.'

'Who?'

The Chief grinned. In fact he almost burst out laughing. 'You,' he crowed.

Pel's fury had to be seen to be believed. It had been so concentrated he had seemed about to take off and whizz round the room.

Darcy had glanced at Nosjean. 'We have lift-off,' he had whispered.

By this time, however, all Pel's excuses were expended, all the bitterness and shrill protestations worn down. All the paperwork he claimed he had to do, all the lists he had to work through, all the computer reports, had been brushed aside in cavalier style. He had to sort out Misset, he had complained, because he always had to sort out Misset. There was Lagé's forthcoming retirement. There was the suggestion that Nosjean ought to be upped to inspector. There was the fraud case at Argente and the jeweller's break-in at Buhilly, the false alarms at Talant, the cars being stolen from the car-park at Métaux de Dijon.

The Chief waved them all away. 'They'll wait,' he announced. 'Darcy can handle them.'

Darcy had smiled and nodded. Much as he admired Pel, he always enjoyed running the show on his own – at least until it grew too difficult, then he was always pleased to see Pel back.

'He has Nosjean,' the Chief said, and this time it was Nosjean, all pale intensity, dark eyes and eagerness, who smiled.

'The rest –' the Chief dismissed them with a wave of his hand ' – they'll survive. Go off, Pel. Take a break. A day or two in a different country might do you good.' It might even, the Chief thought, smooth the little bugger's temper a touch and reduce the everlasting tension between him and Judge Brisard. It might even – though the Chief was none too sanguine about this – make him realize that Burgundy wasn't the only place in the world. 'You'll have De Troq' to do all the running about for you. You'll need a spare hand, anyway, in case you manage to bring the woman back, and De Troq' speaks the language.'

De Troq' straightened up. He was pleased, but he didn't smile because De Troq' was a baron – even if a poverty-stricken baron – and barons didn't go in for letting their hair down by smiling too much. He was slightly built like Nosjean, with a small neat head, beautifully cut hair and an expensive suit, because being poverty stricken was comparative, and poverty-stricken barons always seemed to be able to afford to be less poverty stricken than most people. And he knew his abilities. He spoke three or four languages and had a grand manner which usually squashed self-important people and had often been a great asset to Pel's team. There was just one snag, he thought. He had recently become involved with a girl who worked in Judge Polverari's office. He and Nosjean had been competing for Claudie Darel's favours for a long time but recently their noses had been pushed out by one of the junior advocates and Nosjean had been forced to fall back on girls who looked like Charlotte Rampling, and De Troq' on the girl in Judge Polverari's office. She was attractive, intelligent, and what was more, had a grandmother who was a baroness which, in De Troq's eyes, made her very suitable.

Pel's temper was simmering like a witch's cauldron as he returned to his office. There was nothing unusual in his bad temper. Pel was often in a bad temper. Chief inspectors of the Brigade Criminelle of the Police Judiciaire, those splendid men who pitted their wits against the crooks of the French Republic, had every right to lose their temper occasionally, and often every excuse.

He stared at the future with empty eyes. After remaining

unmarried for far longer than he had ever intended – though he had to admit, looking at himself in the mirror in the bathroom every morning, it was understandable – he had finally been brought to the altar and, to his amazement because he had never believed it possible that anyone could live with him for long without throwing him out, it had been an instant success. And now they were snatching it away from him!

He lit a cigarette, stared at it with disgust, and, wondering why he couldn't give them up, dragged the smoke down to his socks and immediately felt more able to cope with the problem. To Pel, anywhere beyond the bounds of his native province was outer darkness. The Mediterranean coast, so beloved of holiday-makers, to Pel was a hotbed of vice. The north was cold. The west was damp. The east led into the wastes of Russia whence came the winds that petrified him in winter. This time it was worse than that, though. It wasn't merely Paris or Champagne or Alsace. It was thousands of kilometres away. Thousands! Ten? Twenty? It didn't matter much. Pel thought of it with a catch at the breath.

Mexico! In the name of God, Mexico!

Pel's knowledge of Mexico was small and what he'd heard about it he didn't like. It wasn't long since he'd sat shocked and horrified at the television pictures of a devastated Mexico City, destroyed in one of the biggest earthquakes of recent years, and from what he'd read of the rest of the country it was a lawless place suffering from a tendency to battle, murder and sudden death. He was quite prepared to admit that his view was more than likely wrong but nothing he'd read of the place offered much encouragement.

It needed another point of view so he called in Darcy who immediately held out a packet of cigarettes. Pel eyed them with distaste.

'Why do you tempt me, Daniel?' he asked.

Darcy smiled, showing his splendid white teeth. 'I enjoy the expressions that cross your face, *patron*,' he said. 'Greed, anguish, despair, doubt, concern – all of them – and finally relief. It's a whole stage show in one. It's better than *Dallas* on television.'

Pel gave him a sour look. He was well aware of his feelings about cigarettes. For years now he'd been trying to give them up.

Once he'd managed it for a whole half-day. But that had been inspired and he'd never managed it since.

'Mexico,' he said. 'Have you ever been there, Daniel?'

'Never, worse luck.'

'What's it like? Do you know?'

Darcy's handsome teeth flashed again. Darcy's teeth could snap your head off if you moved too close. 'It's hot, *patron*,' he said. 'That is, when it isn't too cold. It's got a lot of desert. And where it isn't desert it's tropical. It's a very difficult country, they say. They have revolutions there, don't they?'

They'd better not, Pel thought. Not while he was there, anyway.

'What about the people?'

'They all look like bandits, I believe. I think, in fact, that up to not very long ago a lot of them were. You must have seen the films, *patron*.'

Pel hadn't. 'I mean,' he said sourly, 'what are the cops like?'

Darcy shrugged. 'I've never met one, *patron*. I don't suppose they're as efficient as we are, but I expect they do their best.'

Breaking the news to Madame wasn't as difficult as Pel had thought. He left the car – the new car she had persuaded him over his agonies at its cost to buy – in the drive. The front door was opened by Madame Routy with such promptness he suspected she had been waiting behind it for him.

'What have you spoiled for supper tonight?' he asked. It was a regular quip and it got a regular answer.

'It wouldn't matter,' she responded. 'You wouldn't know what a good meal is.'

The niceties observed, they both continued on their way. Madame Pel was occupied with lists, because she'd just acquired new premises next to her beauty salon in the Rue de la Liberté and was about to open a boutique – an expensive one to attract the wealthy customers who came to her salon to have their hair styled.

She put the list down and listened carefully, as she always did. She was never too busy for Pel. She smiled at his mingled indignation, disgust and dismay.

'You'll be all right, Pel,' she said.

'It's about 10,000 kilometres away!'

'There are telephones. They're not savages. I've made calls to France from Mexico City. I went there once to a conference. They have taxis and restaurants and hotels and buses just the same as we do. The place even looks a little like Paris because a lot of the older architecture's French in style. After all, the French Army was in Mexico for a long time during the last century. They've even got an opera house like the one in Paris.'

'Nothing from Burgundy?'

'Probably only you.' She smiled. 'How long will you be away?'

'Two days, I suppose. One day there, one day back.'

The smile came again, gentle and chiding. 'I think it might take longer than that. It's an eight-hour flight and you have to allow for jet lag. I should say a week.'

'A week?' Pel stared. It was worse than he'd realized. 'Simply to pick up a villain?'

'Are you going on your own?'

'De Troq's going. To do the talking. He's a linguist. He's also a baron and has the grand manner, and it's necessary to impress people. Make them realize the French police force contains men of dignity. I thought the Paris lot might do the trip. You know what they're like up there. They pick all the best jobs for themselves and leave us the trips to dreary places like Belgium and Holland and England. But, no, this time, they said it was *our* case and *we'd* got to handle it. I expect they've got something better lined up for themselves. Bali or Java or somewhere like that.'

'Why is your man in Mexico?'

Pel, who was stuffing papers into his brief-case, looked up, startled. The question was unexpected.

'Why?'

'Yes, why Mexico?'

'To get away from the murder charge in France.'

'Nothing else?' Madame frowned. 'Well, why not Australia? It's further away. Why not the United States? It must be easy to get lost in the United States. Why not New Orleans? Or Quebec? They speak French there. Or why not Brazil? They're not known to be sympathetic to extradition. I seem to remember reading about the British having some problem over some man they were after. And didn't you say Navarro had a Mexican background?'

Pel looked at his wife with affection. She followed all his cases with great interest and she never missed a trick.

And she had quite a point. *Why* Mexico? Pel considered. Well, Mexico *was* a long way away, which was one good reason. And it *was* inaccessible, parts of it, so he understood, very inaccessible. And he'd heard the Mexicans in the past hadn't been over co-operative, because they hadn't had a lot of love for France since the French invasion in the last century.

He frowned. Had their guess been right? Navarro *did* have a Mexican background. Had he, as they'd thought, found something there worth having and was that the reason why he and Donck had quarrelled violently enough for Navarro to end up dead? And was that why Donck had bolted to Mexico rather than one of the other countries he might have chosen? Was *he* after it now? It was a thought worth investigating.

Pel kissed his wife. 'Geneviève *de mon coeur*,' he said. 'You are a splendid business woman.' Splendid enough, he thought privately, to have removed from Evariste Clovis Désiré Pel the terror of a penniless old age. 'You run the best hairdressing salon and beauty parlour in the city. And I know you have a gift for selling because I haven't failed to notice the things you are about to display in your new boutique. But I think, nevertheless, that you missed your vocation. You would have made a good detective.'

He was pleased to see the delight on her face.

6

What Madame had said provided a very interesting idea.

Sufficiently interesting, in fact, to occupy Pel's mind for the next two days while the documents were prepared and the case he had to offer to the Mexican authorities was set out precisely and clearly. His wife offered advice from her own experience of Mexico City.

'It's warm,' she said. 'But it's very high and can be cold at night, especially this early in the year. I'll make sure to pack a warm sweater for you. You can have the one I knitted.'

Pel smiled to show his thanks, but it was a false smile because he was wondering if it were possible to drop a knitted garment out of the window of an aeroplane over the Atlantic. Madame believed her duty as a wife was not only to provide a good home, good food and good companionship for her husband, but – despite her occupation with business and her ability to acquire through that business vast wealth and the finest sweaters money could buy – also to knit for him. Unfortunately, however, for all her skill with finance, Madame was no knitter and the results of her efforts usually found their way, after one wearing, to the back of Pel's wardrobe and there left until they could decently be forgotten.

'That will be splendid,' Pel said, lying through his teeth.

Because he was going to be away from her side for the first time since their marriage for more than a day or so, he took her for a drink in the Bar du Destin, one of his favourite haunts, and then to a meal in the Relais St Armand where they had first met. Pel had been making one of his periodical attempts to give up smoking at the time and the little gadget he was employing to roll his own had so amused Madame, recently a widow, that she had burst out laughing. There wasn't much Pel's inability to stop smoking had done for him, but at least it had brought him Madame.

'Do you remember,' his wife said as Pel snatched his thoughts back to the present, 'that the first time we came in here, we were sitting over there? You were eating an *andouillette*.'

'A weakness of mine.'

'And when you tried to roll a cigarette, I offered you one of mine. I smoked in those days.'

'I still do,' Pel sighed. 'You thought I was trying to give up because I was an athlete.'

'A little flattery,' she admitted.

'I took to haunting the place after that,' Pel said. 'In the hope of meeting you again.'

'So did I.'

'You did? Why?'

'Because you intrigued me.'

Pel smiled. He didn't often smile and it made him look bilious. But the romantic thought that theirs had been an instant romance – the across-a-crowded-room sort of thing – pleased him, because in his hearts of hearts Pel was an incurable romantic.

'I shall miss you, Pel.'

'And I you.'

'Do be careful. Don't get wet. And remember it's cold at night so if you have to go out put something warm on.'

'I'll also remember to say "please" and "thank you".'

They both laughed and she put her arm through his and hugged it, so that he got a whiff of her perfume. Good God, he realized, we're behaving like a couple of lovesick youngsters! But it was a thought that ought to sustain him during his long absence in Mexico. A week! Holy Mother of God, it was a lifetime!

In fact, it was to turn out longer than that.

Getting Pel away was like launching an expedition to the Antarctic.

He had been walking around for two days looking like Napoleon receiving the news of his defeat at Waterloo, and on the day of his departure he awoke feeling like a martyr – and looking a bit like one, too. Like some wines, he considered, he didn't travel well.

The night before, he had carefully laid out the suit he kept for when he met the President of France or the Queen of England, put out enough shirts and underwear to fit out a regiment, and alongside the file of papers and documents he was taking, made another pile of notebooks, pencils and ballpoints and the assorted cures for the various ailments he considered he suffered from. Finally, he built on the bed a stack of packets of Gauloises as big as the Great Pyramid of Cheops. He had still been at it when Madame, wondering what had happened to him, had appeared alongside him.

She smiled, removed half his shirts and underwear, found something lightweight in case it was hot and something warm for the cold evenings, discarded half the notebooks, pens and pencils on the grounds that they had shops in Mexico where he could buy them, and swept away the largest part of the Gauloises.

'I shall need those,' Pel said in alarm.

'No, you won't.' It was the iron hand in the velvet glove, Pel thought. It happened in the end with all marriages. 'All you need is enough to get you to the airport. You can buy them there in the duty-free shop and they'll be much cheaper, too. Leave these for when you come home.'

The following morning, De Troq' collected him in the great roadster he drove – slimline mudguards, a strap over the bonnet and headlamps like the eyes of a prehistoric monster. Despite being poverty stricken, De Troq' seemed to have more of the good things of life than most people.

Yves Pasquier from next door was there to see them off.

'*Maman* says you're going away.'

'Well –' Pel wondered how he'd heard and how much his affairs were discussed over coffee up and down Leu '– not for long.'

'You're coming back?' The boy sounded disappointed.

'So I hope.'

'Where are you going?'

'Mexico.'

'Where's that?'

'Across the sea. Near America.'

'Do they have guns in Mexico?'

'Without doubt.'

'You could bring me one back.'

The request was made without blinking and without subterfuge. Clearly Yves Pasquier was in the habit of receiving gifts from people who went abroad.

'Do they chew gum as well?' he asked.

'Probably.'

'Perhaps you could ask them if *they* know how to separate it from string and marbles.'

Madame smiled. 'You could bring him something back,' she murmured. 'It would cement the friendship.'

As they stowed the luggage in the car, Pel noticed that, while his own suitcase was unmanageably large, De Troq's seemed to consist only of a small canvas holdall.

'Have you been to Mexico before?' he asked.

'Not exactly, *patron*.'

'What do you mean? Not exactly.'

'Well, my father has. So has my grandfather and my great-grandfather. So it's a special pleasure to be able to do the same.'

'Your family's connected with Mexico, I hear.'

'We have an interest. My great-great-grandfather, the General, was there during the intervention. He was commanding the 137th Regiment of the Line.'

'I don't suppose your great-great-grandfather kept any notes about Mexico, did he?'

'He kept a diary, *patron*.'

Pel sniffed. 'It would have been useful if you'd brought it with you.'

De Troq' smiled his faint superior smile. 'I did, *patron*.'

It was a bright sunny day and France was looking at its best. Because he was leaving it, to Pel, as they crossed the hills towards Paris, the fields looked greener than ever, the trees and hedgerows more lush, the vistas wider.

Inevitably, he managed to get lost among the by-ways of Charles de Gaulle Airport which, at the best of times, was like being in a space city, but De Troq' managed in the end to get him aboard the aircraft. Settling back for the take-off, De Troq' took out a book – *Letters of Madame de Sévigné*, Pel noticed with envy; why couldn't he read intelligent things like that? As the machine began to move, De Troq' noticed that Pel's knuckles were white as he clutched the arm of his seat. It wasn't the take-off, though. He'd realized he'd forgotten to buy his duty-free Gauloises.

Over the Atlantic Pel recovered a little as he remembered that he had managed to rescue some of the packets Madame had swept aside and stuff them into odd corners of his suitcase. 'Do you think I'll have enough?' he asked. 'I wouldn't like to run out of them.'

De Troq' smiled. 'You can have some of mine,' he offered. 'I'm not much of a smoker.'

'I wish I weren't.' Nevertheless, Pel felt relieved, deciding that what he had might now see him through the two or three days he expected to be in Mexico.

He shuffled restlessly in his seat. He was never very good at sitting still. 'What do we do now?' he asked.

De Troq' smiled. Pel's sergeants all admired him in their different ways and were prepared to put up with a lot. 'You can eat, *patron*,' he advised. 'That can occupy some time, so don't rush it. You can watch a film. Usually they're pretty grim. I always have a couple of large whiskies and go to sleep.'

'You've flown the Atlantic before?'

'Once or twice,' De Troq' said casually. 'Relatives in Louisiana.'

There obviously *was* something to being a baron, Pel decided.

True to his word, De Troq' went to sleep. But being in an aircraft to Pel was like being inside a giant vacuum cleaner and he couldn't relax. He lit a cigarette and eventually tried to sleep. It didn't work, so he listened to music on the headphones. But that involved holding the earpiece in so tight he felt it would set up a disease of the inner ear, so he watched the film instead. As De Troq' had warned, however, it was dreadful, so again he tried sleeping. To his surprise he woke up three hours later to find the whisky had worked as De Troq' had said it would and that they were actually beginning their descent to Mexico City.

Getting through customs wasn't difficult because of De Troq's ability to speak Spanish. They ordered a hire car because it was felt it might be necessary and they were driven with their luggage to the car-park where they were introduced to a large grey and rather battered American Dodge. The hire-service operator showed them round it and tried the starter. There was a whirr and nothing else, so he climbed out, kicked the car, and tried it again. This time the engine started.

'Always,' he explained, 'it is necessary to make the kick.'

The operator disappeared and De Troq' climbed into the driving-seat, something Pel firmly backed away from. He wasn't the best of drivers and, when his mind was busy, was known, much to the fury of passing lorry drivers, to drive in the centre of the road, so that the idea of driving in a foreign country terrified him. De Troq' seemed to suffer from no such inhibitions and was just about to let in the clutch when a white car with a red band round it and the word *Policía* on the side, appeared and screeched to a halt alongside them. The driver, tall and running to fat, leapt out and opened the rear door.

The man who climbed out was lean with a brown handsome face and a nose as thin and curved as a sabre. He was dressed in a dark suit, with bright-yellow cowboy boots, a pink tie and a hat such as Pel had seen worn in *Dallas*.

'Don Evaristo Pel,' he said. *'Jefe de Policía Francesa?'*

It was all beyond Pel but De Troq' nodded. *'Sí.'*

The Mexican grinned. *'Jefe de Policía* Barribal. Plutarco Jacinto Barribal. I've been attached to you because I speak English and I was told you did, too.'

Pel had an older sister who had married a British soldier after the war and, after several visits to her home, his command of the language was reasonably good. He answered in the same tongue and introduced De Troq'.

'He speak English, too?'

'Yes.'

'Good. I speak it good. I was educated in the States. People mistake me for a *Norteamericano*. It gets me lots of American girls. We get lots of *Norteamericano* girls down here. I'm to take you to headquarters. You won't want a car. We use mine.'

The hire operator protested that he was losing money but Barribal shut him up quickly and they got their money back and left him muttering as they climbed into the police car. Leaning over the front seat, Barribal kept up a running commentary as they passed through the city streets.

'You'll find it different here,' he said. 'Things don't work as well. So you might as well get what you can out of it.' He jerked a hand. 'That's the National Palace. The *Presidente* lives there. Soon you'll be in the Paseo de la Reforma and see the statue of Cristóbal Colón – Christopher Columbus to you – and Cuautomoc, who's some guy out of the past. Some people like to see him. To me, he don't mean a thing.'

The police car slipped through crowded streets, wide ones full of traffic, hotels and big stores, and narrow ones where the shops were mere holes in the wall surrounded by fruit carts and lounging men. Here and there were cleared gaps as if a bomb had struck.

'Earthquake,' Barribal said. 'Mexico has many sorrows. Not all of them of her own making.'

Police headquarters, Pel was surprised to see, were modern. Barribal gestured to the police driver and led the way inside. A lift carried them through several floors and they were led into an office where a stout grey-haired man with a Spanish face rose from behind an enormous desk.

'*Comisario* Ramón García Granados,' Barribal introduced. 'Chief of Police.'

The introductions accomplished, Pel sat blank-faced, holding the glass of brandy which had been offered while Barribal did the talking. After a while the man behind the desk rose. Since Barribal and De Troq' rose also, Pel rose with them. A minute later he was in a much smaller and far less grand office that he recognized at once as that of a working policeman. It seemed to have the same files on the desk as the ones on his own, and the same furniture. The only difference was a crucifix on the wall over the desk.

'Now,' Barribal said, 'we speak English. It's as easy as Spanish for me and many Mexicans speak English because we have much American tourists. They come because it's cheap in Mexico and I think they hope they might be lucky enough to see something violent.'

He explained that they had been informed that Pel – 'the famous *Jefe* Pel,' he called him – was arriving with an assistant and, in an effort to make him feel that every attempt was being made to be helpful, he, Barribal, had been told to remain with him at all times.

'Sit, Don Evaristo.'

Opening a file, Barribal looked at Pel with a wide smile that showed teeth quite as splendid as Darcy's.

'We have your friend –' Barribal studied the file for a moment '– Marc Donck, safely tucked away. That's not the name he gave, of course. He calls himself Pierre Alaba when he is picked up for the hold-up of the Banco de Atlantico, in the Avenida 16 Septiembre.'

Pel sat up sharply. 'He held up a bank?'

Barribal smiled. 'He hold up the bank and get away with half a million pesos. But, as he make his escape, he hit a car and was knocked unconscious. By the time he'd recovered we'd found out who he was.' The wide smile came again. 'We also found the bag containing the pesos in the car. So we lock him up for safety. He's now at La Cantera, la Penitenciaría de Estado. The State Penitentiary. It's fixed. He's yours. You will be able to see him and take him away.'

'Was he on his own?' Pel was thinking of Navarro's ex-mistress, Jacqueline Hervé.

'One other,' Barribal said. 'The guy who drove the car. Name of Esteván Borillas. Known to us. He's got a record.'

Pel listened carefully. He was thinking that, having bolted from France so fast he was short of funds, Donck had held up the bank in an effort to raise money for something else he had had in mind – the thing that had brought him in Mexico. It wasn't unknown for crooks with big ideas to hold up a bank to fund them.

'You'll be interested in the gaol,' Barribal went on cheerfully. 'Especially Mexican. Inefficient, naturally. Special kind of prison. The guy's not a murderer, of course.'

'He is, in France,' Pel said shortly.

'*Seguramente*. Of course. But you will see him. Then he will be brought back here and handed over to you. He will be placed on the aircraft and after that he will be your concern. I hope he will not escape and do the hijack to Libya.'

'I hope he won't, either,' Pel said.

Having got him, Pel was prepared to handcuff Donck to his seat. But for the wet sort of people who might have objected, he might even have lashed him with strong rope, so thoroughly only his eyes would have been visible above the coils across his chest. Pel wasn't a mean-spirited man. He just didn't like criminals.

'When will this be?' he asked.

'Tomorrow I'll take you to see him. The next day we'll study the documents. Perhaps the day after he will be yours. Or the day after that.'

'Why can't we do it all in one day?'

Barribal smiled. 'Because this is Mexico,' he said cheerfully. 'And we believe in *mañana*. Tonight, I suggest you enjoy yourselves. There are places to visit. Restaurants. Night-clubs. If you would like a dame even –'

Since he was in Mexico City, it seemed to Pel that perhaps they ought at least to see the place so he could talk about it later to his wife. Already the sky was dark, the lights were coming on and the glow on the trees reminded him of the Champs Elysées in Paris or the Cours Général de Gaulle in his own city.

'I'd like to buy a little gold for my wife,' he said to De Troq'. 'Something to wear. I'm told gold's cheap in Mexico. I might be glad of your assistance.'

Feeling dusty after the journeying, and scruffy after sitting so long, he decided on a bath and a change of clothes. Afterwards, he helped himself to a drink from the refrigerator in the bedroom, and sat with his feet up on the bed to drink it.

When he woke he had what felt like a broken neck because he'd been lying with his head at an awkward angle. The glass was empty and on the bedside table but he couldn't remember placing it there.

Then he saw it was daylight. In a panic, he looked at his watch and discovered it was seven a.m. At first he thought he was dreaming, but then he realized that jet lag and caught up on him and he had slept through the night. There had been no sight-seeing, no theatres, no restaurants. Nothing.

Shaving and dressing, he went in search of De Troq', but his room was empty and he finally found him downstairs in the bar drinking chocolate and eating rolls.

'I fell asleep,' he said.

De Troq' grinned. 'So I noticed, *patron*.'

'We missed seeing the city. Why didn't you wake me?'

'I tried, *patron*. But I couldn't.'

Pel stared accusingly. 'What did *you* do? Did you see the sights?'

'Barribal turned up. He tried to wake you, too, and couldn't. We had a meal and he drove me round for a while.'

Pel scowled, deciding he must be growing old, had obviously

passed his peak and was now on the downward slope. Any moment now – he stopped dead before he had himself in a senile old age, and instead ordered coffee and rolls.

'Did Barribal say what time he was coming for us?'

De Troq' looked at his watch. 'Nine o'clock, he said.'

As he spoke, Barribal appeared at their table. He had on a pink shirt and orange tie and was wearing a lightweight suit of pale green. His boots matched his tie. He sat down and gestured to the waiter who arrived with more coffee and rolls. His face showed no smiles and somehow it seemed ominous.

'I have news for you, *mí jefe*.' Barribal frowned. 'And I guess it is not good.'

'Your wife's ill? You can't go with us to the penitentiary?'

'Worse than that,' Barribal said. 'Your guy has escaped.'

7

'What!'

Pel was on his feet, and almost dancing with fury. He'd been imagining arriving back in France with his criminal lashed to the seat and the triumphant cries of the welcoming police in his ears. 'Escaped! How in the name of God did that happen?'

Barribal waved a hand. 'I don' know. *Santa María Purísima,* I go to the office this morning to make sure all is in order and I am told.'

'Who let him go?'

'Again I don' know, I know I tear a strip or two off a few people. I have only the report. All I know is that somehow the guy Borillas get hold of a gun and hold up a guard. They steal his clothes and start to walk out, carrying his rifle. Is very bad, but these goddamn Mexes are sloppy. Fortunately, the guy Borillas don' make it.'

'He didn't make it? Why not?'

'They are spotted and some guy shoot Borillas in the arm.'

'What about Donck? He could be dangerous.'

'He get away. And he has the gun. We got to pick him up. There might be some shooting. Somebody could get killed.'

Pel glared. Not only had they allowed his man to escape, now they were telling him he might get shot. Pel didn't like being shot at and he certainly wasn't used to being killed.

Barribal was gesturing angrily. 'But I don' know the answers, really, *mí jefe,*' he said. 'Not until we arrive at the penitentiary and find out. Let's go.'

The drive south out of the city was hair-raising. Barribal instructed his driver to put on speed and they swung round lorries, trolley cars, carts and pedestrians. They seemed to hurtle past garages, factories, housing estates, all bare and bleak and devoid of any sort of beauty. Pel had always imagined Mexico to be lazy and colourful, with strumming guitars and wide-sombreroed smiling people. What he saw was a land struggling to reach modernity through the ugliness of too-hasty development.

Eventually, the traffic began to thin and they turned off the main road on to a dusty track lined with maguey cactus plants. They drove for a while into the sun, finally coming to a standstill in a wide circle at full speed that threw up dust and grit. They climbed out in a space crowded mostly with women with babies and straw bags and packages wrapped in newspaper. One or two of them were obvious prostitutes and there were dozens of children dashing among the honking cars that drew up and parked. Guards were obvious everywhere, in American-style high-heeled boots and *Dallas* hats. Boys were shouting.

'Twenty cents, señor! I find any man you want. Fifteen cents to you, señor. Special favour, eh? I have intimate knowledge of the whereabouts of Salazar, Eufemio, and the gangster Alamara, Raul-Juan.'

His face grim, Barribal pushed through the crowd to the gate. There was a long argument with an Indian-faced guard carrying a carbine but Barribal started to shout and gesticulate with papers and eventually the guard allowed them to pass through.

'It's the goddamn system,' Barribal growled. 'Liberal-minded guys inflict it on us. They say a goddamn prisoner has the right to see his wife and family. He has the right to his dignity, they say. Even to the point of sex. In bed, too. Me, I'd cut it off, then there'd be no trouble of this sort. There might even not be any crime in the next generation because there wouldn't be a next generation.'

Pel was inclined to agree but at that moment his fury didn't allow him to listen.

Inside, the prisoners were meeting the visitors to hawk pottery, leatherware, novelties, food, drink, home-made toys, hand-tooled purses and belts, balloons, madonnas and bracelets. Several of them, holding begging bowls, grouped together to sing:

Rayando el sol,
Me despedí

Bajo la brisa,
Y ahí me accordé de ti . . .

'They have to learn a trade,' Barribal said. 'That's the idea behind it. So they'll be useful citizens when they are free.' He scowled. 'By the time they come out, Mexico will be full of nothing but gifts for tourists. Everybody in the goddamn country'll know how to make leather belts and purses and sing love-songs.'

The whole place was full of the odours of garlic, sweat, motor-car exhaust fumes, wine and disinfectant. There were men and women in the same gaol, even in neighbouring cells.

'It is better in the old days,' Barribal said. 'Then they stand them up and shoot them. Three-deep to save bullets. Now you have to pay the kids to stop the hub-caps and the windscreen wipers of your car being stolen. Let's go see the governor.'

The prison governor was a small man with a mandarin moustache and spectacles. Though, like every Mexican Pel had so far seen, he looked like a bandit, he also managed to look like a very mild-mannered bandit. Barribal leapt at him, red in the face, and he backed away against his desk as if he expected to fend off blows. The shouting went on for several minutes at the end of which the chastened governor gestured and explained.

'He say he has Borillas in safe custody,' Barribal said.

'A pity he doesn't have Donck,' Pel growled. 'We might have been on our way home tonight.' He could just imagine what the Chief would have to say, what Paris would have to say, when he cabled that the journey, the preparations, the expense, all the work that had gone into the preparation of the documents, had all been for nothing.

Borrillas was in a single dark cell in the main block. There were no other men near him, no sign here of the free-and-easy atmosphere of the rest of the prison, and no concessions for his wound.

'We can be as cruel as the next guy when we want to be.' Barribal explained.

Borillas, a gorilla of a man wearing his arm in a sling, was still indignant and understandably bitter that Donck had escaped and he had not.

'Who produced the gun?' Barribal asked. 'Donck's girl-friend?'

'No. Mine.'

This was unexpected because they had been convinced, since

Donck had escaped, that Jacqueline Hervé had smuggled the gun in.

'My girl-friend visited me,' Borillas said. 'The next time she came, she slipped me a gun, and we got out. But some bastard took a shot at me as we went over the wall and got me in the arm. So I'm here and the other guy got away.'

'Did *his* woman ever come to see him here?'

'You mean the woman who helped set up the bank robbery?' Borillas frowned. 'No, she never came. He was mad about that. He said she was cheating him. Something to do with her getting away with some money of his or something like that. Something valuable, anyway. He said if she hadn't visited him, that was the only explanation. She'd bolted.'

'Did he mention her name?'

'*Sí*. He called her Jacquelina. Something like that. Her other name was Hervo or something.'

'Why did he set up the bank job?' De Troq' asked.

'To get money, I suppose. That's why *I* robbed it.'

'Did they say why they wanted the money?'

'To spend.' Borrillas looked at them as if they were stupid.

'Did they mention any project they had in mind? Were they simply raising funds for something else bigger?'

'Bigger?' Borillas frowned. 'What's bigger than a bank job?'

Pel looked at De Troq'. It seemed to him that, since Donck and Hervé had bolted from France at full speed, the hold-up was either to supply them with the money they needed to carry out whatever it was that had resulted from the Navarro-Martin meeting, or else to buy airline tickets to somewhere like Brazil where there was no extradition arrangement.

'They'd either got something planned, or else they'd carried out something they'd planned,' he said. 'Did you know what it was?'

Borillas frowned. 'They didn't tell me. Some treasure they'd found maybe? They didn't tell me anything at all. Whenever I appeared they always stopped talking. I think it was something that had been hidden. I think it was old.'

'Old?'

'*Sí*. Old.'

'So where will they have gone, *peón*?' Barribal snapped.

'I think they were aiming north. Maybe the American border.

They mentioned going to Querétaro. They also mentioned San Miguel de Allende.'

'What's that?' Pel asked.

'It's a place near Querétaro,' Barribal explained. 'Not far north of Mexico City. Just off the main road. Old colonial town popular with tourists.'

'Why would they go there?'

'They mentioned some guy who was going there,' Borillas said. 'Some book-writing type.'

'A professor?'

'They mentioned a professor.'

Even Pel's limited knowledge of Spanish had enabled him to pick up the word. 'Professor, did he say? Which professor? Ask him, De Troq'.'

There was a short jabbered conversation in hurried Spanish then De Troq' turned.

'He says he wasn't Mexican. He was asking questions.'

'When?'

'When they met him.'

'Did he see him?'

'Once, briefly. With Donck and the woman. Borillas was there but he doesn't know what they were up to because he couldn't speak their language. He thinks it was Portuguese but I expect it was French.'

'Where's this professor now?'

There was another long exchange of words, and De Troq' turned again.

'He doesn't know but he had a bag with him and he saw the hotel label. It was called the Tepentitla.'

'I know it.' Barribal was recovering his spirits now that they were making progress again. Somehow he seemed to feel that the questioning of Borillas was redeeming the mistake of the prison authorities. 'It's near the Alameda Gardens in Mexico City.'

'This professor,' Pel said. 'What was he like?'

The professor, it seemed, was thin and dark-haired and wore horn-rimmed spectacles.

'Sounds like Professor Martin, *patron*,' De Troq' said. 'It looks very much as though the place *he* disappeared to is also in Mexico.'

'And that there *is* something here that was of interest to

Navarro,' Pel growled. 'And now, doubtless, to Donck and the woman.'

Barribal was taking the initiative again now. 'We go to the Hotel Tepentitla,' he announced. 'We will talk to this professor. And –' he added ominously '– he had better have something to tell us.'

8

Unfortunately, he hadn't.

Because he wasn't there and hadn't been there for some time.

There seemed little doubt that the man who had taken a room at the Tepentitla was Professor Henri Martin, the French historian – his name was in the register – but the hotel hadn't seen him for several weeks and didn't know where he was. At first, they had assumed he had been doing his research – they knew this was why he was in Mexico, because he had told them so – but they had no idea where. They hadn't worried for a day or two but then, after a week without any sign of him, they had removed his luggage to the basement and let the room.

'You still have the luggage?' De Troq' asked.

'We have it, señor. He had two suitcases, a camera case and a small canvas holdall. He took all but one suitcase.'

'Did he say where he was going?'

'No, señor. But he had hired a car. We know that because the porter had to fetch it for him each day. We do not have a car-park here and the cars are kept in a vacant lot at the back of the hotel. Under guard, of course.'

'Is the car there now?'

'No, señor. He took it the morning he last appeared, and neither the car nor the professor has been seen since.'

'Didn't he tell *anyone* where he was going?'

'I questioned everyone, señor.'

'We will see the porter,' Barribal said.

The manager shrugged. 'I regret he is not here, señor. It is his day off.'

'He lives in Mexico City, doesn't he?'

'Yes, of course.'

'Then send a car for him.'

The manager sighed, made gestures and spoke rapidly to an assistant manager and a porter went running for the front door.

'In the meantime,' Barribal said, 'which is his room?'

'*Cinquente-siete*. Fifty-seven.'

'We'll see it.'

The manager spread his hands as if he were showing them the stigmata. 'I regret, señores. It is now taken by a married couple.'

'We'll still see it.'

The hotel manager protested that, since the key was not in its place, it might well be occupied, but Barribal was insistent. They took the lift to the fifth floor and Barribal knocked on the door. There was a startled cry from inside.

'*Quien?*'

'*Policía.*'

Even through the door, they could hear the hurried scrambling beyond and eventually it was opened by a small bald-headed man with lipstick smeared across his mouth. Beyond him, a woman was hurriedly zipping up her dress.

'*Documentos!*' Barribal snapped.

The man fished out his papers nervously and Barribal turned to the woman who dug into a handbag and offered them with a wail of despair. Barribal took one look at them then flung them back at her.

There was a lot of self-important shouting by Barribal and loud apologies by the manager until the woman burst into tears and the man looked as though he'd soon follow. It soon became evident that the woman was not the man's wife and he thought the presence of the police was because his wife had found out about his transgression. The manager explained and then the man began to grow indignant. Shouting at the manager, he grew red in the face with anger and the woman burst into a fresh paroxysm of sobbing. It all went clean over Barribal's head as he opened wardrobe doors and looked in the bathroom.

When it was over, Barribal marched out – followed by the embarrassed Frenchmen – putting on a big show of Mexican macho to hide the fact that he was embarrassed, too.

'*Libertinos*,' he said disgustedly. '*Hombre disoluto. Desgraciados animales.*' He turned to Pel. 'The world's full of guys like him. I expect he's got a faithful wife waiting with the children at home. We'll examine the luggage.'

They were conducted to a room near the manager's office which looked as though it were a staff rest-room and within a short time the suitcase arrived. It was locked, but the label – in a leather container attached to the handle – said 'Professeur Henri Martin'. His address in France followed.

'We'll open it,' Barribal announced portentously.

He was looking round for something large and sharp when De Troq' produced a bunch of keys and got to work on the lock. As he threw the lid back, Barribal turned to the manager.

'You see?' he said, gesturing. 'The efficiency of the French. Why don't you have keys?'

The suitcase contained little but clothes, though there were a few scribbled sheets of paper and a notebook.

Barribal took the notebook and turned again to the manager. 'Have you no idea at all where he went?'

The manager shrugged. 'There is the Mayan site at Tula,' he said. 'If he is a historian he could have gone there. It is very interesting. It is also an interesting town. I believe he also visited the Biblioteca Nacional, or the National History Museum, which is housed in the Castle of Chapultepec.'

'We will visit them.'

As they closed the case, the porter was ushered in. He was an old man with grey flecks of beard on his dark unshaven chin. He wore a rumpled cotton uniform with green collar and cuffs.

'Tula, señor,' he agreed when they questioned him. 'Yes, he mentioned Tula.'

'In what context?'

'He asked me the road to Tula.'

'Did he say why?'

'No, señor.'

'You can add nothing more than that?'

'Nothing, señor.'

Barribal dismissed the old man with a wave of his hand and the porter disappeared, looking bewildered and clearly wondering what it was all about.

'We'll take the suitcase,' Barribal said. 'And now we'll go to the library.'

In the reading and reference room of the library, they found another trace of Professor Martin. The assistant, who spoke good English with an American accent, recognized him from De Troq's description and, reaching behind her, fished a pile of cards from a drawer.

'Request cards,' she said in English. 'This is an important library and when people wish to read here, they have first to fill out a card with their names and professions.' She sorted out the cards and removed one. 'Martin,' he said. 'Henri. Professor of Modern History. University of Dijon. He is vouched for by the Hotel Tepentitla. Will that be him?'

Pel nodded and, replacing the cards, the assistant produced another batch. 'Here we are,' he said. 'When they wish to have books, they must fill in request cards. Too many books have been stolen by students. Now, if one is missing, we know where to look. It is now difficult to steal.' She studied the cards for a moment. 'I remember he did not speak much Spanish and the books he requested were largely in French. De La Gorce's *Histoire du Second Empire. Expédition du Mexique*, by J. Niox. An English one, *The Mexican Adventure* by D. Dawson. Bibesco's *Combats et Retraite des Six Mille*, Kératry's *La Contre-Guérilla Française au Mexique*. Général Brancourt's *Lettres*. There is also *La Intervención Francesa en Mexico sugun el Archivo del Mariscal Bazaine*, published here in Mexico in 1907.'

Here it was again, the French intervention in Mexico to put the unwanted Austrian Archduke Maximilian on the throne.

'Was Tula involved in the battles of the French intervention?' De Troq' asked.

The assistant shrugged. 'I don't think so, señor. Tula is only the site of Mayan remains. Pyramids. Figures. That sort of thing. There's little there, and in those days it would be no more than a small village. It would have no importance and no value. It wouldn't be worth fighting for.'

'So why did Martin want to go to Tula?' Pel said. 'It doesn't seem to have anything to do with what he was researching.'

They drove back to police headquarters and joined Barribal in his room. Pel was hot, angry and frustrated and by this time had come to the conclusion that Barribal was a lunatic.

The appearance of three bottles of cold beer cheered him and eased his view of Barribal a little as they began to examine the suitcase. The clothing gave no indication of what Martin had been up to, so they turned their attention to the sheets of paper and the notebook. Most of the contents were in shorthand which De Troq' recognized as the Sloan-Duployan system, often used in France.

A court shorthand expert summoned by Barribal identified it at once. 'People here tend to use an adaptation of the Gregg system or the Marti system,' he said. 'But there are other systems, of course, for different languages.'

He couldn't read the Sloan-Duployan shorthand easily but turned up during the afternoon with a man who could. Chiefly, the notebook consisted of notes that seemed to deal with the career and travels of the Emperor Maximilian after his arrival in Mexico. There were a lot of what appeared to be meaningless dates and place names – San Miguel de Allende, Acapulco, Veracruz, Mexico City, Zacatecas, Querétaro, Chapultepec – and names of Mexicans De Troq' recognized from his reading – Juárez, Mejía, Miramón, Escobedo; even Bazaine, once even De Troquereau – and names of European royalty. But none of it seemed to lead anywhere and it seemed more like disconnected notes made to refresh Martin's memory rather than a connected diary which would indicate his movements.

But there were also passages in longhand that indicated Martin was contemplating a journey to the north of the capital, and once there was the word, *'cama'* – bed – written in pencil as if it were a reminder. Alongside it, in ballpoint, were the words, *'Pilar'* and *'Las Rosas'*. There were also at several points among the shorthand, the letters, 'ASS'.

'Pilar's a girl's name, *mí jefe,*' Barribal explained. 'Perhaps it explains "*Las Rosas*" – roses – and bed. He is reminding himself to send her roses and intends to get her into bed. Or maybe he has *got* her into bed and is sending the roses as a delicate memento.'

'And ASS?'

Barribal shrugged. 'Asociación de Seguridad Secundaria? Or Secreta?' He grinned. 'Or maybe Sexual? I will check.'

There was also a roll of film in a small plastic cylinder with a self-seal lid.

'Could this have been used?' Pel asked.

'If it hadn't, it would be in a box, *patron,*' De Troq' pointed out. 'You don't take them out of the cardboard container until you're going to put them in the camera. Afterwards, you put them in the cylinder to keep the light from them. I think it has been used.'

'Then it might be of interest to see what's on it.'

'I'll fix it,' Barribal said.

Pel watched the door close behind him and fished for his cigarettes. He had run out but De Troq' produced a packet of Gauloise.

Pel lit one and stared moodily at the rising smoke. 'One day,' he promised, 'I know I shall give them up. In the meantime I smoke less and less, but not *much* less, so it becomes a race against time. Which will come first? Me giving them up or cancer of the lungs?' He drew on the cigarette and looked up. 'This French intervention in Mexico. What do you know about it?'

'A little, *patron*. My family has always known about it because of my great-great-grandfather.'

'I was never very good at history,' Pel admitted. 'Inform me. And make it so it's finished before that lunatic returns.'

De Troq' drew a deep breath, clearly enjoying himself. 'I'm not sure of the reasons for it all, *patron*,' he said. 'I think there was a lot of French investment here in the 1860s but the country was in a chronic state of civil war and it seemed to Napoleon III that a good solution would be to get rid of the president and put a French puppet in his place. He also thought it might be a good idea to have a solid Latin bloc to the south of the United States who at the time were engaged with their own civil war. They persuaded the brother of the Emperor Franz Josef of Austria that it would suit him, and he was brought to Mexico and landed at Veracruz, backed by the French Army and Navy. There were battles because the Mexicans didn't want him, and the elected president, Benito Juárez, never wavered in his opposition. Maximilian was established in Mexico City but there were a great many casualties from the fighting.'

'How did it end?'

'*Alors* –' De Troq' shrugged '– although Maximilian was very decorative, he was far from bright and when the American Civil War ended, the Americans made it clear that they didn't want Europeans interfering on their side of the Atlantic. I expect you've heard of the Monroe Doctrine, which says exactly that. It also began to seem to Napoleon III that he'd rather put his foot in it, because things had started to go wrong. To cut the story short, he withdrew his troops, Maximilian's wife, Carlota, went mad, and in the end Maximilian was besieged with a few loyal troops at Querétaro where he eventually surrendered. He was shot. You'll have seen Goya's painting of his death.'

Pel hadn't but he muttered something, hoping that De Troq', who was known to be a bit of an intellectual and a little frightening, would think he had.

'Anything else?'

De Troq' shrugged. 'That's all I know, *patron*. A sordid sort of business. It ought never to have happened, and when it failed nobody was very surprised.'

De Troq's summary had been neat and succinct. 'Why would Martin be interested in that?' Pel asked. 'Other than the reason we've already considered – profit? We have no information that he's writing anything about it, though he might well be. And if he is, why is he visiting this place, Tula? That doesn't sound like him. Martin's a man who likes the limelight. *And* the money that goes with it. So is his interest in Tula because he's found something there that has a bearing on the French intervention? Something nobody knows about and would be worth investigating? Or is it simply that he'd found something that would produce money? Mayan relics or something of that sort? It must have been something like that, because Serrano Navarro wasn't the sort to be interested in limelight for Professor Martin, was he?'

They tossed it back and forth until Barribal returned. 'I had them check those letters, ASS,' he said. 'They went through the directories, but nothing that would interest us turned up. They're still looking, though.'

He had a fistful of large photographs in colour, fresh from the dark-room. He spread them on the table and they leaned over them.

Two of them were of a girl, obviously Mexican because she was dark-haired and beautiful and was wearing a brightly coloured dress. She appeared to be standing on some sort of high platform that showed the countryside all around. In the background they could see a huge strange stone figure, like a column with a crude head cut in it.

'That'll be Pilar, whoever she is, I suppose,' De Troq' said, indicating the girl.

'Perhaps,' Pel suggested dryly, 'the reason Martin went to Tula was more simple than we imagine – to meet her. What else do we have?'

There were two pictures of Martin himself, wearing sandals, a wide-brimmed straw hat and a red shirt, but they were not as good as the ones of the girl. He was not in the centre of the pictures and one of them was slightly lopsided.

Most of the rest of the reel consisted of straightforward pictures – Mayan remains; a country cart; a splendid church.

'The Church of San Francisco Xavier at Tepozatlán,' Barribal said. 'It's near Tula. Dates back to the early seventeenth century.'

The end of the reel showed houses, ordinary undistinguished wooden houses which weren't Mexican in style, with flat façades and stoops, and the last pictures of all showed a deep valley containing what appeared to be a town. Beyond the town the plain stretched away to distant hills and in the centre they could see a tall church and a stadium which looked like a bullring. In the foreground was what appeared to be part of another building, a wall of pink bricks, its summit built in a series of graceful downward arcs with pointed peaks. There were two or three other pictures taken in a town, showing a church, a square surrounded by clubbed jacarandas full of magpies, and what appeared to be a hotel.

De Troq' indicated the indifferent pictures of Martin. 'It looks as if the girl took those,' he said.

'Women can't be relied on,' Barribal said with all the arrogance of a Mexican male that they'd already noticed wherever they'd gone. 'And they were taken at Tula. The big statue is Mayan. I once take my sons there to see their history. I think they are taken on top of the pyramid.' He moved the pictures about and they saw close-ups of the carved heads, and of what appeared to be small chambers.

'Something could have been hidden there,' Pel said, indicating the strange wooden houses.

Barribal frowned. 'They're not Mexican,' he said.

'They don't even look occupied,' Pel said.

But Barribal placed his finger on a row of figures sitting in the sun alongside one of the houses, heads down, wide-brimmed hats over their eyes. 'Men,' he said. 'Sleeping Mexican men. *Some* guy lives there.'

Pel indicated the other pictures. 'And these?'

'San Miguel de Allende,' Barribal said immediately. He indicated the view of the wide valley. 'That is a famous picture. Everybody takes it. You approach from the plain and pass a large modern motel and you're just wondering whether to spend the night there or try a little further when the road drops away. It is narrow and winds much, so you have no choice except to continue. Then you come to this view as you turn the corner. You have the whole plain and the town before you and you stop to take the photograph because just at that point the road widens enough to park your car and there is a little balustrade where you can lean your camera to hold it steady. Also the sun is over your shoulder and the picture is perfect. Everybody does this. I've seen dozens of that photograph. It is in all the brochures. All the guys in the force taking their family north, stop and take it. Visitors take it. Americans looking for old Mexico take it. They go there because San Miguel is a fine example of colonial Mexico and it is very popular because it's easy to reach from Mexico City and tourists like easy trips. It has good hotels and an American art school and the wealthy *Norteamericano* mammas and papas come to visit their children there. Good bars. Good restaurants that sell *Norteamericano* food. Lotsa shops where you buy gifts to take home to grandmamma.'

'Gold, for instance?' Pel asked.

Barribal grinned. 'Good Mexican gold. Beautifully worked. *Rebozos* – shawls – hats and *sarapes*. That's the all-purpose garment in Mexico; you wear it against the cold, sleep under it, even make a tent of it. Except that nowadays they all wear blue jeans. And the old sombrero have disappear because you cannot get two in the front seat of a motor car without blinding the driver. You can buy all these in San Miguel and the Americans like it easy.'

'Tula,' Pel said thoughtfully. 'Tepozatlán. San Miguel de Allende. How far away are they?'

'Tula. Hour and a half from Mexico City. San Miguel. Just to the north of Querétaro. Two hundred kilometres. Both off the main road but there is a fast highway north.'

'Could we do them both in a day?'

'We do Tepozotlán and Tula in the morning and arrive at San Miguel in the afternoon. You stay the night but there is a good hotel. It'll be full of Americans, I guess, but –' Barribal shrugged '– a word from the chief of police there will get us in. I fix it.'

Pel closed Martin's notebook and, pushing the photographs into a neat pile, indicated to De Troq' to place them in his brief-case.

'We ought to go there,' he said. 'If we find nothing, I think we'll go home.'

9

'What are you expecting to find, *patron*?' De Troq' asked as they sat over a beer in their hotel.

'I don't know,' Pel admitted. 'With luck, Donck and the Hervé woman. After all, they're the reason for us being here. We're supposed to be taking them back. Perhaps even the missing Professor Martin. He's probably just in bed with this Pilar, but we might be intrigued to discover what he's after, because it looks very much to me as if he's after *something*. And that, *mon brave*, might lead to an explanation of why Navarro was murdered. Donck and Hervé are linked with Navarro, and Navarro is linked with Martin, so it seems to me they're all involved, somehow or other, and the explanation lies somewhere between them. Martin's obviously been visiting Tula and this San Miguel place, so it's more than likely Donck and the woman have also gone there. We might even bump into them in the street. It's been known.'

It had, too. When Pel had been a young cop he had worked with an old sergeant who had been on the track of a wanted man for twenty years – ever since he'd been a young cop himself – and then one day in Dijon his car had collided with that of another driver on a corner and, when they had exchanged addresses, it had dawned on him he was face to face with the man he'd been seeking throughout his whole career.

That evening, Pel tried to telephone his wife, who had assured him she had telephoned France from Mexico without difficulty. Obviously things were different for Pel – things were always different for Pel – and there was a long wait. Eventually, just when he had fallen asleep on the bed, the telephone rang and the operator announced he was through.

'Pel!' The delight in his wife's voice almost brought tears to his eyes. 'Where are you?'

'Still in Mexico City.'

'You sound so close. I thought you must be back in Paris.'

'Not yet. Our man's disappeared. A fool of a policeman called Barribal let them escape.' It hadn't really been Barribal's fault but it salved Pel's fury to lay the blame on him.

'When will you be back?'

Pel considered. Since the Mexican police had allowed his quarry to escape and had no idea where he was, it wouldn't appear to be good sense to go on hanging around. No self-respecting police chief was going to keep two men in a foreign country at great expense on the off chance their quarry would turn up.

'I don't know,' he admitted. 'But since our man's disappeared, probably very soon.'

'Oh, Pel, I'm so pleased!'

It did Pel's crusty heart good to think his wife was missing him.

His cheerfulness evaporated, however, as he wrote out the cable that was to be sent to the Chief, informing him of the disappearance of Donck and Hervé. He tried to make out that there was still hope that they might be picked up but he didn't really believe it and could just imagine the shout of rage when the Chief was informed. For the rest of that day, he suspected, Darcy was going to have a rough time.

He had just finished getting the facts down, and De Troq' was preparing to send it off when Barribal arrived. García Granados, the Chief of Police, had a request to make, he said, and he'd been ordered to bring Pel to the police chief's presence.

'At this time of night?'

'I guess so.'

'What on earth for? I've just been preparing a cable to my own Chief informing him that we hope to take a plane home within the next day or so.'

'Don't send it, Don Evaristo,' Barribal said. 'Not yet.'

'In the name of God, why not?'

Barribal ignored the question. 'I have my car outside. The Chief wait and he has a large bottle of brandy and four glasses on his desk.'

Puzzled, they allowed themselves to be driven to police headquarters. With the day staff and the typists all gone, it seemed quiet, but here and there uniformed and plain clothes men were still at work. In one of the rooms, they could see men in civilian suits, whom they assumed to be detectives, playing cards.

García Granados rose from behind his desk as Pel was ushered in with De Troq'. He was considerably more friendly than he had been when they'd first arrived, gestured expansively at the chairs which had been arranged in a half-circle, and began to slosh out large helpings of brandy. Picking up a glass, he held it out to Pel. '*A su salud, señor*,' he said.

'*Bon santé*,' Pel said shortly. 'Ask him to come to the point, Plutarco.'

Barribal spoke to the Chief who began to deliver what appeared to be a long address. Several times he tapped his head, twice he clutched his heart, and once he clapped both hands. When he had finished he sat back, looked at Barribal and gestured at Pel.

'The *Comisario*,' Barribal said, 'says me to explain to you that he's in a great dilemma. A guy's disappeared – your Professor Martin – and today he receives a message from the famous University of Dijon in France asking where he's gone to. He says he has no idea and neither has anyone else. He does not know this guy, Professor Martin, but he point out that *you* do and he make the request –' he grinned '– with the greatest concern for the inconvenience it must cause you, that you will help us find him.' Pel frowned and he went on hurriedly. 'He also point out, again with great distress, of course, that if you should find it impossible, he would also find it impossible to permit the extradition of the criminal, Donck, even if he's found, and it is possible he may be, because we have find that he hire a car from the Hertz Agency in Mexico City who say that, as we thought, he heads north. He finally point out that it might be possible to kill two birds with one stone, and suggest you cable your Chief that you agree.'

Pel stared at De Troq'. 'In the name of God –' he began, then he stopped and shut his mouth again. He had just been promising his wife that he'd be home as soon as possible. Now it looked as though he might be in Mexico for the rest of his life, because Mexico was as big as Europe, full of desert and mountain and tropical forest where the chances of finding Donck, Jacqueline Hervé or Professor Martin looked remarkable slim.

'The *Comisario*,' Barribal went on, 'say that he offer you all the facilities of our telephone service and that, with a police prefix demanding swift action, it should not be difficult.'

Nor was it. The answer was back by midnight. It was short and to the point, but Pel could just imagine the Chief's face as he realized they had *him* over a barrel just as much as Pel. There would inevitably be interest at a superior level and the questions would come down from the highest of high altars. Where are Donck and Jacqueline Hervé? Why haven't they been returned to face trial? Who allowed them to escape? No matter what they said, it would be firmly believed that it would be Pel's fault and, through Pel, the Chief's.

'*Allez*,' the cable said. '*Et bonne chance.*' Go ahead. And good luck. It didn't say much but Pel knew what lay behind it.

They showed the cable to García Granados, who smiled and poured more brandy.

'*A su salud*,' he said. Pel didn't bother to reply.

Barribal drove them back to the hotel. 'I have been ordered to stick with you,' he announced as he dropped them at the door. 'And give every assistance.'

Pel gave him a sour look. Barribal constantly at his side was something which, at that moment, he felt he could do without. And just then he was missing Burgundy as he'd never missed it before and he found himself itching to be back in his own office with its swivel chair, large window and splendid carpet – choice of three colours for chief inspectors and above. Nostalgically, he wondered what was happening there – if Darcy was coping, and what Nosjean was up to, even if the supermarket at Talant had been broken into again.

In fact, Darcy was quite enjoying himself. Despite the fact that he admired Pel, normally he always had him standing somewhere in the shadows just behind him and Pel could be a frightening superior at times. Though Darcy affected a cheerful indifference, he wasn't quite as indifferent as he pretended, and he had no wish to have Pel return in a bad temper to discover he had missed something.

The supermarket at Talant was still puzzling Bardolle. There had been another alarm and, after the uniformed cops had taken a look at it, Bardolle had gone along also. Police dogs had been sent and the place had been examined, but they seemed to have got nowhere and achieved nothing, except the horse laugh from L'Estropié, Edouard Fousse. Aimedieu still wasn't quite sure what he was looking for at Fontenay because he had checked the 500-franc notes, and they had *all* proved genuine. Every one.

Nosjean, however, seemed to be making progress. He had picked at random three car owners who had claimed insurance on their stolen vehicles but had not reported them to the police: one François Orain, a Roger Pelaut, and a man by the name of Dugaste, and it seemed to be time to get down to particulars. François Orain he knew about, but when Nosjean called to see him again he was just about to drive off in a Peugeot 304.

'New car?' Nosjean asked.

'Second-hand,' Orain explained. 'To take the place of the other one. Just got it, I had to scratch round a bit to raise the money but I expect the insurance company will pay up eventually.'

'Nice buy,' Nosjean said. 'Where did you get it?'

'Garage Moissin at Ferouelle. I was told they were good and they were.'

Nosjean watched him disappear with his wife and family to do the shopping. He was certain there was something fishy going on but he couldn't put his finger on it. Perhaps Pelaut might let drop whatever it was, because he was one step up on Orain and had had his replacement second-hand car for a few weeks now.

He was in the street outside his house cleaning it when Nosjean arrived. It was a reasonable-looking Renault and he was putting a good shine on it.

'Thought I might sell it,' he said. 'And buy a new one. It's in good shape but it's not like the one I had, and you get used to a car, don't you?'

'Yes, you do,' Nosjean agreed. 'But it's not bad-looking. Where did you get it?'

'Garage at Tubours near Lyons. Marc Moissin, who has the garage at Ferouelle, put me on to it. He's good with second-hand cars but he hadn't got what I wanted when I went to see him, so he put me on to this other place.'

'Same value?'

'About the same. Hundred or two in it. After all, I'm not rich so I had to use the money I got from the insurance company after the old one was pinched.'

Nosjean gestured at his own battered vehicle. 'I'm thinking of swapping that,' he said. 'I'll try them. Who told you about Moissin?'

Pelaut frowned. 'Some type at work,' he said. 'I can't remember exactly.'

Since the thefts of cars from Métaux de Dijon had been going on for three years on and off, Nosjean decided that perhaps it might be a good idea to go back a little further in time, and Josephe Dugaste, who had had his car stolen the previous winter, seemed a likely subject because he was now the owner of a brand-new Citroën. He was a small thin-faced man with a beard, which made him look like a ferret peering through a hedge, and he seemed to have adjusted very well to his loss.

'I've got a new one, now,' he said. 'I got hold of a second-hand Toyota at first, to tide me over after I was paid the insurance money for the stolen one, and I did quite well out of it. In fact, I got a bit more than I expected so I got rid of it and bought a new Citroën BX instead. It's nice to have a new car. Especially without paying much extra.'

'When did you buy it?' Nosjean asked.

Dugaste thought for a while. '8th March,' he said eventually. 'As soon as I got the insurance money. It happened to be my wife's birthday so I thought it would be a nice surprise for her. I traded the Toyota in – the one I bought to tide me over when my original Citroën was stolen. I'd kept it for a while but then I decided to go mad and have a new one. The insurance company had written they were going to pay up.' He grinned. 'My wife thought it was a good birthday present, though I'm the one who really benefits.'

Nosjean thought for a moment. 'Where did you get your second-hand car?' he asked. 'The one that replaced the stolen one.'

'Garage Moissin at Ferouelle.'

Same as Orain, Nosjean noticed at once. Same place that had advised Pelaut to go to Tubours. 'Why there?' he asked.

'A type at work told me about him. He got a second-hand car there and got a good deal.'

'Would it have been François Orain?'

'Might have been. I can't remember now.' Dugaste's eyes flickered. 'I think it was Marcel Morice, in fact. He works alongside me.'

'Is Moissin a Citroën agent?'

'He deals in everything. If you want it, he can get it for you.'

'That must cost a bit more, because he'd have to get a car he didn't normally sell from an agent who did, who'd also want a profit.'

Dugaste shrugged. 'He says it's worth it for the trade it brings.'

'He must do very well somewhere,' Nosjean commented shrewdly. 'Good value for second-hand cars. Any kind of replacement.'

Dugaste smiled. 'Perhaps he charges a lot for repairs.'

It turned out that Marcel Morice, in fact, didn't know Dugaste and that started Nosjean wondering afresh. If Morice didn't know Dugaste, how had he come to tell him? Morice couldn't remember telling him and, in any case, he had bought his own car in Dole. Dugaste was obviously lying.

Somehow, Nosjean hadn't quite taken to Dugaste, anyway. He seemed a little sharper than he ought to have been and, learning that he had been insured with Aubineau, Nosjean went to see the insurance manager again.

'Yes,' Aubineau admited. 'We paid him. Thirty-three thousand francs for the Citroën. He seemed very satisfied. I gather he bought a Toyota to replace it.'

'That's right,' Nosjean said. '8th March.'

Aubineau grinned. 'Well, he must have sold the wife and kids,' he said. 'We didn't pay him until 10th May. Two months later.'

It seemed odd enough for Nosjean to visit Dugaste again. This time Dugaste had the same sort of shifty expression Nosjean had noticed with Orain and he was on the alert at once, convinced by this time that there was more to the theft of cars than he'd realized.

'How did you manage to buy it?' he asked. 'On tick? After all, 33,000 francs is a lot to lose. But you managed to buy a new car before you received the insurance.'

'Oh, no, I'd received it.'

'Two months afterwards,' Nosjean said quietly. 'I got that from Assurances Mutuelles.'

Dugaste frowned. 'That's right,' he said. 'I did. I forgot. I got it on a down payment with some money my wife let me have. I remember now. The insurance company had agreed to pay, so I told her I wouldn't have to owe her for long. She took some convincing, believe me.' Dugaste laughed. 'You know how women are – suspicious.'

Nosjean was still not satisfied. It was Nosjean's gift for not being satisfied that made him a good detective. Everything, he knew, had to lock together like a jigsaw and if it didn't, it was no good trying to shove it into place so that it *appeared* to fit. It *had* to fit. Full stop. Fit. F-I-T. No argument. And this didn't seem to. Nosjean went back to Aubineau.

Aubineau was puzzled. He sent for the files and the girl who looked like Charlotte Rampling brought them into him, giving Nosjean a shy smile as she passed to let him know she hadn't forgotten him.

Aubineau was peering at the papers now. '10th May,' he said. 'That's when we paid. It's down here. Complete with cheque number and everything.'

'He said he got it on 8th March.'

'Not with our money.'

'But you did pay him?'

'Oh, yes. 10th May. Our computer didn't make a mistake. Computers don't.' Aubineau grinned. 'At least, most of the time they don't. There was one occasion when it told us to pay out 2 million francs on a 20,000-franc claim. But you always know, and there was nothing wrong with the computer on 10th May. And we never – repeat, never – pay out until the last moment anyway, in case the car turns up. Once the computer says pay, you might never get it to change its mind.'

'Did you tell him in March that you intended to pay?'

'We don't do that.' Aubineau shrugged. 'We might find we have to change our minds, and once you have it down on paper you can't back away from it. We pay at the last possible moment and only after giving plenty of time for the stolen car to turn up. We never say ahead we're going to pay just in case we don't have to.'

Nosjean was growing more and more puzzled. Dugaste's brand-new car worried him because he couldn't understand where he had found the money for it. What was more, he had a suspicion that before long Pelaut would be buying one and, after him, Orain. Then, when Aimedieu reported that he had found the source of the strange 500-franc notes was at Ferouelle, which was near Cloing where he'd been making enquiries, he suddenly wondered if the two were connected. Stolen cars – unexpected large-denomination notes. It was very possible. Ferouelle was the place where the Garage Moissin, where Dugaste and Orain had bought their replacement cars, was situated.

'Ferouelle's a funny place for a car-repair depot, isn't it?' Nosjean said. 'Up in the hills. Nowhere near anywhere. Most of the successful ones are here – in or around the city. Places tucked away out of sight get overlooked, I've found. Are they doing well enough to be chucking 500-franc notes about?'

Aimedieu frowned. 'Since you mention it, it does seem a bit strange, doesn't it? I don't know of any repair depots stuck out in the wilds either. Perhaps I should do a bit more checking.'

Nosjean took the problem to Darcy and the two of them went to the Bar Transvaal for a beer to talk it over. Finding a corner out of the way where they couldn't be heard, they discussed the case in undertones as they toyed with a sandwich.

'There's something fishy going on,' Nosjean insisted. 'I'm sure of it. I don't know where it starts or how deep it goes but I bet it's there.'

They confessed themselves baffled and Darcy gave Nosjean a sheepish look.

'Better get it cleared up before the Old Man comes back,' he said. 'Or, at least, on the way to being cleared up. It'll please him.'

Nosjean grinned. 'I wonder what he's up to,' he said. 'I bet he's hating it.'

10

Nosjean wasn't far wrong.

While Mexico City wasn't exactly what Pel would have chosen as somewhere to lay his head, it was civilized or, at least, had civilized areas to it which could just be made acceptable to someone brought up in the culture of what he felt was the most civilized province of the most civilized nation in the world. Nevertheless, it still wasn't what Pel would have chosen.

He didn't like Mexico. He missed the greenness of France, the good wines, the good food, the bronze evening sunshine, the long straight roads through fertile fields. So far, what he had seen of Mexico indicated only poverty and harshness. The fact that it was a backward country struggling to haul itself up by its bootstraps missed him entirely.

In addition, he had realized that he was facing a major crisis. It looked now as if they were to stay in Mexico much longer than he had expected and, fully intending to be on his way home within a matter of a day or two, complete with criminals, he had gone at his Gauloise as if there were no tomorrow. Now he was counting them like a miser counting his gold.

Barribal was also constantly knocking on his door with information he had unearthed. His department had thoroughly checked the letters 'ASS' but had found nothing that might be relevant. They had covered everything from grain cleaning and sea-shell collections to a gay-lib group, and Pel had had to admit that Barribal had left no stone unturned. He had tried all that might be relevant and not one of them had heard of Professor Martin.

The following morning, dressed in a gaudy mixture of colours, his handsome face smiling, his splendid white teeth showing, he was outside the hotel with a large and expensive Mercedes car.

'It is at your disposal, Don Evaristo,' he announced.

With the assistance of Barribal's police driver, they tossed their luggage into the boot with Barribal's and set off out of the city. As they left, they went through the same drab areas of factories, garages and warehouses, then, as they began to leave the capital behind, the shabby ugly sprawl of buildings grew less compacted and they began to see small dusty patches surrounded by cactus. Tepozotlán was close to the eastern side of the main highway and Barribal turned off on to an unbelievably bumpy cobbled road. There was a splendid square in front of the church they had seen in the photographs and, opposite, a drab-looking fair complete with roundabouts and stalls and faded flags. They found the police station not far away where two policemen in dusty uniforms were lounging on a bench, and asked to see the sergeant in command.

He turned out to be a long lean, languid individual in a faded blue tunic, dusty shoes and a revolver hanging limply from the belt at his waist.

Barribal produced the picture they had of Professor Martin and a mug shot of Donck which had been prepared in Mexico City on his arrest. Overnight Barribal had had the photographic department reproduce them many times with the photograph of Jacqueline Hervé Pel had acquired from Navarro's home, and they had a folder full of them in the car.

The sergeant had seen no one even faintly resembling any of them and it occurred to Pel that perhaps he didn't ever bother to look.

'It would be difficult not to see them here in Tepozotlán,' the sergeant explained. 'It is not very big.'

'You will watch for them, nevertheless,' Barribal instructed sternly. 'If you see them you will contact police headquarters in Mexico City. *Al instante!* At once! You understand?'

The sergeant saluted and saw them to the door. The road to Tula turned east off the main highway and, for a large part, it was unmetalled so that they towed behind them an enormous cloud of yellow dust. Skinny cows, goats and horses watched them as they tried to graze where there was no grass, and occasionally they roared through poverty-stricken villages where the chickens screeched as they fled to safety.

It was a brown land, and here and there they caught glimpses of what it was like further north, harsh and unforgiving with an abrasive wind blowing into their faces. Most of the time, it was covered with low scrubby bush with occasional hedges of the maguey from which the Mexicans made their pulque. Pel stared at it gloomily. All the pictures he'd seen of Mexico had indicated a romantic land of flowers and exhilarating music and had shown nothing of the emptiness, the dust and the harsh wind. Nor, he thought bitterly, had it shown him the acres of rubbish, the cans, the bottles, the blowing paper, and the flags of torn plastic stuck on the cactus plants, that lay outside every town they passed. Mexico's rubbish-clearance schemes seemed to consist of dumping everything in the desert and leaving it to take its chance in the wind.

Finally swinging off the road, they passed through a deep dip, turned right and began to climb again. At the top of the rise they came to an enormous flat-topped man-made pyramid on which were about half-a-dozen colossal figures, blunt, square and ugly, that appeared to be carved out of solid blocks of stone. Surrounding it were the remains of square columns which appeared once to have supported the roof of a huge temple. Nearby were what appeared to be small covered chambers.

As the car stopped, a thin old man in jeans and a cowboy hat came out of an adobe dwelling and handed each of them a crumpled ticket and demanded the entrance fee. Barribal paid and De Troq' produced the pictures they'd found on Martin's film. The custodian shook his head. The pictures showed the site sure enough, he agreed, but he didn't recognize Martin. The pictures of the girl aroused some interest, however. He was sure he'd seen her somewhere before.

'Here?' De Troq' asked.

The old man shook his head and gestured towards the town in the valley below them. 'There,' he said. 'There somewhere.'

The old man was unable to help them any further so Barribal insisted they see the site instead. 'Now you're here,' he said, 'why not? Tula is very popular with the Americans.'

Pel allowed himself to be persuaded to climb to the flat top of the pyramid, but he hadn't come to Mexico to see the relics of

Mayan civilization and soon lost interest. The town of Tula itself was similar to Tepozotlán, with cobbled streets, narrow alleys and high pavements. It smelled of food and drains and was busy with traffic – small cars, the pick-up trucks the Mexicans seemed to like, and large country buses, all of which seemed to have faulty exhausts so that they sounded like jets taking off every time they moved. But Pel was also not slow to notice that there were plenty of pretty girls about and that they looked as if they could be related to the girl in the pictures they had.

The officer in command of the police station looked not unlike the man at Tepozotlán. He knew no one in the photographs they offered.

It was hot and dusty, and Barribal suggested a drink and a meal. In a square surrounded by jacarandas in full purple bloom over a pink bandstand, they found a little restaurant next to a funeral parlour displaying blue-painted coffins covered against the dust with stretched plastic. The landlord of the restaurant spoke some English and, as a long shot, De Troq' tried the pictures on him as he brought them a mess of beans, minced meat and tortillas. To their surprise, his eyebrows shot up and he almost dropped the food.

'You know them?' Barribal said.

The landlord slapped the plates down, then the bottle of wine and waved his hand.

'Dios mio, sí!' He gestured wildly at the pictures of Donck and Jacqueline Hervé. 'Not those two. That one.'

'Which one?'

He pointed at the picture of Professor Martin. 'He came here. In here.' He pointed at the floor between his feet. 'He had a meal. She served him.'

'Who did?'

'That one.' The proprietor's hand was flapping at the picture of the unknown girl. '*She* served him.'

Their long shot had brought a bonus.

'Here?' De Troq' asked.

'Yes! Yes!' The landlord gestured excitedly. 'Here! She work for me. That is Pilar Hernandez. She is not a good girl. She –' he gestured at his knees '– the skirts. Too short, señores. *La blusa* –

the blouse –' his hand flapped near his chest '– too low. She is too fond of the men.'

'And she served *this* man?'

'Yes, your honour. They talk much. I hear them laughing. Then he go away. The next day she does not come to work and when I go to her home, she is not there. She has disappear.'

'With this man?'

The landlord shrugged. '*Quién sabe?* How do we know? I never see her since. Her parents are worried. But not *too* worried because she has disappear before. Once to Mexico City. Also with a man.'

'This man?'

'No, señor. That was Salazar Gómez, who keeps the store by the main road. He is a goat, that one, and he has nine children.'

They seemed to have struck gold.

'She lives here then?' Pel asked.

'*Sí*, señor. Though whether she is here now, I don' know. Perhaps she has go off again with the man in the picture. She is mad, that one. Always talking about films. Some man she go off with give her an extra's part in a film he is making near Durango and after that she thinks she is going to be a film star. But he leave her flat and she come back.'

Once more Pel jabbed a finger at the picture of Martin. 'What about this one?'

'He was here, señor. On the 17th. I remember. It is my wife's day off and she doesn't work that day so that Pilar serve him his meal. They talk a lot. I hear them laughing. I don' mind. He is the only customer and he buy a large bottle of wine. Later he go and the next day she doesn't appear. I tell you.'

'Do her family live in Tula?'

'*Sí señor. Calle Vicenza, numero – momento, señor*, I have the number in the kitchen.' The landlord shot off and came back with a large number seven written on a piece of torn card. '*Numero siete*. It is behind the Franciscan church.'

They finished their meal in a hurry. It was so heavily spiced, to Pel it was like eating fire.

The Calle Vicenza was a narrow winding street behind a market where Indian women crouched with a dozen beans on a piece of newspaper, hoping for a sale. It was noisy, scruffy and littered with fragments of old vegetables, but there were a few surprisingly modern shops. As the Mercedes slowed to a stop, a lorry was delivering carboys of what looked like acid.

'Water,' Barribal said. 'You have to buy it. When God created the world, He left Mexico until last and, after six days of hard labour and looking forward to a Sunday with His feet up, He allowed His hand to slip. He forgot the water. There is never enough.'

The Hernandez house was a flat-fronted, flat-roofed, terraced dwelling with its green-painted plank door opening directly on to the street because there was no pavement. When they told the owner what they were seeking, he gestured to them to enter.

'La casa a Usted,' he said. 'The house is yours.'

The room they entered was empty of furniture but full of pictures in small frames – madonnas, crucifixes, and photographs of men in uniform. Through another door they could see a small sun-bright yard.

Both Pilar Hernandez's parents were good-looking which, they supposed, was why their daughter was beautiful, but they had no idea where she was because she was always disappearing and reappearing without explanation.

'She learn English,' her mother said in careful precise words. 'That is trouble. She is also too pretty. Too many men want her.'

'She is film mad,' she went on. 'Always she talk about becoming a film star.'

She jerked aside a curtain to reveal a small alcove with a single iron bedstead in it, covered with a threadbare blanket and faded coverlet. The walls were plastered with pictures of film stars. Most of them were Mexicans Pel had never heard of but there were a few Americans – even one French one – that he recognized.

The woman fished under the bed and produced a pile of magazines which she tossed down with a gesture. *Las Películas,* Pel noticed, and *Las Estrellas de Cine.* Even he could translate those. *Films. Film stars.*

Señora Hernandez sighed. 'Always she talk about it,' she said. 'She is beautiful, of course. But she have no chance. She cannot act.'

She had never seen Martin, whose photographs she studied through a magnifying glass, so they had to assume that Pilar Hernandez had never brought him home.

Outside again, they debated whether to try any further. Barribal was in favour of getting the local police on the job but Pel had not been impressed by the Mexican local police and suggested trying San Miguel instead, because quite obviously Martin had been there – and judging by the order of the pictures on the reel they had found – after he'd been to Tula.

'OK, it is easy from here,' Barribal said. 'We take the road out of Tula to the main highway and then head north past Querétaro to San Miguel. A few minutes. No more.'

Unfortunately it wasn't as easy as they'd expected. Barribal's map failed to agree with the signs and the signs were loose in their sockets and often pointed the wrong way, so that eventually they found themselves in Querétaro. There was some sort of procession taking place and the police were out in force closing streets to the traffic so that they went round in circles for half an hour before Barribal lost his temper and made a police sergeant remove barriers so they could pass.

By this time Pel was sunk in gloom, certain he was on a wild goose chase and more than ever convinced that he ought never to have come to Mexico. As they stopped for lunch at a restaurant alongside the road, built and operated in American style, he spread the photographs they had taken from Martin's reel in front of them on the table.

'The girl's interest in the case is nothing,' he said, heavily. 'She's obviously just some little tart Martin picked up and used to enjoy himself. They're probably tucked away somewhere now in a hotel. The pictures he took of the remains at Tula also have no significance whatsoever. She simply took him there to have a look at them.'

'But why did he go to Tula anyway, *patron*?' De Troq' said. 'It's off the main road. Why go there?'

'Not to look at the Mayan remains.'

'They did, though, *patron*.'

'I think she wanted to. He picked her up. That's what she was – a pick-up. He fancied her in the restaurant and arranged to meet her the next day, and then, or soon after, they went to the Mayan remains. He wanted to see them – not because there was anything there for him but because they just happened to be there. She'd probably never seen them.'

'She lived in Tula, *patron*.'

'All the more reason why she'd never seen them. Have you ever been up the Eiffel Tower in Paris?'

'No.'

'Have you ever been in the Ducal Palace at home?'

'On duty. An enquiry. That's all.'

'The last thing anyone ever looks at is what's under their nose. She'd probably lived in Tula all her life and never bothered to visit the place until Martin turned up. She was feeling full of beans and he fancied looking at the remains, so she suggested it. But it isn't the Mayan remains *he* was interested in. If they had been, there'd have been better photographs. He knew how to use a camera but he never seemed to focus on the antiquities.' Pel spread the pictures out for them to see. 'Just the girl. The Mayan remains just happened to be there. No, it was something else.'

He stared at the photographs again, eventually concentrating on the pictures of the strange wooden houses. One of them had curtains blowing through the window and there was what appeared to be a well in the centre of the street, and what seemed to be a saloon, but, apart from the row of men sleeping in the sun, there was no sign of life.

'You know what these remind me of,' he said. 'Films of the Wild West. Built of wood, flat-fronted with boardwalks.'

'As in Arizona or Kansas,' Barribal agreed. 'Dodge City. Somewhere like that. With John Wayne. I have see them, too. But they don't build houses like that any longer, not even in Kansas or Arizona or Dodge City. They need somewhere for the air-conditioner and the icebox and the washing-machine and the Coca Cola. American towns don't look like that these days. And the numbers, Don Evaristo.' He fished out the negatives and looked at the numbers. 'They come on the reel before the pictures of Tula. And we know he was in Tula on the 17th. So if they're pictures of Arizona or Kansas, he probably went to America. But he wouldn't go up there then come back to Mexico. *Madonna* –' he studied the pictures for a long time, frowning deeply, then he rose. 'I got a magnifying glass in my brief-case,' he said flashing his magnificent teeth at them. 'Let us take a closer look.'

Returning with the magnifying glass, Barribal studied Pel through it, one huge magnified eye staring at him. Pel glared back at him.

'Sherlock Holmes, Don Evaristo,' he said. 'You ever read about that guy?'

Pel had and he didn't think much of him. 'A very English detective,' he said coldly. 'Not very clever.'

They bent over the pictures and Barribal suddenly gestured. 'Those goddamn buildings have got no backs to them!' he said, lifting his head to stare at Pel.

He passed over the magnifying glass and Pel studied the pictures. Sure enough, it was possible to see sunshine behind the windows of the houses in the pictures.

'They don't have roofs, either,' he said. 'They're nothing but façades. Just the front walls. Nothing else.'

Barribal frowned. 'Who builds a house without a back to it?' he asked. For a long time he studied the prints. 'It says on this one, "Wesley's Emporium",' he announced. 'That don't sound very Mexican.' He studied the prints again, then he slapped his thigh.

'*Madonna!*' he said. 'I've got it! This isn't a Mexican village! It's a film set.'

Pel gaped at him.

'There are several in Mexico, *mí jefe,*' Barribal explained. 'There are two I know of – both near Durango. There's also one near Taxco in Morelos. The *Norteamericanos* often make films here because it is cheaper. The extras don't ask so much. They eat tortillas and minced beef instead of steaks. Several films are shot. They build the sets. Whole streets of houses like this. A church. A saloon. The heroine's home. The heroine's always the schoolmistress. You know the *Norteamericanos* – very sentimental about schoolmistresses. The territory is right also, because Mexico look like Arizona or Texas. There's more than one place like this.'

'And which is this?'

Barribal grinned his wide white-toothed smile. 'Not the one in Morelos. The country's wrong. This is the one near San Miguel. That hill in the background's the Cerro del Mercado. Two hundred metres high and solid iron ore. I am up there two years ago when some guy murders the manager of the mine for the petty cash. It is near the village of Chapadores. That is why there are guys in the picture. It is right alongside the main road to San Miguel, after you turn off the highway past Querétaro. They got steers there. It's a staging post because the railway runs close by and on to the slaughter yards. Very interesting.'

Pel frowned. 'I think,' he said thoughtfully, 'that it would be as well if we went there.'

11

They filled up at a petrol station operated by an entire family. While Father pumped in the petrol, Mother and children washed and polished with rags or merely with their sleeves. An hour later they had stopped by the film set.

It wasn't easy to distinguish it at first because it lay well back off the main road and there was no sign to indicate where it was. The village of Chapadores was there, though, a long straggly adobe village with the usual church, and with sheep and goats and pigs and chickens in the street. Raisin-eyed children in rags studied them solemnly as they passed, moving slowly and trailing the inevitable cloud of dust.

Finally Barribal jerked a hand. 'There it is!'

Higher up the slope, connected by the winding dirt road through the village, they could see what looked like wooden-frame houses and a church spire.

'This is the place,' Barribal said at once. 'That's not a Mexican church. Our bishops always built them big and imposing. They preferred to spend money on buildings instead of on people.'

After a while they came to cattle milling round in a corral, and two or three men with a truck lashing a gate in place with ropes. They took no notice of them as they passed, not even lifting their heads to look at them. They had obviously taken over the corral built by the film makers for their film and were totally absorbed in what they were doing. Then they passed a row of houses where dusty curtains blew in the breeze, past the 'Wesley's Emporium' of the photograph with its stoop, and a place signed as the 'Bar 2', its swing doors hanging awry on their hinges.

As Barribal stopped the car, they peered out, warily almost, as if they expected a posse of lawmen in stetsons on horses to swing out from behind the wooden façades and arrest them. Now they were close, they could see the emptiness beyond the doors and windows. Here and there, where filming had obviously taken place, crude shelters had been built behind them to throw the windows into darkness and give the impression of living homes beyond.

Outside the car it was cold in the wind despite the sunshine, and Pel even found himself wishing he had brought Madame Pel's knitted sweater.

'It is the height,' Barribal said. 'We have left the bowl of Mexico for the highlands.'

It was an eerie sensation to stand in the middle of the empty street, surrounded by the ghosts of a long-dead film. No one had stopped them, no one had shown any interest, and the people of Chapadores had clearly made no attempt to use any of the old buildings.

'Why was he interested in *this* place?' Barribal mused. 'Why did he take photographs of it?'

As they stood among the empty buildings, they heard a motor vehicle start, then, at the end of the street, a car shot away. Barribal's head jerked round.

'That's a police truck,' he snapped. 'What's happening?'

He set off on his long legs down the dusty street between the empty façades, followed by Pel and De Troq'. At the end, near the wooden mock-up of the church, there was the well they'd seen in the photographs and, to the left, hidden by the wooden frames of the buildings, a small square, where there was an impression of a stable and a group of dwelling houses. A group of men stood by a pick-up truck, and a police car was parked in front of one of the 'houses'. With them was a group of ragged children. As Barribal marched up to them, a policeman in the usual dusty blue uniform, his peaked cap pulled down over his eyes, looked up, then turned and marched self-importantly towards them.

'*Alto*,' he said. '*Policía!*'

Barribal didn't argue. He simply fished out his identity card and flipped it. The policeman immediately backed away, stiffened and tossed up what was meant to be a salute. For a second, the two of them talked quietly, then Barribal turned to Pel.

'Something queer here,' he said. 'Someone – a woman, they

say – telephone – they think long-distance – to let them know there is a body under one of the stoops. She leave no name and she is very brief. At the same time some of the *muchachos* from Chapadores come up here. They do sometimes. They pick up a bad smell and inform the father of one of the kids. He come up and recognize the smell at once and tell the police. His call comes just after the other.'

The men standing in a group had spades, Pel noticed, and he moved closer, his nostrils wrinkling at the unmistakable sweetish smell that came out at him.

'I think we've probably found Martin,' he said.

Barribal crossed himself, quick dabs at his breast with his finger tips. 'I think we have,' he agreed.

An hour later, they stood back, holding their noses. Around them were the remains of the wooden stoop on one of the houses. The men had ripped the planks up and were now staring into the hole they'd dug beneath the frame.

'That him?' Barribal asked.

'That's him,' Pel said.

'Somebody tortured him, *patron*,' De Troq' said. 'His hands are tied and you can see cigarette burns. They beat him up and shot him. Why?'

'He was beaten to find out something,' Pel said. 'And he was shot because then he'd become dangerous. He might have gone to the police.'

Barribal was busy organizing the removal of the body. The police truck had returned with a police officer to whom Barribal turned over the whole affair.

'It is not my business,' he explained to Pel. 'He is here a long time. Only because nobody come here is he not found. But I don' want to be tied down here. I've ask for a full report and I come back here tomorrow. It's late in the day now and we must be in San Miguel before it is dark. We can leave the local guys in charge.'

As Barribal moved away, De Troq' moved closer to Pel. 'Who was it informed the police, *patron*? Pilar Hernandez?'

'Or Jacqueline Hervé?'

De Troq' looked puzzled. 'Why her?'

Pel shrugged. 'Well, it wouldn't be Pilar Hernandez, would it? *She* strikes me as a rather dim, film-struck girl and *she* wouldn't wish to be involved in this. And she certainly wouldn't kill Martin, because she had no reason to torture him and certainly wouldn't want him dead. He was giving her too good a time. That was Donck.'

'So why would Jacqueline Hervé telephone the police and put them on to it?'

'Was she dumping Donck?' Pel lit a cigarette and blew out smoke. 'It's odd, don't you think, that although she was prepared to help Donck get rid of Navarro and was willing to bolt from France with him, she never visited him in prison? Could it be that she'd had enough of murder and was scared – probably of Donck, too, by this time. After all, with this one, he'd killed three people and that's enough to scare most women. Perhaps she wanted to bolt. She's probably in Brazil now.' Pel paused. 'Mind you,' he admitted, 'that's only a guess.'

De Troq' studied him. 'All the same, *patron*,' he said, 'it's probably not a bad one.'

When Barribal returned, Pel stopped him. 'You know who did it, don't you?' Pel said.

'Sure. This Donck. You know what this means, don't you?' Barribal grinned. 'We now have a murderer here in Mexico. And that means that *we* want that guy, too, so *you* can't have him. We also have to show results, to provide good statistics, and I shall want to see him on charges in Mexico. Here. In the San Miguel district. It will be good for promotion.'

'I have two murders to your one,' Pel pointed out coldly.

Barribal grinned. 'But this is Mexico,' he said. 'You know the saying. Anything can happen in Mexico, and usually does.'

'We'll discuss that later.'

'Sure. Right now I want to know why they kill him and why they torture him.'

'To get something they were after,' Pel said.

'Proceeds of a big hold-up perhaps?' Barribal suggested. 'But we haven't had any. Not lately. There may be some that have been forgotten that this Donck has learned about. But we've been doing well lately. We have a good record. A few guys are murdered. A few are arrested. But nobody get any loot we don' know about and haven't recovered.'

Pel studied the Mexican for a moment. 'Donck and the woman came up here,' he said. 'Borrillas told us they were coming to Querétaro. Why? To meet Martin? Perhaps they were looking for him. Perhaps they found his hotel in Querétaro and learned where he'd gone. They followed him and finally came up with him here.'

'We check,' Barribal said. 'I'll tell the police in Querétaro to ask at the hotels.'

'I'd rather know *why* they wanted him,' Pel pointed out. 'And what this "treasure" was that Borillas heard them talking about, Borillas said he thought it was something old.'

'We don' have a record of hidden loot that far back.'

'Did these Mayans and Aztecs have gold?'

Barribal grinned. 'Sure did. But I guess it's all been found now.'

'Could some have been missed?'

'Could, I think. But how would Donck know about it?'

'Martin? He was a historian. Donck obviously forced him to tell them.'

'Antique civilizations weren't his interest, *patron*,' De Troq' insisted. 'Historians have to cover a lot of ground and most of them specialize. Martin's interest wasn't Mayan civilization. That we know.'

Pel turned and he explained. 'In France, for instance, one historian will know about the Revolution. One will deal with Louis XIV. One with De Gaulle. In Mexico, it'll be the same. One will deal with the antique civilizations, one with the war of independence, one with the great revolution. Navarro was checking on the French intervention.'

The hotel in San Miguel de Allende was right opposite the main square, an old colonial house with the rooms built above a courtyard containing trees, bougainvillaea and a fountain. Clearly it was aimed at the Americans. It was spotless, efficient and well-ordered and, as Barribal had promised, a call at the police station fixed it so that rooms were available without argument. Pel's was at the back but, as he didn't fancy missing what was going on at the front, he insisted on exchanging with Barribal. Barribal smiled, shrugged and didn't argue.

It was late afternoon by this time and all the shops appeared to be shut.

'The siesta,' Barribal explained. 'They open in the evening.'

The Comisaría de Policía was just up the road, in a flat-faced building with a wide opening leading into a room where several uniformed men lounged. They were shown through to the officer in command and introduced.

'*El Jefe* Don Evaristo Pel,' Barribal said. '*El Sargento* De Troquereau. They are famous policemen from Europe involved in a case here in Mexico.'

The Chief of Police rose and shook hands, and in faultless English with an American accent offered chairs and drinks.

'British?' he asked.

Pel was indignant. 'French,' he snapped.

They produced Martin's photographs and the police chief stared at them. They didn't ring a bell of any sort and he summoned his secretary and asked for the chief of detectives. The chief of detectives was a small man in green trousers, a yellow shirt and a white tie. His jacket was American in style with loud check.

They studied the pictures again. Nobody, it appeared had seen either Professor Martin or Donck or Jacqueline Hervé, but the Chief of Police frowned.

'The girl,' he said, pointing to the photograph of Pilar Hernandez. 'Who is she? *Una turista Norteamericano?*'

'She's some little *mujercilla* from Tula,' Barribal said. 'She's left there more than once and returned. This time she went off with the man in the photographs whom my French *compañeros* are looking for. A Professor Henri Martin who's been found dead under the stoop of one of the houses in the film set at Chapadores.'

The police chief looked up. 'I've just heard of that.'

'It's murder,' Barribal said. His finger touched the pictures of Donck and Jacqueline Hervé. 'We think these two – also French – were responsible, and that –' the thick spatulate finger rested on the picture of Pilar Hernandez '– that this woman might know something about it.'

The police chief picked up the picture of the girl and stared at it.

'I know this girl,' he said. 'I've seen her somewhere.'

Everybody it seemed, had seen Pilar Hernandez.

'I wish I could think where,' the police chief said. 'I've seen that face.' He smiled. 'She is beautiful enough to be memorable.'

During the evening the loudspeakers attached to the bandstand in the square came to life. At first what they had to offer was dance music then abruptly it changed, and a high tenor voice broke into 'Che gelida manina', from *La Bohème*.

Barribal grinned. 'The band only play at the weekend,' he said. 'The rest of the week they play tapes from the mayor's office and the mayor like opera. His secretary like jazz but when he comes in he makes him take off the tape and put on opera.'

Barribal seemed happy enough and so did De Troq', but Pel had no ear for music and considered opera consisted of rugby-forward-sized people yelling across a stage at each other. But it was a case of like it or lump it and the singing went on all evening.

By this time, Pel was tired of Mexican food, which he felt burned away his palate so that he would never enjoy real food – Burgundian food – ever again, so Barribal found a small restaurant down a side street that ran from the main square opposite the hotel. It was suffocatingly hot and was full of Americans, and the food, not Mexican food, was dreadful, while the proprietor, a saintly faced New Yorker, told them he served only non-alcoholic drinks. Pel sat through the meal glowering with disgust. A Frenchman didn't eat steak – however indifferent – with coffee or Coca Cola. Afterwards, they sat in a bar in the main street drinking brandy. The opera had finished – obviously the mayor had gone home – and the loudspeakers were broadcasting a brass band. It was different from French bands, more tinny, more shrill, more ear-piercing.

Barribal struck up a conversation with an American girl and, as they whispered in a corner, Pel leaned towards De Troq'. 'What's he saying?' he asked.

De Troq' smiled his careful smile. 'Sweet nothings, *patron*. The usual clichés. Good Spanish compliments. *Vida de mi vida. Alma de mi alma. Amor de mi amor.*'

'What's that mean?'

'Life of my life, soul of my soul, love of my love.'

'People don't still speak like that.'

'They seem to in Mexico. Barribal certainly does.'

'After only a couple of drinks, too!' Pel pulled a face then he nodded solemnly, noting the words for future use. They would please his wife. He stared at Barribal, who had straightened up now, handsome, immaculate – even if gaudy – in his dress, and was flashing his splendid white teeth at the girl.

'Who does he remind you of?' Pel asked.

De Troq' grinned. 'Inspector Darcy, *patron*.'

'I'm glad you noticed, too.'

De Troq' smiled. 'Have you also noticed, *patron*, that his driver looks like Misset?'

Pel's eyebrows rose. That was a thought. Were policemen duplicated in other countries? Were there Darcys and Missets – even Pels – all over the world? Were there such people as Daniel Aleksandrovich Darcyskis? Were there English, Russian and Italian Missets? It was a terrifying prospect.

After a while, the girl rose and left and soon afterwards Barribal discovered he had business to attend to at the police station. They noticed, however, that he went in the direction the girl had taken, which was opposite to that which would have led him to the police station.

Since the shops were still open, Pel felt it was time to buy the gold necklace he had promised his wife. He had tried sending a postcard to her but the post office had been out of every kind of stamp but the lowest denomination and he had had to stick on so many there had been room only for the words, *Love, Pel*.

He found the right shop without difficulty. No one spoke either French or English but it didn't worry him. He had never had any doubts how to pronounce foreign words. You simply decided, pronounced them, and stood by your decision, and if there were problems you just shouted louder.

Returning to the hotel, he had a last drink with De Troq' in the courtyard and went to his room. As he started to undress, he realized why Barribal had offered no objection when he had insisted on changing rooms. While the sun was out, the flocks of magpies which inhabited the jacarandas in the square had made the daylight hideous with their chatter. Now it was the brass band. Car horns also sounded constantly, as if the owners were driving round and round the square, honking at the girls, while the chatter of the magpies had been replaced by the shouts and shrieks of young men and women.

It was long after midnight when he fell into a shallow sleep. He remembered hearing three dogfights during the night, with what appeared to be about ten Alsatians on each side and three-minute rounds. Drowsily he wondered why sixty Alsatians would want to start a fight at three o'clock in the morning.

Now there was a youth singing – *'Y si Adelita se fuera con otro'* – for some unknown reason in the street outside and then – perhaps because of it – he found he had a severe case of indigestion and was convinced he was dying, but couldn't conceive how it had happened, because he had been well aware of the dangers of Mexican food and had chewed everything he had eaten thirty-two times before swallowing it. It hadn't been easy to make minced meat go that far but he had managed it, and he felt twinges of resentment that it hadn't worked.

The girl, Pilar Hernandez, kept coming to his mind, and he dreamed he was chasing her round the old film set but could never catch her.

As he came to consciousness it seemed everyone else in the place, every other man, woman, child, beast and cockerel, to say nothing of the lorry drivers, who were already moving their jet-propelled vehicles about the town, had also awakened and there was a cocktail of calling voices, braying, crowing and barking and the high revving of engines. To the last moment he had been dreaming of chasing Pilar Hernandez, then somebody had levelled a shot-gun at him, but instead of the crash of a shot it was the jarring of a bell.

He sat bolt upright in bed to realize it was daylight and that the first vehicles of the new day were moving up and down the hill past the hotel. Bells were going like mad all over the town and he decided that St Paulinus, who was reputed to have invented the church bell, had a lot to answer for. As he stared about him, the telephone bell rang again and he snatched it up.

'Don Evaristo Pel?' the voice said. *'Jefe de Policía Francesa.'*

It was enough like *Chef de Police* for Pel to be able to answer. *'Sí,'* he said. 'Pel.'

'Momento.'

There was a series of clicks and buzzes then a voice came on the line. It was speaking Spanish and Pel looked round in a panic for help. Then it changed and he heard English with a thick American accent.

'Chief Inspector Don Evaristo Pel?'

'Yes.'

'Ah, Don Evaristo. This is Police Chief Cardeñas. We met yesterday.'

What in God's name, Pel wondered, was the Chief of Police wanting at this time of the morning? Surely not to say it wasn't Martin they'd found the previous afternoon.

'I have thought thoughts, Don Evaristo.'

'Oh?'

'The girl. I have tried to contact Inspector Barribal, but I am informed he is out.'

He would be, Pel thought.

'I have therefore decided to speak to you. *Momento.*' Pel heard pages rattling, then the voice came again. 'Pilar Hernandez. I have remembered where I saw her.'

'What?' Pel scrambled for a piece of paper and a pencil to write down the address. 'Where?'

'The Posada San Francisco.'

'Posada San Francisco?' Pel muttered the words as he scrawled them frantically. What in God's name was the Posada San Francisco, he wondered. A bar? A brothel?

'The Posada San Francisco,' he said. 'Where is it?'

There was a laugh from the other end of the line and the police chief's fruity voice came again. 'Right there, señor. You're on top of it. It's the hotel where you're staying. She works there.'

12

Normally, Pel liked to start the day with a smile and – if you were lucky – a breezy comment. He knew the mood wouldn't last long so he always felt it would be best to get it out of the way and then he could forget it for the next twenty-four hours and go about his business, concentrating on what was happening. But that was in normal circumstances, when he came to consciousness normally, slowly, anticipating his breakfast and his first cigarette of the day.

This was different. He glanced at the clock and saw it was the unearthly hour of 7.30. He couldn't imagine what the Chief of Police was doing about at that hour of the morning – and cheerful too! – and his reaction was twice as strong. De Troq', still dozing in a room along the corridor, leapt to life at the thunderous knocking on his door, then, ignoring all the niceties, Pel burst in.

He was in his dressing-gown and was unshaven, and a few thin strands of hair stood straight up on his head like the crest of a cockatoo.

'*Patron!* What's wrong?'

'That woman! Pilar Hernandez! I've found her! She's here! In this hotel! She works here!'

'What?'

'Get up! Get dressed! We need to get on to this before she disappears again.'

De Troq' had been thinking of his breakfast coffee and rolls and he didn't take kindly to the suggestion of immediacy. 'I'll get dressed and get some breakfast, *patron*.'

'There's no time,' Pel snapped. 'We might lose her.'

De Troq' picked up the telephone. 'I'll have a word with the manager, *patron*,' he said. 'I'll tell him to get hold of her and hang on to her, *then* we'll get dressed and have breakfast.'

Pel scowled, wondering why he hadn't thought of that, and he listened as De Troq' spoke in Spanish into the phone. The phone clattered back at him, then De Troq' smiled and replaced the receiver.

'We've lost her again, *patron*,' he said quietly.

'What?'

'She's not here any more.'

'Where is she?'

'That was the assistant manager,' De Troq' said. 'The manager doesn't appear until later and the place is run in his absence by three under-managers. That was the early shift. He knows the girl and says, yes, she did work here. But not any more.'

'Why not?'

'She just left. She didn't let them know. She didn't turn up. It seems to be a habit of hers.'

Pel glared. This, he felt, was cheating, and he began to think horrible things about the police chief for waking him up so unnecessarily. But then, as De Troq' held out a packet of cigarettes and he drew the first lungful of smoke down, he came to his senses and realized that, though their quarry had disappeared again, at least they had picked up her trail.

'So what's happened?'

'The under-manager says he'll make enquiries. He suggests we take breakfast and then call on him and he'll supply us with whatever he's found out. It seems sensible, *patron*.'

Even Pel had to admit that it was.

They were finishing their coffee when Barribal appeared. He looked a little hung-over.

He ordered coffee, lit a cigarette and brushed a hand across his forehead. 'I have quite a night,' he said. 'American girls!' He kissed his fingertips. '*Mucho caliente*! Very hot.'

He chattered about the girl he'd seen the night before, the state of the economy, the police chief in Mexico City, whom he seemed to hold in great contempt, and the number of American girls in Mexico.

'They got the post-mortem report on this *hombre*, Professor Martin,' he said. 'He'd been tortured all right. Cigarette burns on his chest, just like we say. His fingers are broken. And he is beaten up. Whoever put him there want something from him very bad. I'll see you get a copy of the report.'

He was still talking with his mouth full when Pel told him what they'd learned about Pilar Hernandez.

'*Qué?*' Crumbs exploded from Barribal's mouth as he sat bolt upright. 'What? You find her?'

'*We* didn't. The police chief did. She was here. In this hotel.'

'Living here?'

'Not quite. Working here.'

'Then why don't we go talk to her?'

'Because she isn't here any more. She's left. She's always one step in front of us. We're due to see the under-manager. He's making enquiries. We can go as soon as you've finished.'

'I've finished!' Barribal swallowed the rest of his coffee and clattered the cup back to the saucer. 'Let's go!'

'Agostino P. Vey', the triangular strip of wood on the desk announced, and Pel noticed that on the other upright side, facing away from them, it said 'Calo H. Fernandez'. Doubtless the bottom of the three sides, the side on which it rested, carried the name of the third under-manager. It seemed a good idea and a great saving in expense.

Agostino P. Vey was a slim young man, beautifully dressed in a dark suit with an immaculate white shirt and sombre tie. Obviously the Posada San Francisco, conscious of its American visitors, liked to put on a good front.

'Pilar Hernandez,' he said in American-accented English. 'She came here three weeks ago and asked for a job. The housekeeper, Señora Ramirez, took her on. She was an attractive girl and she said she had come from Mexico City looking for work.'

'She hadn't,' Pel said. 'She came from Tula with a man. He probably left her, to do some business he was occupied on, and he was murdered. His body was found at Chapadores yesterday. He's a Frenchman. That's why I'm here.'

Agostino P. Vey listened carefully, then he nodded. 'I heard about that. Inspector Barribal spoke to me about it.'

He would, Pel thought. 'When did she leave?' he asked.

'One week ago. She wasn't satisfactory and Señora Ramirez suspected her of going to the rooms of male guests at night. Then, during the day a week ago, she was seen talking to a Señor Arkwright. He's an American who has a house up the hill. They seemed to be deep in conversation. The following day she didn't appear.'

Pilar Hernandez's habit of talking to men and then disappearing obviously hadn't left her.

'After twenty-four hours we replaced her,' Vey said.

'This Arkwright? Who is he?'

Vey turned to a pad by his elbow. 'George R. Arkwright. An American. Very wealthy. He doesn't have a good reputation here. He's often in town. He comes in here to drink occasionally. We don't like him but we can't forbid him because the bar's open to the public. She isn't the first girl we've lost in this way.'

'To Arkwright?'

'*Sí*, señor. They go to work at his house. At least, that's what is said. Then we hear of them back in the town working somewhere. It seems he tires of them quickly.'

'This *hombre* got a bad reputation?' Barribal asked.

'I have heard that the police have made enquiries about him. I understand he's been warned.'

'I think we better go see Señor Arkwright.' Barribal smiled grimly. 'But first we call on the police and see what they know of him. It might help.'

He borrowed Vey's phone and spoke into it for a few minutes, then he rose and gestured. 'We got him,' he said. 'They know him.'

Outside the police station, they stopped while Barribal disappeared. He came back with a sheet of paper in his hand and a wide grin on his face.

'He's been warned about young girls,' he said. 'Under-age girls. It is not hard in Mexico to tempt girls with money. There's not a lot of it about. Let's go.'

Climbing from the town, they soon found Arkwright's house. It stood at the top of the steep hill above the town, close to a modern motel called La Ermita and set back from the road behind a white-painted board fence that was entirely American. Around it, it had a hectare of land, the outer edges of which seemed to consist largely of rocks and cactus, though close to the house there were green lawns, flowering shrubs and potted cactus. The veranda was ablaze with bougainvillaea.

George R. Arkwright certainly seemed to be very wealthy because there appeared to be an army of servants working on the garden and another army busy with dusters, feather mops and vacuum cleaners in the spacious interior. The house was built in Spanish style with barred windows, white walls, dark furniture and brightly coloured rugs and furnishings.

They announced themselves and asked to see Arkwright. The elderly Mexican woman who let them in nodded, bobbed a curtsey and turned away. A moment or two later, Arkwright himself appeared. He was middle-aged, large, fat, and full of smiles. He wore linen trousers, a red shirt and sandals.

'Police, hey?' he boomed. 'Don't often get a visit from the police. What have I done wrong?'

Barribal hastened to point out that he'd done nothing wrong but that they were making enquiries about a body which had been found on the film set at Chapadores.

'Hell, I read about that. Nothing to do with me.' Arkwright gestured. 'Siddown. Make yourselves at home. Lemme get you a drink.' As he busied himself at a table where the bottles stood he talked over his shoulder. 'Nice place I got here, don't you think, hey? My Dad spent all his life making money and expected me to. Pet food. That was his line. It wasn't for me. I didn't even like the smell. But he kept me at it, teaching me the business, showing me how to watch costs and cut corners. When he died, I sold it within a month. National chain. Glad to have it. Me, I was glad to get out.'

He handed them their drinks, his face wreathed in smiles. 'Didn't even like Chicago where we lived. Moved around some. Ended up here. Here, I can live as well as my old man did without lifting a finger. Mex's cheap. The greasers work for nothing. I can live without hardly disturbing my capital. Hardly bites into the interest the bank makes for me.'

'Pilar Hernandez,' Pel said quietly.

Immediately Arkwright's face changed. 'What's that?'

'Pilar Hernandez. You know her, I believe.'

Holding his glass in his hand, Arkwright studied them for some time. Then he took a quick swallow and stared at them again, this time aggressively.

'So what? It's no business of the police.'

'It might be,' Barribal said.

'Hell, I know these folk here don't like me none. They think I got too much money. They think because I have parties up here and invite a few local girls, I'm dangerous. Sump'n wrong with havin' parties, havin' a few dames in?'

Barribal said nothing and Arkwright went on. 'OK,' he said. 'There've been complaints but they all got sorted out.'

'The girl, Pilar Hernandez.'

'She's above age. She's twenty-one. Nothin' wrong with that, is there? She came of her own free will and accord. I didn't lasso her, tie her up and bring her up in the back of the estate wagon.'

'We think she knew the man who was found dead at Chapadores.' Pel said. 'He was a French professor and she met him in Tula as he was on his way north from Mexico City.'

'So what? I didn't ask what her background was. I'm not a judge of morals. I ain't got that many myself.'

'Is she here?'

Arkwright stared at them, then swallowed the rest of his drink. 'I don't have to answer that,' he said.

'Yes, you do, señor,' Barribal snapped, and for the first time Pel began to concede to himself that perhaps Barribal was not mad after all and, in fact, was probably a good policeman who hid his efficiency behind a façade of light-heartedness. 'If you don't, in fact, I arrange for your residence permit to be taken away from you.'

Arkwright sneered. 'Listen, cop, I've got enough money to fix you any time.'

'I don' think so, señor. Mexicans are poor compared with your country but some of them are honest. You don' answer our questions, I will have you declared an undesirable alien. Then you will have to go back to the States. Or maybe you prefer Brazil or Uruguay?'

Arkwright's stare had become a glare. 'That's the trouble with this goddamn country,' he said. 'Too goddamn moral. All those goddamn priests. They're everywhere and –'

'Señor –' Barribal's voice cut sharply into the diatribe so that Arkwright stopped dead '– we wish to see the girl. Is she here?'

Arkwright was silent for a while, obviously considering the pros and cons. 'Yeah,' he admitted at last. 'An' you guys had better take her away. I don' want nothin' to do with girls who're involved with the law. I gotta clean record.'

'Not all that clean,' Barribal said, smiling. 'Would you like to see it? I take the precaution of bringing a copy with me.'

Arkwright muttered to himself and dragged at a bell pull. When the old woman appeared, he gestured with his glass. 'Pilar,' he said. 'Tell Pilar to come here.'

The girl entered quickly then, as she saw the three policemen, she seemed to sense danger. Her quick stride faltered and she entered the room slowly. Arkwright, who was busy filling himself a fresh glass, gestured.

'You damn floozie!' he said. 'You got me into trouble with the police!'

'Police?' She looked at the three policemen. 'What I do?'

'What didn't you do?' Arkwright exploded. 'I wish to Christ I'd never seen you.'

'I do nothing wrong. I'm a good girl.'

'Tell that to the Marines.'

Barribal interposed his big frame between them. 'Sit down, señorita,' he said. 'You speak English?'

'Yes.'

'She speaks it well,' Arkwright said. 'I guess all the guys she's been with taught her.'

'Be quiet,' Barribal snapped. He gestured at Pel.

'Henri Martin,' Pel said quietly to the girl. 'French. A professor of history. Did you know him?'

Her eyes flickered to Arkwright, then to Barribal, to De Troq', and back to Pel. 'Yes,' she said warily. 'I have meet this man.'

'Did you know he's been found dead.'

'On the film set at Chapadores,' Arkwright said. 'These guys found him.'

'I have not see him for five weeks. I not know where he is.' She didn't seem upset and Pel guessed she found it easy to transfer her affections.

'When did you see him last?'

'Long time ago. He give me his luggage to look after.'

'What sort of luggage?'

'Jus' a suitcase and a holdall.'

'He also had a camera. I think it was a good one. What happened to that?'

Her eyes flickered and he guessed she'd sold it and kept the money. 'I don' see no camera,' she said.

'What happened to Martin?'

'He say he has business. We come here. In a car. Then he put me down, give me his bag to look after, and say he will be back later in the day. He give me money for a meal and say, "Buy yourself something."'

'Tell me exactly what happened. From the time you met him in the restaurant at Tula.'

She sighed. 'I work there. Just for the time being, you understand. Until I get a job in films. One day I am going to be an actress. I know about films. I act in one once.'

'A walk-on part,' Barribal said cruelly.

'That is just a beginning. I have learn a lot.'

'How?' Pel asked. 'Acting?'

'I have read the magazines. *Films. Film Stars.* I know how to act.'

Pel doubted it. She couldn't even lie convincingly. 'Go on,' he said. 'Why did you go to the Mayan remains at Tula?'

'Because I have never see them. I have live in Tula all my life and I have *never* see them. So we go. Enrico – Henri – he is quite happy. He take photographs of me. He promise to send them to a friend of his who is a film producer. Then we go on to Chapadores.'

'Because it was a film set and you wanted to see it?'

'Yes. One day, I think. One day, this will be me. We are very happy. We come to San Miguel and we stay at the Motel La Ermita. But we also go to other places. We eat a good meal at a hotel on the road west out of San Miguel. Enrico is much excited there, because it has things there which he is interested in.'

'What things?'

She shrugged indifferently. 'Furniture. The hotel register which was once the family visitors' book. Nothing I understand. He make notes. Then later he say he must go back to Mexico City. To pick up some books, he say. I think he dumps me. But he does not. He comes back in two days. Then he tell me he has to meet a man. Business, he say. He go off in the evening and this time he never come back. He dumps me after all.'

'What was your relationship with Martin?'

She tossed her head defiantly. 'What you think?'

'Have you reported his absence to the police?'
'Why? He leave me. I think he has gone back to Mexico City.'
'Weren't you interested?'
'Men have leave me before. Other men.'
'Why was he killed? Do you know?'
'I not know this.'
'What happened to the notebook he had?'
'I leave it with his luggage. There is not much in it. I look. I think perhaps there is an address where I can find him. But there is not. Just a lot of lines I can't understand. I buy myself a shawl.'
'Go on.'
'He does not come back. I think when it is late I must find somewhere to sleep.'
'Didn't you go to the police and report his disappearance?'
'I think he will not want this.'
'Why?'
'I think he is doing something he do not want them to see?'
'Why did you think that?'
She shrugged. 'The way he talk. The things he does. He has this notebook. A new one. A fresh one. For new discoveries, he says. He puts things in it.'
'Go on.'
'I think I go to the hotel, but then I think I have not much money. So I find somewhere more cheap. I must have somewhere. I go there with the suitcase. I sleep there. And wait. He doesn't come back. I think he leave me. I get a job at Posada San Francisco.'
'Until this guy –' Barribal jerked a hand at Arkwright '– persuaded you to move in here.'
'I think so, yes.'
'What happened to his luggage? This suitcase you said he left.'
'I leave it at the house where I find to sleep. Before I get work at Posada San Francisco.'
'Where is it? Here? In San Miguel?'
'Of course.'
'Address?'
'Calle Julian de los Reyes, 14. It is small house. Not good. I don' like.'
'You'd better show us.'
She looked at Arkwright. 'I go?'

'You go,' he said. 'Get the hell outa here! I don't want no involvement with the fuzz. Beat it. Take your things and go. I can soon get someone else.'

Barribal smiled. 'When you do, señor, make sure she comes willingly, and that she is of mature age and sound mind. It would give me great pleasure to arrest you.'

13

They checked Pilar Hernandez's story at the Motel La Ermita. Sure enough, there was no sign of Martin's luggage there but the register showed a Señor y Señora Enrico Martin, of Mexico City, as having stayed there, which seemed to indicate she had told them the truth.

Number 14, Calle Julian de los Reyes looked exactly like Number 7, Calle Vicenza, in Tula, where Pilar Hernandez had grown up. It was small, flat-fronted, flat-roofed, with a plank door painted with peeling green paint that opened on to the street, so that you stepped from the living-room into any traffic that happened to be passing. Nearby was a little square with a stand where women were filling gaudy plastic buckets with water, and a few children sat round with their feet in the puddles they made.

The woman who opened the door saw Pilar Hernandez first and gave her a glare. She seemed on the point of setting about her, in fact, but Barribal pushed her back. As he made clear what they were after, the woman disappeared, returning with a suitcase and a canvas holdall.

'*Todo?*' Barribal asked. 'This is everything?'

'*Todo!*' The woman gestured them aaway. 'There is nothing more!'

Barribal refused to be put off and pushed his way inside, into a room exactly like the one in Tula, with walls full of pictures and just four chairs and a table on which was stretched a gaudily coloured runner centred by a plastic container holding a single flower. The barrage of questions was beyond Pel and it seemed to produce nothing.

Barribal shrugged and they headed for the street, followed by the imprecations of the woman against Pilar Hernandez.

They opened the suitcase in the car. There was nothing of any particular interest. Once more, mostly it was clothes. Then, at the bottom under the clothes, they unearthed what looked like a pair of tweezers. They were very long and narrow and the pincer end worked like scissors with a wire attached to a trigger on the handle. The hinged part was short, hooked and with prongs that had been roughened, presumably to make their grip better.

Barribal held them up. 'What are these for?'

The girl shrugged. 'I have never see them before.'

'For barbecuing steaks? For pulling teeth? For extracting nails from planks?' Barribal handed them to Pel who noticed that they looked as though they had been hurriedly and crudely made.

Again the girl shrugged. 'I don' know,' she said. 'He does not show them to me.'

There were also several books. Barribal picked one up.

'*La Intervención Francesa*,' he read. He looked at the girl. 'Did he get you to read this to him?'

'Some of it. He does not speak much Spanish.'

'Which part did you read?'

It was obvious that what she had read had not sunk in. 'I don' know,' she said. 'Something about an emperor. He want to pay his soldiers and he cannot. At Querétaro.' She dismissed him with a shrug. 'He is a silly man, I think, this emperor.'

Pel picked up another book. '*Expédition du Mexique*,' he read. 'In French. It'll bear studying.'

The notebook they found, like the one they had found in Mexico City, seemed of little value. There was a great deal more of the shorthand writing, several of the 'ASS' letters in the margin, and '*cama de matrimonio, de madera, de nupcias*'.

Barribal looked puzzled. 'Double bed, wooden bed, marriage bed?' He looked up at Pel. 'What's he trying to find out? He seems very interested in beds.'

The girl was unable to help them and knew no reason why the dead Henri Martin should have been interested in double beds.

'Perhaps for me?' she asked.

They dropped the girl in the town. 'What am I to do?' she asked.

'Go home to Tula,' Barribal said shortly.

He slipped her a small denomination note, but she stared at it contemptuously, stuffed it into her skirt pocket, then turned on her heel and strode away, a fine, defiant figure, her black hair floating in the warm breeze.

Studied again over beers in a bar off the main street, the notebooks produced nothing.

'He wasn't interested in the Mayans, *patron*,' De Troq' said, deciphering some of the shorthand. 'He seems to be entirely interested in the Emperor Maximilian. It's all down here. How he was put on the throne of Mexico but was later captured by the Mexicans under Juárez and after the siege and capture of Querétaro, was forced to surrender and finally shot by a firing-squad. It's just a lot of notes about his travels.'

'Nothing else?'

'It's a new notebook. There's very little in it. Perhaps Donck and Hervé have another notebook.'

'Any reference to "treasure"?'

'No, *patron*. There are the notes on "bed" and the words "*Las Rosas*" again. "Pilar" is here again, too. Just the word. Nothing more. As well as "ASS".'

'Well, we've explained "Pilar" and "bed" and probably "roses",' Barribal said. 'They seem to go together. But what does "ASS" mean and what was this "treasure" Borillas heard Donck and Hervé talking about?'

'*Patron* –' De Troq's expression was faraway, as if he were deep in thought '– treasure.'

'What about it?'

'In those days, armies carried their pay around with them. Would Maximilian have had a war chest with him? To pay his troops?'

'Would he? Inform me.'

'I think it would be fairly normal. If he did, in 1861 it would surely be in silver or gold. Pesos, napoléons, dollars or Maria Theresas. Something like that.'

Pel's eyes met De Troq's. 'It's not impossible,' he agreed quietly. 'What would be the value of such a war chest?'

De Troq' shrugged. 'Hard to say. How do we know what a gold peso piece, a napoléon, a silver dollar or a Maria Theresa's worth? A lot these days, I imagine. A war chest full of coins like that could be worth a million francs or more. There'd have to be enough to pay his soldiers, and an army – even a small one – would need a lot. And it would be in silver or gold, *patron*. It could be worth a fortune these days.'

'Worth getting your hands on?'

'Martin might well have come across documents mentioning it.'

'And if he had, to Donck it would be well worth taking a risk for. He's known to be willing to take risks, and gold or silver to that value would be worth chancing your arm for.'

'I think we ought to find out more about this war chest of Maximilian's,' Pel said.

'If there was one.'

Pel agreed. 'If,' he agreed. 'At the moment, though, I can't think what else it could be.'

There was not only an American art school in San Miguel, there was also an American library for the use of American visitors. What was more, on its staff it had a Frenchwoman who twenty years before had married a Mexican called Méndez, an elderly lady with a face deeply lined by the sun but with hair dyed so red it looked as if it had been chosen from a decorator's colour chart. However, she knew everything the library contained and spoke French, Spanish and English perfectly. What was more, because they were so close to Querétaro, where Maximilian had made his last stand and finally met his death, she was sound on her history of the French intervention in Mexico.

'Maximilian came here towards the end of his reign in Mexico,' she said, reaching for files. 'Early in 1867. The French were on the point of evacuating the country. Paris had come to the conclusion that nothing further was to be gained from the Mexican adventure and the French troops were being withdrawn. That meant that Maximilian was trying to support the Mexican Empire solely with a few loyal Mexican troops, and that was hopeless because on the whole the Mexicans – apart from a few wealthy families who hoped to gain from it – didn't want an emperor, and Juárez had passed a law which said that any Mexican offering help or assistance to an enemy of the country was liable to the death sentence. It didn't encourage anybody to give assistance.'

'Anything known about the last days, Madame?' Pel asked.

'Quite a lot. Plenty was written. There's José Blasio, Blanchot,

Buffin, Emmanuel Dommenech, Luisa Gasperini, Kératry, Baron de Troquereau Tournay-Turenne –'

'We have De Troquereau,' De Troq' said.

'Oh!' The librarian stopped. 'I'm surprised. There can't be many copies. His mémoirs were privately printed and only about fifty copies found their way into libraries. It was produced chiefly for members of his family.'

Pel could guess why, too. The Baron de Troquereau Tournay-Turenne, if he were anything like his descendant, would assume that the French intervention in Mexico, despite the fact that it concerned thousands of French soldiers, was really only a private matter that concerned the De Troquereaus.

He indicated De Troq' with a small feeling of pride. 'This is the present Baron de Troquereau,' he said. 'He is the General's great-great-grandson.'

'Oh!' Señora Méndez went pink and became flustered. 'I'm so pleased to meet you. A splendid writer, the General.'

'I always thought him a crashing bore,' De Troq' said solemnly.

'Oh! Oh, did you? Oh! Well, perhaps he was. People were in those days, weren't they? All the same –' the librarian struggled to recover her composure '– we've got lots of material here. They all put their thoughts on paper about what happened. We have a pretty clear picture.'

'What we're interested in,' Pel said, 'is how Maximilian paid his troops.'

'With gold, I expect.'

'Did this gold disappear?'

The woman stared at Pel for a moment then she gestured. 'One moment,' she said.

She vanished through a door behind her desk and re-emerged some minutes later with a book.

'Baron Alfred van der Smissen,' she said. 'He was a soldier. It's said he became the lover of the Empress Carlota when Maximilian neglected her. It was quite a scandal.'

She began turning pages, then looked up. 'He refers to Walton – *Souvenirs d'un Officier Belge au Mexico*.'

Another book appeared and she riffled through it and looked up again. 'One moment more. I must find something else. You see, the Mexicans wrote very little themselves on the subject.'

Another leather-bound book appeared and she looked up again.

'5th February 1867,' she said. 'The French troops departed from Mexico City, leaving Maximilian on his own.' Her finger traced the words down the page. 'But the same day he received news from Miguel de Miramón, one of his generals, that he had attacked Zacatecas and forced the Juárez Government to flee.' Her spectacles slid down her nose as she peered excitedly at the print. 'It seems Maximilian was delighted by the news but within hours he learned that Miramón and his troops had in fact been outflanked by General Escobedo and cut to pieces. It was known as the Massacre of San Jacinto.' She looked up apologetically. 'It was a battle of unparalleled ferocity with all the worst elements of a civil war. Juárez ordered that no mercy should be shown and over 100 Frenchmen who had volunteered to remain behind after the French Army left were summarily executed. Miramón's fight had cost Maximilian over 3,000 men and –' she paused, her finger on the print, then she looked up '– and part of his war chest, a sum of 25,000 pesos.'

'Which would go where?'

Señora Méndez smiled. 'Who knows? Escobedo was a Juárista general and would turn it over to Juárez, I suppose. Probably he kept a little back for himself, of course. It wasn't unknown. It never has been in Mexico's history.'

'What about the rest of the war chest?'

The librarian turned more pages and came up again with a bright fluttery smile. 'It seems that what was lost was about a quarter of the normal war chest. What remained were the remaining three-quarters. That would be held at Querétaro, I suppose, and, because Maximilian was besieged there, it would remain there.'

'Was it ever found?'

She looked startled. 'Found?'

'Is there any record of it appearing after the surrender?'

Another book appeared. By this time they could barely see Señora Méndez for books.

'I think there is,' she said. 'There is a list made out by General Escobedo of the spoils collected after Maximilian's defeat. It lists the number of rifles and cannon, the amount of ammunition, the gunpowder, the horses –' she frowned '– but not the war chest.

That's strange. Normally they always stated the amount found, and even at Querétaro they mention the money found in Maximilian's personal possession. It wasn't much. But no mention of any 75,000 pesos which must have been there.'

'And that,' Pel said, 'would be worth how much today?'

The librarian shrugged, frowned, thought for a while, then shrugged again. 'I have no idea. It would undoubtedly have been in gold and silver. It's impossible to estimate. With the rise in the price of gold and the present inflation rates – millions of pesos. It could be two or three million dollars. Perhaps more – much more.'

'At the present rate of exchange,' Pel said slowly. 'Around several million dollars. Donck wouldn't hesitate to murder for that.' He frowned. 'We begin at last to see some reason for all that happened. Why Donck was interested in Martin. Why Hervé betrayed Navarro. Why Navarro is dead. Martin discovered something and somehow Navarro found out – perhaps Martin asked his advice. Navarro made enquiries of his own. Through Hervé, Donck found out what he was up to and went to see him, probably to persuade him to allow him to join in. Navarro didn't want that. He wanted the money for himself. There was a quarrel. Navarro and his bodyguard, Desgeorges, were shot and Donck and Hervé turned up in Mexico, which is a sensible place to turn up if the treasure they're after's there. They found out – or already knew – where Martin was, and followed him.'

He paused. 'It's my guess,' he went on, 'that they arranged somehow to meet him at Chapadores – although the village's handy, the film set's deserted, and it would be at night. They torture Martin to get the facts, then murder him and bury him there. They unearth the treasure. Having got what they want, all they have to do now is leave for somewhere safe like Brazil. But they'd left France in a hurry and the money they'd managed to bring wasn't enough and even in Mexico you need money – especially if you need an airline ticket to Brazil. So Donck picks up Borillas and tries to knock off a bank in Mexico City. He pulls it off all right, but he doesn't allow for the fact that there are bad drivers everywhere in the world. There's a collision and he ends up in gaol with Borillas.'

De Troq' frowned. 'And while he's there,' he said, 'Hervé gets the wind up and bolts.'

Pel sighed and rubbed his nose, trying to marshal his thoughts. 'That's the way it seems, *mon brave*,' he agreed. 'But, unfortunately, it leaves one question unanswered. *Why* did she shop Donck to the police for Martin's murder?'

That evening they received an agitated and excited telephone call from Señora Méndez. 'I have found out about the disappearance of the war chest,' she said cheerfully. 'It seems to have vanished before Maximilian reached Querétaro and was besieged there. I grew quite worried and looked up our records. Quite a job. Very dusty. There's a lot of dust in Mexico and most of it seems to be in our papers. There is a reference in a letter from Miramón to Mejía – they were the imperialist generals who were captured with Maximilian and shot alongside him. It's dated 20 February 1867, soon after Maximilian left Mexico City to join his troops at Querétaro and roughly a month before the Juáristas started their siege. It states quite firmly, "Twenty-five thousand pesos to Escobedo at San Jacinto. The other 75,000 – where? The Emperor has nothing and, now, neither have we. We can expect desertions." I've looked through other letters and turned up no reference to it being found and it's well known that the Emperor had no money of his own because attempts were made to bribe his captors to bargain for his life, but it was impossible to raise the money because he had none.'

Pel put the telephone down and looked at De Troq'. 'Seventy-five thousand pesos in gold. Worth three million francs or more,' he said. 'It disappeared sometime between the battle at San Jacinto and the time when Maximilian was captured at Querétaro.' He lit a cigarette. 'This Maximilian doesn't seem to have taken care of things very well, does he?'

De Troq' grinned. 'My great-great-grandfather considered he wasn't very clever, *patron*. He felt he had an idea that because he was a member of a European monarchy he only had to appear and the Mexicans would worship him. He ended up pretty well disillusioned and fell back on fathering a child by the wife of one of his gardeners, while his own wife, who was probably bored stiff with him by that time, had the affair with this General van der Smissen we heard about and returned to France where she appealed for help, and finally went off her head.'

Pel was silent for a while. After a moment or two he looked up. 'Donck and Hervé came here,' he said. 'To San Miguel de Allende. So did Martin. Why?'

'The library, *patron*?' De Troq' looked excited. 'To look things up? To check where the war chest went to?'

'Señora Méndez looked things up. For us. She says there's no indication of what happened to the war chest. So they didn't get very far.'

'Perhaps Martin had found out elsewhere and knew where to look.'

'Señora Méndez could find nothing.'

'They might have removed it, *patron*. Cut it out with a razor blade from a book. It's been done before.'

Señora Méndez was delighted to see them back, and gave a giggle of excitement.

'I'm growing quite interested,' she said. 'I've been spending all my spare time checking.' Her face fell. 'Unfortunately, I've found nothing.'

'Have you had anybody else in here recently enquiring about Maximilian's last weeks?' Pel asked.

She looked puzzled. 'Mostly they check in Querétaro. That's where he was shot. They have a lot of material there.' She frowned. 'But there *was* a man who came in. Just over a month ago. I can check.'

'Please do.'

She disappeared and came back with a box of request cards. 'Five weeks ago,' she said.

'He sounds like our man. What was his name?'

'Martin. Professor Martin. Henri Martin. It's here on the cards. Can you talk to him?'

Pel frowned. 'I doubt it, Madame,' he said. 'He's dead.' He fished out the photographs Pilar Hernandez had taken at Tula. 'Is that him, do you think?'

Señora Méndez went into a flutter of excitement. 'I really couldn't say. I expect so. I'll check. I wasn't here at the time, you see, so I don't know. I also don't know what he was after. I see he requested a book called *Da Miramar a Mexico. Viaje del Emperador Massimiliano y de la Emperadora Carlota.* Miramar to Mexico. The journey of Maximilian and Carlota. It's a privately printed work. He also asked to see the papers of General Calles, who was an imperialist who survived the siege, and the diary of Prince Felix Salm. He was a Prussian officer who was captured with Maximilian. He also survived. Perhaps he found some clues there.'

'Did any of these people ever mention San Miguel? This place?'

'I don't think so. It was quite a long way from Querétaro in those days. Not nowadays, of course, with motor cars. But with only coaches and bad roads, it would be quite a journey. Maximilian came here before being besieged at Querétaro. We know that. There's a stone set in the wall of the Posada San Miguel. You can see it. It mentions that he did.'

They decided they were in need of a drink and that the best place to have it was in the Posada San Miguel, which was at the other side of the square from their own hotel. It was a similar place to the Posada San Francisco with a square courtyard, a fountain, creepers, trees, shrubs and bougainvillaea. As they drank, they searched about them and eventually, on one of the walls, half-hidden by the creepers, they came on a small marble plaque. It was in Spanish and Pel saw the name, Maximilian.

'What's it say?' he asked.

De Troq' squinted upwards. '"In this courtyard,"' he translated, "the Emperor Maximilian I, puppet ruler of Mexico, 1863–1867, stopped on February 26th to take a glass of wine before proceeding to Querétaro where he was besieged, captured and on June 19th shot by a firing-squad."'

Pel reached for a cigarette. 'So he *did* come to San Miguel,' he said thoughtfully.

He sat for a while in silence then he held up his thumb, 'Known facts. Seventy-five thousand pesos – between three or more million French francs – in gold disappeared somewhere after the massacre at San Jacinto on 13 February 1867, and the defeat at Querétaro on 15 May.' He lifted his first finger. 'Nobody seems to know where it went.' Up went his middle finger. 'But Maximilian stopped *here*. On 26 February after San Jacinto and before reaching Querétaro, in this very courtyard, I suppose.' Up went his third finger. 'It was after that when this General Miramón mentioned that the money had disappeared.' His little finger rose. 'So it's more than likely that the money was handed over to someone for safe keeping at that meeting here, was hidden, perhaps buried, and has remained so ever since, until Martin found out something somewhere in his reading about where it was and set out to find it.'

14

There was another telephone call that evening. Señora Méndez had taken the trouble to go round to the home of the assistant who had been on duty when Martin had appeared to request books, and he had identified the photograph. She was delighted with her success and in a twitter of excitement.

'It's all so thrilling. A sort of detective search through history.'

Pel preferred to call it simply a detective search. Yet she was right. For the first time since they had found Navarro and his bodyguard, Desgeorges, dead on the floor of his library at Sorgeay two months before, they had finally begun to understand why it had happened. It explained why Donck and Jacqueline Hervé had fled not to Brazil where they might have been safe, but to Mexico, and why Professor Martin had been found dead under the stoop of the film set at Chapadores.

Pel was so pleased with their progress he felt he had to post a letter to his wife to tell her how right she was in her estimate of the reason for Donck's flight. He was homesick for Burgundy – even, damn it, for Madame Routy. He was also sick of the sight of De Troq'. Good as he was, he was inclined to be a little humourless and Pel missed Darcy's sharp comments and the asides of Judge Polverari. In addition, having been well brought up as a baron should be, De Troq' was always polite, never rude, always calm, never in a panic, always in control – in a way Pel could never hope to be – and it had begun to irritate. Pel had worked with De Troq' before but had never been thrown into such close contact, and by this time he was almost wishing he could be run over by one of the Mexican buses that sounded so much like spacecraft taking off.

On the other hand – he tried to be fair – down now to his last packet of French cigarettes, Pel had been offered two more by De Troq', so he couldn't be all that bad. And – Pel had to admit it to himself – no other member of his team could have been so useful. De Troq' had been what he liked to call 'expensively uneducated' but, uneducated or not, he had a knowledge of the world, had travelled, spoke three or four languages more or less fluently, and seemed also to have a knowledge of art, music, literature and history which had proved immensely useful on many occasions. It wasn't much good looking for something that had happened in the past when you had no idea what century it had happened in, or where, or to whom. And, Pel felt, the fact that his great-great-grandfather, the General Baron de Troquereau Tournay-Turenne, whom God preserve, had served in Mexico during the French intervention, seemed to give his great-great-grandson a sort of in-built awareness of the period, a feeling for it which had more than once been very valuable. Thank God for barons, Pel thought. Though he liked to think it made no difference how a man was born, he was a snob at heart and had often thought how nice it would be to be elevated himself to the nobility.

The following day Pel was back at the library. Señora Méndez, who by this time was in a tizzy of excitement at the thought that she was involved in a murder enquiry, produced evidence that Maximilian's treasure in his war chest was indeed in Austrian Maria Theresas, napoléons, American silver dollars and gold peso pieces.

'The evidence is here,' she said. 'In the book by Prince Felix Salm. He was a prisoner with Maximilian at Querétaro and would have been shot but for his wife, the princess. She was American but she had a French background and she started life as a circus bareback rider. She engineered his release and he published his memoirs the following year. In English in London. Two volumes. *My Diary in Mexico.*' Señora Méndez indicated a passage in the book in front of her. 'He writes that Maximilian was very upset that nothing could be done for him. "He told me", he says, "that he had deposited his treasure in a safe place." He had always felt that he might be defeated and had hoped to bargain with it for his life because he knew the Juáristas were in desperate need of money. He goes on, "*I* don't think they would ever have bargained, but Maximilian thought so. I was about to ask him where the money was, so my wife could find it and use it on his behalf, but just then there was an alarm that the Juáristas were breaking through the defences and from that moment we were engaged in a wild fight and I never got the chance again to ask him."'

'So there *was* a treasure?' Pel said.

'It looks like it.'

Pel frowned. Was Professor Martin after the money? Had he learned of it, as they believed, and had Navarro also learned? And was that why Navarro and Martin were dead? Because Donck had learned through Jacqueline Hervé, Navarro's mistress, who was also Donck's mistress? Where, though, was Donck now? Come to that, where was Jacqueline Hervé?

And that brought up another question: Why, if they were in the thing together, hadn't Jacqueline Hervé helped Donck to escape? Was it after all just as he had thought, that she had lost her nerve and bolted? Surely, after three murders and with the 'treasure' within reach, she would be able to steel herself sufficiently to carry the plan through? Or was it because, knowing where the treasure was, she had deliberately left Donck in the penitentiary and gone off to collect the treasure herself? It suddenly seemed a possibility.

'I think,' he said, 'that Hervé dumped Donck for the loot. When he made his attempt on the bank to raise honest-to-God cash to pay for airline tickets to Brazil or somewhere and it went wrong and he was put behind bars, it dawned on her that she was suddenly on to a good thing. She wasn't going to have to share the spoils with him. They were hers – all of them. That's why she shopped him for the murder of Martin. So the police would hang on to him and make it safer for her. Unfortunately, she didn't allow for him escaping. However, she had plenty of time before then to bolt for Brazil and he'll not find it easy to turn her up again there. And neither will we. I supposed we can write "Finish" to it all. We've lost Hervé and Donck *and* the treasure and it doesn't look to me now as though we're going to find any of them.'

Back at the Posada San Francisco, Pel was brooding over a beer when Barribal appeared.

'Information,' he said. 'I find a young cop here called Fontano, whose grandfather fight with Pancho Villa.'

'Against Maximilian or for him?' Pel asked.

Barribal gave him a cold look. 'Villa is born long after Maximilian is shot,' he said. 'Villa is an ex-bandit and one of the leaders in the revolution of 1910 to 1920.'

'If Villa wasn't born until years after Maximilian was killed, how does he interest us?'

'Because the revolution of 1910 is to overthrow a man called Porfirio Díaz who manages to remain dictator and President of Mexico for over thirty years. And Díaz, as a young soldier, fights for Juárez against Maximilian.'

'And what does this cop have to tell us?'

'He says his grandfather was one of Villa's *Dorados* –'

Pel looked puzzled and Barribal explained. 'Villa is always impressed by Napoleon's Old Guard so he creates an élite force of his own. They are called *Dorados* – the Golden Boys – because of the gold badges on their uniforms. Most of them are killed in Villa's last battles before the revolution ends.'

'But not this one?'

'This one wisely keeps his head down and survives. He later acquires land and becomes a wealthy farmer.'

'And – ?' Pel was wondering where it was leading to.

'The cop, the guy called Fontano, say he's hear the old man talk about being one of a party which go to search for Maximilian's treasure.'

The old grandfather, a patriarch with a white beard and a lean straight figure still, was a handsome old man remarkably alert despite his ninety-one years. He lived in a splendid large house furnished in magnificent style.

'There was a lot of property going spare after the revolution,' he explained to Barribal. 'A lot of it was abandoned and nobody wanted this place because it had been burned. I got it for a song and worked hard. Now I am rich.' His mouth widened in a grin. 'I pray there will be no more revolutions.'

'*Agente de Policía* Fontano says you were one of Villa's *Dorados* who were sent to pick up Maximilian's treasure.'

'That's right. Villa had heard of it and, like all rebels, he was always desperate for money to buy guns.'

'Where was it?'

'Hacienda de las Rosas.'

Pel glanced at De Troq'.

'Las Rosas, patron,' De Troq' said.

'Where is this Hacienda de las Rosas?'

'Not far away. Just west of San Miguel.'

Barribal turned to the old man. 'What happened when you got there?'

The old man grinned, showing a magnificent set of false teeth that looked as if they'd been made out of porcelain. 'Nothing,' he said. 'We didn't find anything.'

'What?'

'We'd been told it was buried in the floor of one of the stables. We dug them all up. Every one. There was no treasure.'

'So it might still be there somewhere?'

The old man grinned again and shook his head. 'I shouldn't think so. We heard later that Porfirio Díaz had heard about it too. Long before he became *presidente*. We heard *he'd* dug it up.'

'But he might *not* have done?'

The old man shrugged. 'It's just possible. But, knowing Porfirio Díaz, I think he would have.'

'Is this hacienda still standing?'

'Oh, yes. Of course. It's a hotel now. Splendid. Very popular with Americans. It was converted in 1970. Some American put money into it and they created a museum and hotel out of it.'

It seemed well worth visiting the Hacienda de las Rosas. It was a huge place, with what had been the houses of the peons employed at the *grande casa* – the big house – surrounding the four sides of a huge square. They had been turned into motel dwellings and the whole interior of the square changed into parking lots and gardens. The house had been turned into a hotel for non-motel visitors, with a huge dining-room, bars and swimming-pool, and the stables had been turned into a museum.

The house had originally been built as a monastery with enormously thick walls which kept out the heat in summer and the cold in winter. At the back near the pool there was a sunken garden which had been built out of the original stone swimming-bath. With its long corridors, numerous chambers, odd balconies, its own church, shop, great yards and outbuildings, the place was a small town in itself and was perfect for conversion to a hotel and motel.

The museum, dark and cool like the rest of the buildings, was open to non-residents and contained magnificent examples of Spanish furniture, far too large for a modern hotel. It was kept in air-conditioned rooms, among other exhibits such as revolutionary and Juárista weapons, a cannon, a stage-coach, farm wagons, and a whole array of pictures of both Maximilian and Juárez and the heroes of the 1910 revolution.

There was no attendant because there were free printed guides in several languages and all the photographs were in frames and screwed to the walls; all the weapons and smaller memorabilia were in glass cases, while the rest of the exhibits were too big and too heavy to be removed. They wandered among them for some time, not quite certain what they were seeking, studied the ancient furniture, most of it black with age and with its secret panels and drawers exposed, and the uglier furniture of the last century which had still been in use at the time of the 1910 revolution.

Outside again, for a long time, Pel stood in the courtyard blinking in the glare and staring about him, wondering where in this vast space the treasure could have been planted. It had to be here somewhere – but where? Fontano's grandfather and his group had dug up the whole interior of the stables and found nothing, but that didn't mean it wasn't still there. Yet there was so much land enclosed by the four walls of the hacienda, the chance of digging it up again was very slight indeed. Certainly impossible during Pel's stay in Mexico. It began to look as if his theory that Jacqueline Hervé had made off with it was wrong because nobody would be able to recover a buried treasure without a major operation and with tourists and cars constantly going in and out.

Barribal seemed to think the same. He pushed his hat back and lit a cigarillo. '*Oyeme, muchachos,*' he said. 'I think a drink's called for,'

They sat on a veranda outside the hotel, chatting desultorily while a waiter took their order for beers.

'We'll talk to the manager,' Barribal said. 'He might know something. He might even have documents.'

When the beers arrived they were surprised to find that the waitress who brought them was Pilar Hernandez, dressed now in a cream dress with a green apron. She stopped dead as she saw them, plonked the beers on the table and turned away hurriedly.

'*Alto!*' Barribal yelled. 'Stop right there!'

As the girl stopped, rigid with terror, the head waiter appeared and hurried towards them.

'Is something wrong, señores?'

'No,' Barribal said. 'Not yet.'

'Then, please sir, may I ask you not to raise your voice.'

Barribal took out his identity card and flipped it at the waiter. '*Policía*,' he said. 'I want to talk to this girl.'

'She has done something wrong?'

'Not that we know about. But she was questioned two days ago about the disappearance of someone we were interested in. I'd like to talk to her again.'

'Señor –'

'Don't argue,' Barribal snapped. 'Just find another waitress and tell us where we can talk.'

'I must see the manager.'

The manager, who was American, arrived soon afterwards. He was not looking for trouble and acceded to Barribal's request at once.

'I have to know, gentlemen,' he said, 'if you are about to bring charges against the girl. We have to think of our guests and we cannot afford to have doubtful characters among our staff. Is she suspected of dishonesty?'

Barribal looked at Pel. There was a lot Pilar Hernandez was guilty of but most of it seemed to concern loose morals rather than theft. They had no proof of dishonesty.

Barribal gestured. 'Nothing. It's simply that she was on the fringe of a case we're investigating and knew the man involved. We've nothing against her. You needn't have, either.'

The manager nodded. 'I'm pleased to hear it. This way, gentlemen.'

He showed them into a room which looked like the staff dining-room. It contained none of the splendid furniture of the rest of the hotel, simply Formica-topped tables and tubular chairs. As the door closed behind the manager, Pilar Hernandez sank into one of the chairs.

'Thank you for what you said,' she whispered. 'I don' want to lose my job.'

Pel said nothing, because he suspected that, despite Barribal's assurances, the manager would use the first opportunity he could to get rid of her – if she didn't first disappear with one of his customers.

'What are you doing here?' Barribal asked.

It was too much of a coincidence to think she was there by sheer chance but that was how it appeared.

'I needed work,' she said. 'I needed money. I hear of this job. One of the girls from the Posada San Francisco tell me about it. I walk all the way here to get it.'

Barribal gestured. 'All right, all right,' he said. 'Just a few questions then you can go. This is the place where you stayed with Martin, isn't it? The hotel you mentioned near San Miguel!'

She nodded. 'Yes,' she whispered. 'This is it.'

'Did Professor Martin ever talk of treasure?'

She frowned. 'Once.'

'Maximilian's treasure?'

'Maximilian?' Her knowledge of history was not deep.

'The Emperor Maximilian.'

'Ah! No, he didn't. He just said "treasure". But I think it had something to do with this Maximilian. I remember the name.'

'Did Martin ever come back here after your first visit?'

'He was going to bring me to stay here again. But then he disappears and now I'm here as a waitress.'

'*Was* he looking for a treasure?'

'He don' say so.'

'Was he going to dig it up somehow?'

'I don' know. I don' think so. He has nothing to dig it up with. I ask him once but he don' say. He just say it don' have to be dug up. So I ask him how he is going to get it away because treasure is heavy. He say I needn't worry about that. He has all the tools he need.'

They let her go and went to see the manager. He seemed satisfied with their explanations but Pel knew he would never take his eyes off her.

'How old is this place?' Pel asked.

The manager shrugged. 'Perhaps two hundred years. The land was bought in 1750 and originally it was to have been a monastery. We have all the deeds. But then the plans were changed.' He smiled. 'I guess somebody did some horse-trading and built a house instead. The Church in Mexico in those days wasn't noted for its honesty. He made a hacienda of it. His name was Juan Ramírez y Róbles. His family lived here until the revolution, when his descendant was shot. They nailed him to his own front door and used him for target practice. After that it was taken over by one of the rebel generals and allowed to deteriorate. It went down in value, the land was sold to raise money, until eventually there wasn't much more than the buildings and the land they surrounded. We acquired it in 1970.'

'Apart from improvements, is it exactly as it was?'

'Exactly.'

'No new buildings?'

'We had more than enough.'

'So no foundations were dug for new walls?'

'None at all. What are you looking for?'

'Treasure. Maximilian's treasure.'

'Here?' The manager was interested at once and, as he listened to their story, they could see his brain working over the possibility of publicity.

'I guess we should have a new prospectus printed,' he said as they explained. 'With pictures. We were due to and I'm sure glad I've learned this before we went ahead. We'll have to think again now. You'd be surprised how Americans enjoy something old, a bit of history, a bit of tragedy. We also have a hotel in Querétaro, so the two can be linked. We could run trips between them. They'll love it. Especially as we still have all the original furniture. You'll have seen it in the museum. Original beds, chairs, tables. Magnificent. Some of it even has small hidden drawers and compartments. You'll have seen those too. Still and all, that was often the case in those days here in Mexico. In the States and in Europe, too, I guess. Because there weren't many banks and people needed somewhere safe for their valuables. Somehow the furniture survived all the revolutions and we even have all the visitors' books from as far back as 1770. Ramírez y Róbles kept them. They're in the museum. They show everybody who stayed in the house almost from the beginning.'

'Did the Emperor Maximilian stay here?'

The manager nodded. 'Yes, sir! So did a few of the people who tried to bail him out at Querétaro. Perhaps you'd like to see the records.'

They would, and the manager proudly indicated Maximilian's entry. It was dated 1867 and said simply *'Camara Azule, Lado Oriente. El Emperado Massimiliano y su Acompañamiente.'*

'"Blue Room, East Wing. The Emperor Maximilian and his suite",' he translated for Pel's benefit. 'Judging by the number of bedrooms they took, there were twelve of them, unless they doubled up, in which case there might have been twenty, which I guess, is probably a more likely figure for an emperor.'

He led them into the museum and indicated a brass bedstead. It was old, flecked with rust and topped with brass balls. 'That's the very bed he used when he stayed here before going on to Querétaro,' he said. 'Not very pretty and, of course, it was replaced in what was the Blue Room when we took over the hotel. Modern beds. Spring mattresses. I guess you know the way it goes. But the Ramírez y Róbles Family would have used this, because it was new then and brass bedsteads were *de rigueur* in the nineteenth century. Looks ugly to us now, I guess, though they *are* coming back into fashion, but in those days they were all the rage. It was an age of cast iron and brass, wasn't it? Several other famous people also slept here – probably also in that bed – en route to or from Mexico City. The Blue Room was one of the best in the place. Juárez slept there, for instance. So did Princess Salm, who tried to bribe the guards to let her husband escape after his capture. Even offered herself, so the story goes, to the guard to allow him to go free. I guess that's true heroism and true love. She stayed here while she was working on the attempt. She finally managed it, too. American girl,' the manager said proudly. 'Porfirio Díaz, who became dictator-President of Mexico, also slept in it. About the same time. Later, Pancho Villa slept in it. I think they chose this bed because it has a steel bed-spring while most of the old ones have nothing but wide strips of leather and weren't as comfortable.'

He paused. 'Funny you should be interested in beds,' he said. 'We had a guy here interested in them a few weeks back. We've never had anybody interested in them before and now we have two in two months. Are you connected?'

'In a way,' Pel said. 'What was *his* interest.'

'Why, he was unscrewing the brass knobs off. He said he

collected them and could he buy the bed for them? Now that's a funny thing to collect, isn't it, though I guess some of 'em might be called decorative. All the same, I had to tell him no. They weren't for sale.'

They left the hotel deep in thought, Barribal wondering if he could obtain permission to dig up the ground inside the walls and, if he could, if the management of the hotel would slap on an injunction to protect their property. Pel was occupied with wondering how much his brief covered. He wasn't concerned with recovering long-lost treasure. He'd been sent to bring back Donck, and Donck had disappeared.

As it happened, the matter was settled for him when he returned to San Miguel de Allende. A cable was waiting for him at the desk in the hotel, signed by the Chief.

'Return at once,' it said. 'Hervé found murdered at Fontenay L'Église.'

15

Pel's face, when he appeared in the Hôtel de Police, didn't encourage questions. Darcy tried a couple, nevertheless, to get the lie of the land and the pressure of Pel's temper.

'Enjoy the trip, *patron*?' he asked.

'No,' Pel snapped.

'Got over the jet lag?'

'No.'

Darcy gave up and went back to his office to pass the word round that Pel's voice would peel paint and he was best left alone. Sitting in his office, Pel stared at the files on his desk awaiting his attention. The last forty-eight hours in Mexico had been grim. He had used up every French cigarette he had brought with him, plus the rest of De Troq's, and he had found Mexican cigarettes so appalling he had even tried to roll them, with the same success he had had in France. Either they were too tight and the effort to draw on them caused his eyes to bulge, or too loose, in which case, at the application of a match, they disappeared in a puff of smoke and a flare of flame that almost singed his eyebrows.

He was convinced his health had gone down the drain and that he needed an overhaul – perhaps even a wheel change and a respray. He had a headache and felt as if he'd been trampled on by a herd of wild elephants. In addition, he felt he was about to fall asleep at any minute with his head in the 'Pending' tray. This time it wasn't his first experience of jet lag and he was determined not to enjoy it.

He had not been able to sleep at all on the return flight across the Atlantic. He had tried whisky in the hope that it would lull him off but this time his mind had been too busy. Why had Jacqueline Hervé been found murdered in France, he was wondering. There could only be one reason: As he'd suspected, she had utilized Donck's stay in the penitentiary to find the treasure they'd talked about. And that seemed to indicate that Donck, who seemed to have disappeared off the face of the earth since his escape from prison, had discovered that unacceptable fact and had promptly followed her home – with the false passport that Pel had no doubt he possessed. But that set up another question: Why risk coming back to France where he was wanted for the murder of Navarro and Desgeorges? There could be only one reason: Because he knew that Jacqueline Hervé *had* found the treasure and returned with it. And that set up yet another question? *How had Jacqueline Hervé got the treasure across the Atlantic and back into France without questions being asked?*

Everybody they'd talked to had believed the treasure consisted of gold and silver coins, but the amount they had mentioned would have weighed a great deal and been impossible to hide. So could the people they'd interviewed have been wrong? Could the treasure they'd talked about have consisted of something much lighter? Diamonds, for instance? The palm of a hand could contain enough diamonds to account for the amount mentioned? Had Maximilian, unknown to his contemporaries, exchanged his gold and silver for diamonds? It seemed unlikely, because you couldn't pay soldiers with diamonds. And again there was that story of the old *Dorado* that the treasure had been found decades ago by Porfirio Díaz, who could well have known about it because he was a contemporary of Maximilian's.

Pel had worried and fretted over the questions all the way across the Atlantic until he had finally fallen into an exhausted sleep just as the pilot was lowering his flaps for the descent to the west of Paris. He had tottered from the aeroplane feeling a wreck, almost forgetting the Mexican toy gun he had brought back for Yves Pasquier next door, the two large bottles of whisky, the cigarettes, the gold necklace, the large bottle of perfume and the magnificent Mexican sarape he had found in the duty-free shop.

Sensing his mood, De Troq' had said little on the journey south and the French countryside had been so achingly beautiful Pel had wondered how the Chief had dared send him away, especially to somewhere as harsh and un-French as Mexico. Here the land was not tawny but green, there were no dust storms, no abrasive wind to chap the lips, and the sun was mellow, not harsh and cruel. When they stopped for a beer, De Troq', knowing Pel, chose a country bar with a large garden alongside. It was warm enough for two old men to be playing a slow game of boule, watched by a stout middle-aged woman with a long loaf sticking out of her shopping bag. The whole place, under the fading sign for Byrrh painted on the gable-end, smelled of coffee and Gauloises and wine, and brought back a little of Pel's spirit. He looked like a man coming up after almost drowning.

As they headed south, his cynical old heart began to thump. Soon be in Burgundy, he thought, land of Vauban, Bussy Rabutin, Madame de Sévigné and Colette. The first sight of the cracked tower of Sémur-en-Auxois as they turned off the motorway brought it all back and he arrived at Leu full of joy at his native land and intending to show all his affection for his wife. After a preliminary clutch at her, he had murmured his newly acquired endearments, '*Vida de mi vida. Alma de mi alma,*' but she had obviously had no idea what he was talking about and, steering him to a chair, had given him a large whisky and sent him straight to bed. He had awakened that morning feeling that after a sleep everything would be all right. But it wasn't. The lack of sleep and the strange effects of jet lag had caught up with him again.

After a while, Claudie Darel pushed her nose round the door of his room. The only woman in Pel's group, he always swore she'd been picked deliberately by Darcy because, in addition to being efficient, she was also pretty and charming. Pel managed to erase his scowl as she smiled at him because that was the effect she had on him.

'How do you feel, *patron*?' she asked.

'Like death,' Pel said. He made a brave effort. 'Probably, soon I'll just feel as if I'm dying.'

'You need a *café-fine*.'

She smiled again and even Pel's hard heart melted. She had that effect on everybody in the Hôtel de Police and Pel didn't know that she'd just been sent in by Darcy to bring him round. There were matters which needed Pel's attention and they couldn't wait all day until he'd recovered what passed with him as good temper.

Claudie fussed round him, bringing the coffee and brandy. 'Make you feel better, *patron*,' she said.

After a while, she tried him on the outstanding mail Darcy hadn't been able to handle, then she laid a file on his desk. It said 'Talant Supermarket Enquiries' on the outside. Always Talant supermarket, he thought. When he didn't throw it at her, she tried another one a few minutes later. This one said 'Métaux de Dijon: Stolen Vehicles Enquiry'. When that didn't appear to rouse him to fury, she left the room and reported to Darcy that it might be possible to speak to him.

'Mind,' she said, 'I can't guarantee it.'

Darcy grinned, patted her backside as she passed, picked up a few more files, put on his best smile – all white teeth and wrinkles round the eyes – and decided to take a chance.

Pel was staring at the files with a deep frown on his face. Darcy studied him for a moment, decided it was safe, and offered a cigarette.

Pel stared at it reproachfully. One of the precepts of the societies that preached ways and means to stop smoking was 'Ask your friends not to offer you cigarettes.' But that was impossible: Policemen didn't have friends. Only colleagues. He took the cigarette and Darcy, knowing a cigarette could work wonders on Pel, had his lighter to it before he could change his mind.

'Millions stop,' Pel said bitterly. 'Why can't I? I often wonder what my wife thinks of me. I've even thought of having a small fan fitted to me so that the smoke's always blown away from her.' He sighed. 'I even brought back with me enough cigarettes to fill a lorry. Duty free.'

Darcy nodded sympathetically. 'I know how it is, *patron*,' he said.

'I went to buy some perfume for my wife,' Pel went on. 'I'd bought her some gold and a thing called a *sarape* – a sort of blanket with a hole in it – but then I thought I'd try some perfume. And there they were. Thousands of them. All kinds. British. American. French. Mexican. Staring me in the face. How do you get round a situation like that? I bought as many as I could carry without breaking my arm.'

He sighed again. It was a hopeless situation. Even his natural meanness – he preferred to call it carefulness – made him buy things he didn't want. But, after all, no good Burgundian would ignore the opportunity to buy at knock-down prices enough cigarettes to fill a *bar-tabac*.

He tapped the ash from the cigarette, realizing he was suddenly feeling better. Darcy spotted the improvement at once.

'Jacqueline Hervé,' he said. 'Found strangled. Doc Minet's report's in the file.'

'Where did it happen?'

'In the cottage Navarro gave her. We found the deeds there. She was known to the neighbours as Jacqueline Dubois.'

'Didn't they see the picture of her in the papers and on television?'

'It seems she was a bit crafty. She did her hair differently and wore no make-up and it changed her appearance. They spotted Navarro at once when I produced pictures. He was there occasionally. It seems they liked to go there for weekends. Donck went there, too, I think. They couldn't be certain, but they thought it might be him.'

'But they didn't report it?'

'You know what people are like, *patron*. If they're not certain, they do nothing. They're afraid of making fools of themselves.'

'A pity more don't chance it. Why wasn't she spotted as she passed through Immigration Control at the airport? We've never withdrawn our request for them to look out for her.'

Darcy placed a small hard-backed folding document on the desk. 'Passport, *patron*,' he said.

The words, *Estados Unidos Mexicanos*, caught Pel's eye at once.

'Mexican,' he said. 'I thought they must have had them.'

Darcy opened the passport. The picture of Jacqueline Hervé bore no resemblance to the sophisticated girl in the photograph that had appeared on television, and showed instead a plain-looking girl with straight hair. The name on the passport was Ramona Flores Guzmán.

Pel nodded. 'Donck was known as Pierre Alaba. I expect he had a Mexican passport, too, from the same source.'

As he laid down the passport, Darcy produced a small coloured folder. Inside was an airline ticket to Morocco.

'One way, *patron*,' Darcy said. 'We found it in her handbag. She was intending to bolt again and this time she wasn't coming back.'

'Where is she now?'

'In the morgue. I suppose you'd like to visit the cottage.'

Pel was already reaching for his hat and coat.

Darcy gave him the details as he drove. The house had been gone over. It had been obvious at once that somebody had been searching for something.

'Yes,' Pel said. 'Treasure.'

'Treasure? What treasure?'

Pel gave Darcy a run down on the Mexican trip, and explained just what had taken place.

'But no sign of any treasure?' Darcy asked.

'No treasure,' Pel said. 'None at all.'

Fontenay L'Église was a quiet village in the hills and Jacqueline Hervé's cottage was just outside in a lane along the edge of a clump of trees. Nothing had been changed and the chalk outline of where she'd been found was still there.

They moved about the rooms, opening drawers and checking things.

'No treasure here, *patron*,' Darcy said.

'She had *something*,' Pel insisted, and went on to explain the ideas that had been in his mind as he'd flown home. 'Jacqueline Hervé was in Mexico. We know that. But she came home. Why? Because they'd forced Martin to tell them where the treasure was and I think they'd picked it up and she had it in her possession.'

He sniffed and lit a cigarette. 'It's not hard to work it out,' he went on. 'Martin met Pilar Hernandez at Tula and she shared his bed, entertained him during the day and acted as interpreter when needed. She made him take her to the film set because she'd once acted in a film and was nuts about them. After Chapadores they went on to San Miguel de Allende. During this time, Martin had found the treasure or at least where it was. He didn't intend to share it with the girl because she was just an extra detail. He returned to Mexico City to pick up what he needed – probably maps, something of that sort – and about that time Donck contacted him and told him some story that persuaded him to go to Chapadores. I expect he chose the film set because it was out of the way and never visited after dark. In the meantime, Pilar Hernandez was waiting for him, but he never turned up because he was dead, and after a day or two she decided that, like other men, he'd dropped her and she took a job.'

They turned the facts over for a while then Darcy looked up.

'And the treasure, *patron*?'

Pel paused. 'I think Donck must have pulled off one or two

small jobs to raise money,' he said. 'And they were able to pick up the treasure, whose whereabouts they'd got from Martin before they killed him. Then, because they needed money to get out of the country, Donck pulled the bank job that went wrong. While he was in gaol, Hervé shopped him for Martin's murder and bolted with the loot. Unfortunately, Donck escaped and he guessed where she'd gone. He must have known she had a false passport and no doubt he was able to check her destination with the airlines. So he came back to France, too, to find her, because he'd guessed where she'd hole up – here.'

Darcy frowned. 'There's only one question, though, *patron*,' he said. '*Why*, when she had the treasure and the whole world at her feet, did she do something that was so obviously dangerous and come back to France?'

On the way back to the city, they stopped at a bar and sat under the trees with a beer. Darcy was still frowning.

'What beats me, *patron*,' he said slowly, 'is, if they had the treasure, and it seems they *must* have had it, why did Donck hold up the bank? I know you can't pay for an airline ticket with a handful of doubloons, but you can *always* sell old coins. There's a ready market for them and they're easily handled. And there's another thing. Treasure's big. *And heavy*. A war chest to pay an army would weigh too much to get it back here without questions being asked.'

'She obviously did get it back,' Pel said.

'*Patron*, a woman couldn't carry all that money. Not in coins. It's not possible.'

'Could she disguise it?'

'What as, *patron*? Farm machinery?'

Pel gave him a cold look. While he considered sarcasm a very effective weapon, in his office there was only one person who was entitled to use it.

'It's possible, of course, that they changed the coins for something smaller of equal value,' he admitted. 'But, whatever it is now, it's either still in Mexico and Jacqueline Hervé intended to go back for it after coming here, or else – and more likely – she had it here with her and Donck found it and took it.'

16

Pel was studying himself in the mirror in his office when Darcy appeared. Mexico had aged him, he decided. There were new lines about the eyes, and his hair-line had receded so far it looked as if the tide had gone out.

As Darcy sat down, they lit cigarettes, Pel for once not feeling guilty because he considered it could be claimed he was under the stress of work. The pictures, including a not very satisfactory new one of a plainer Jacqueline Hervé blown up from her passport photograph, went out again – to the Press and the television people, requesting anyone who had seen either of the subjects to inform the police at once.

It brought the Press to Pel's door immediately – Sarrazin, the freelance; Henriot, of *Le Bien Public*, the local rag; and Fiabon, of *France Dimanche*. They wanted to know what was going on and why Pel had been to Mexico.

Pel talked to them for half an hour, managing to tell them nothing more than he wished to, giving them only the details he wanted making public in the hope that they might be able to help. It was normal enough for the Press to work closely with the police and, while sometimes it brought some strange stories to light, it sometimes also brought information.

Pel looked more normal now, probably because now that he was absorbed in something he no longer had the time to think of his own complaints. Darcy decided to chance his arm.

'Talant supermarket,' he said.

Pel glared. 'Hasn't that been cleared up?'

'Bardolle's been out there three times since you left for Mexico, the last time yesterday. Before that four times.'

'Have we complained to them?'

'Yes. It's been rewired.'

'Perhaps it needs rebuilding.'

'Yes, *patron.* We've told them that unless they can get their alarm system right, we're going to have to make them pay not just for the fact that they have the alarm connected to the Hôtel de Police but also for the fact that we go out about once a week for false alarms. They've promised to look into it and get the system replaced with a better one.'

'So what's the problem?'

'That type, Edouard Fousse – L'Estropié. The bastard's always there grinning his head off and shouting abuse at Bardolle. Bardolle's sworn he'll hit him one of these days.'

'He'd better not,' Pel said. 'Bardolle's fists are as big as sacks of coal. If he hit Edouard Fousse, he'd disappear into outer space.'

Darcy grinned. 'Bardolle's a surprisingly gentle type normally,' he said. 'He loves kids and dogs.'

'Is he the best man for the job?'

Darcy considered. 'He's a countryman and he's best employed in the countryside.' He looked at Pel. 'He confessed the other day that he'd done a little poaching as a boy.'

'I hope he stopped when he became a cop.'

Darcy grinned. 'All the same, he has to take his whack at town jobs like the rest of us.' He glanced at his file. 'Other outstanding things. One *aggression nocturne* – in the Rue de la Liberté. Kid aged eighteen. Fortunately for us, as he bolted he ran straight into Brochard who was there by sheer chance, returning that way to the Hôtel de Police after making an enquiry about an assault at Amicourt. It's my opinion he'd been to see a girl-friend but I can hardly haul him up for it when he picked up the mugger. There was also an intruder in the Nouvelles Galéries. Wino called Raymond Ellice. He found the door unlocked and walked in because it was warm and he was looking for somewhere snug to sleep. Naturally he became interested in their wines and spirits department. But why was it open? It seems that one Jacques Delmar had opened it and got away with a brand-new racing bicycle that was on display. Carried it down from the third flour without being spotted from the road or by one of the security men. We picked up Raymonde Ellice the same day. Drunk. With a case of brandy stolen from the Nouvelles Galéries under the bed. Jacques Delmar was picked up an hour later. He was just giving the bike a bit of a polish and thinking of trying to find a backer so he could enter the Tour de France next year.' Darcy grinned. 'Not too bad, *patron*. We're well up on the list. After all, Lyons had two shot in a bar last week. They were teasing the landlord for not standing his round, so he got out his shot-gun and blew them through the wall.'

'It doesn't pay to tease landlords.'

Darcy laughed. 'Paris is in a mess, of course. The latest crime report says it's the least safe city in the world, with a burglary every eight minutes, a 640 per cent increase over six years in the use of heroin, a 270 per cent increase in five years in aggression on the Métro, and a great need for another 3,000 cops. It's like a Sunday School here by comparison.'

Pel nodded, his mind far away. He stubbed out his cigarette. 'What's De Troq' on?'

'I've told him to help Nosjean.'

'Take him off it. I need him. Tell him I want him.'

De Troq' entered warily. The news that Pel was in a bad temper had permeated the Hôtel de Police and everybody was being wary. He opened the door slowly, closing it quietly behind him, a small neat figure completely untouched, Pel noticed bitterly, by his trip across the Atlantic.

'De Troquereau,' he said. 'Victor-Charles de Troquereau Tournay-Turenne. Also known as the Baron de Troquereau.'

De Troq' eyed him narrowly. 'That's right, *patron*.'

'Descendant, of one Armande-Pierre de Troquereau Tournay-Turenne, General of the Empire.' He paused. 'Second Empire,' he added, because Napoleon III's Second Empire was a shabby imitation of the Great Napoleon's First Empire. Theirs had called them Napoleon the Great and Napoleon the Small, and there was a lot of truth in the comment.

'His grandfather,' De Troq said, coldly, never one to take cheek, not even from Pel, 'was a brigadier-general in the First Empire and *his* title came from the old regime, not one of Bonapartes.'

Pel didn't argue. It was something he already knew because he'd looked it up. 'Armande-Pierre,' he said. '1815 to 1891.

Served, if I'm not mistaken, in the Crimea, Algeria, Mexico and at Sedan in the Franco-Prussian War.'

'That's right, *patron*. Something wrong with that?' De Troq's voice was cold because he suffered quite a lot of leg-pulling in the sergeants' room.

'None whatsoever,' Pel said. 'I'm still interested in the intervention in Mexico and he might have had something to say about it. Knowing your absorption in your background, I thought you might be able to help. You're off Nosjean's car case and on the Navarro-Martin-Hervé case.'

De Troq' sat in silence.

'I learned a lot about General de Troquereau while we were in Mexico,' Pel went on. 'He had a lot of things to say about what happened.'

'I think he came out of it with some shreds of honour left,' De Troq' said. 'He was one of the few who did.'

'That I'm not denying. Do you have much information on him?'

'There's a lot in the military museums, *patron*. In the Musée de l'Armée at the Invalides in Paris, there's a portrait. They also have his papers.'

'When we were in Mexico we found people tended to bring out his book *Mes Aventures en Mexique* and quote it at us.'

De Troq' grinned. 'He fancied himself as a writer, *patron*.'

'You have a copy, I know. And I imagine you know his papers in the Musée de l'Armée.'

'Like the back of my hand, *patron*. In families like mine it's the habit to grow up with such things. We had money enough then to do so. Unfortunately, by the time I was adult the money was no longer there.'

'Nevertheless, you know your way about his papers. So! You will now go home, *mon brave*, take your copy of *Mes Aventure en Mexique* from the shelf and you will read it. Carefully. From end to end. You will then go to Paris and go through the papers in the Musée de l'Armée.'

'What am I looking for, *patron*?'

'References to treasure. As we know, the Emperor Maximilian hid three-quarters of his war chest and it has never been seen since. There are stories that it's been found. Others that it has not. I think Donck and Hervé – for that matter Navarro and Professor Martin, from whom all this started – certainly thought that it had not, and guessed where it was. So go home. Read everything you can that was written on the Mexican intervention, then come back here and tell me if you've found any reference to treasure.'

De Troq' rose slowly, a little puzzled. He had a date for the following evening with Judge Polverari's secretary. He'd been away a long time and had a lot to catch up on. He had been wondering, in fact, how he could wangle the night off and now, it seemed, he had no need to. On the other hand, he knew Pel would be waiting and he would need to be back in the office after a reasonable lapse of time with the facts at his fingertips. He had better, he decided, get busy at once.

'Very well, *patron*,' he said. 'I'll find out all I can.'

After he'd gone, studying the files, Pel had a sudden wish to know more of the man they had heard so much about. So far, he realized, he'd never really met him face to face.

'Maximilian, Emperor of Mexico,' he said to Claudie Darel, when she appeared in answer to his call. 'Know anything about him?'

'No, *patron*. Not a thing.' At least she was honest. Most people, unwilling to admit lack of knowledge, would have hummed and hah-ed and made guesses.

'Bring me the encyclopaedia,' he said. 'Let's have a look at him.'

The volume was deposited on his desk, a slip of paper between the appropriate pages, and he opened it and stared at the small print:

> **Maximilian Ferdinand Joseph, Archduke (1831–1867). Emperor of Mexico.** Brother of Emperor Franz Joseph of Austria and son-in-law of King Leopold I, of the Belgians, whose daughter, Charlotte, he married in 1857. Born Schönbrunn, Vienna; governor of Lombardo-Venetia. When French troops invaded Mexico, he was offered the Mexican throne. He arrived in Mexico 1864. Juárez, the elected Mexican president opposed him and civil war followed. In 1867 the Fr. troops were withdrawn and M. was captured at Querétaro and shot. See E. Corti, *Die Tragödie eines Kaisers*, 1933; M. Hyde, *Mexican Empire*, 1945; *La Tragédie Mexicaine*, Camille Buffin, Brussels, 1925.

Maximilian, Pel decided, seemed to be the sort who never managed to come to terms with reality and was easily taken in by a bunch of political shysters. Nowadays, he'd be chosen as the front man by a bunch of swindlers to given an impression of honesty. At the very least, he would be the man who allowed himself to be taken in by door-to-door bond salesmen.

There was a picture, flattering no doubt in the way of royal portraits, of a tall young man with a blank visage adorned by a luxuriant beard, but to a policeman's cynical eye, he looked exactly like the idealistic type of young man who might well get himself shot. He had the look of a born victim.

Other things in addition to the Donck-Hervé case were also moving and Aimedieu's checking the rash of 500-franc notes in Cloing had brought an unexpected bonus.

'The Moissin repair depot,' he told Nosjean. 'The garage at Ferouelle nearby. Run by a type called Marc Moissin. They seem to come from there. We thought they might. Mind, the place seems straightforward. It takes a lot of vehicles for repair and overhaul, and there's a steady sale of new cars. I expect a lot of ready cash changes hands. There are plenty of little fiddles. Cars are like that. They breed fiddles.'

Nosjean frowned. 'What's known about this place?' he asked. 'I still think Ferouelle's a funny place to have a repair depot. What about this Marc Moisson, for instance? Is he honest?'

'He has no record.'

'Doesn't mean a thing. There's always a first time. What do you know of him?'

'He has a brother who helps him at weekends. He doesn't live at Ferouelle, though. Lives in Dijon. Works at Métaux de Dijon.'

Nosjean's ears pricked. 'Does he now?' he said slowly. 'What's *his* name?'

'Claude. Claude Moissin. The father owned the garage before Marc Moissin, and the sons were taught the trade before the old man died.'

'The *sons*?' Nosjean asked.

'There are others as well. One lives in Nantes –'

'Does he work there?' Nosjean was bolt upright at once.

'Yes.'

'Where exactly?'

'Produits Métallurgiques.'

'Aren't they the firm who've been having cars stolen like Métaux de Dijon?' Nosjean was turning sheets of paper over at great speed. He slapped the pile. 'That's right. Here it is. What do we know about *this* Moissin? What's *his* name?'

'Georges. He married a girl from Nantes whose brother runs a garage, and Georges went over there to live. He also helps in the garage at weekends.'

'Name of *this* garage?'

'Garage Tourdin.'

'Lot of garages around, aren't there? Tell me more.'

Aimedieu shrugged. 'There are four Moissins altogether. Marc, Claude, Georges and Bruno. Three are fitters. The other – Bruno – is a clerk. Civil Service, I think.'

'Three fitters. One runs a garage at Ferouelle and tosses around 500-franc notes as if they're confetti. One works at Métaux de Dijon, which is suffering from a rash of stolen cars, and helps his brother at Ferouelle. Another brother at Produits Métallurgiques de Nantes, which is also suffering from the same rash of stolen cars, and at weekends he, too, helps his brother-in-law, who owns the Garage Tourdin. A big coincidence, don't you think, *mon vieux*?'

Aimedieu did think, and Nosjean leaned across the desk.

'Get out there,' he advised. 'Have another look round. I'm sure you'll come up with something more.'

Going to see Dugaste again, Nosjean found him with his head in the engine of the new Citroën he'd bought.

'Got it near Lyons,' he said.

'At Tubours?' Nosjean asked innocently.

Dugaste looked startled. 'How did you know?'

'Heard about that place. I'm after a new car and I'm told they're good.'

Dugaste's relief was obvious. Nosjean's question had clearly frightened him but he seemed satisfied with the explanation. He smiled. 'Went off for the weekend with the wife and went mad. Marc Moissin put me on to the place. He's clever with cars.'

Indeed he was, Nosjean thought. Very clever. Too clever for his own good, in fact.

Going back to the lists of stolen cars, it didn't take him long to spot a strange similarity between the cars stolen from Métaux de Dijon and those stolen from Produits Métallurgiques de Nantes. Within a day or two of a car being reported stolen at Nantes, he noticed, one was reported to the insurance companies as being stolen at Métaux de Dijon, or within a day or two of one being reported lost at Dijon, one was reported stolen at Nantes. And oddly enough, though the cars were never the same model, they were always roughly the same size and always roughly the same value.

'Are they swapping them?' Aimedieu asked.

'If they are,' Nosjean said, 'who's profiting? Let's dig a bit more deeply. What about this fourth brother, who works for the Civil Service?'

Surprise, surprise.

It didn't startle them very much when they learned that Moissin Number Four, by name Bruno, worked in the Vehicle Registration Department in the Préfecture in the city. 'Now *that*,' Nosjean said, 'is very interesting, isn't it? I think you'd better have a full-time watch put on that place at Ferouelle while I go to see the top boy at the Préfecture.'

The top boy in the Vehicle Registration Office in the Préfecture was a stiff-necked Civil Servant who looked faintly dessicated. At first he denied to Nosjean the slightest possibility of anything going wrong with the system of registering vehicles.

'It's foolproof,' he insisted.

'Foolproof?' Nosjean's eyebrows lifted.

'Absolutely.'

'Are you suggesting that there are never cases of registration forms being damaged, crumpled torn or lost before they go through the computer so that they have to be written off.'

'Absolutely.' A deep frown of disapproval changed to one of anxiety. 'Well, of course, there are always one or two. It's inevitable, isn't it? Nobody and nothing is foolproof.'

'You just said *your* system was.'

'Well, perhaps I was being over-enthusiastic. A few are always lost.'

'Many?'

'Of course not. One or two each month.'

'Which would add up to quite a few in the course of a year, wouldn't it?'

Leaving the desiccated gentleman somewhat shaken but promising to keep the enquiry firmly under his hat, Nosjean contacted Aimedieu and, telling him to draw on Brochard, Lacocq or Morell, said he wanted to know everywhere that Marc Moissin, of the garage at Ferouelle, went.

Meanwhile, however, there was no sign of Donck and no one could remember seeing Jacqueline Hervé, save the neighbours at Fontenay l'Église. However, all was not lost because a fortnight later, Aubineau reported another theft from the car-park of Métaux de Dijon. 'Not ours,' he told Nosjean. 'Assurances Gau. *They* told me. Type called Baudon. Hilaire Baudon, 17, Rue Petite Baratte, Talant. He's claimed for a stolen green Renault. Number 67 RH 39.'

'Thanks,' Nosjean said.

'Are you getting anywhere?'

'We might surprise you yet,' Nosjean said and promptly got on to the police at Nantes.

Two days later he was far from surprised to learn that a yellow Citroën, number 14 PT 33, owned by one Alain Tessler and of roughly the same value as Baudon's Renault, had disappeared from the car-park at Produits Métallurgiques de Nantes.

He smiled. Things were beginning to come together. After all, Dijon and Nantes couldn't be much further apart without going outside France. It seemed a very amicable arrangement for a scheme which was finally beginning to take shape in his mind.

It came as no surprise when Aimedieu appeared in the office.

'Marc Moisson,' he said. 'He drove to Nantes in a green Renault number 43 BH 67 – a Bas Rhin number. I followed with Brochard.'

'Could it have been the stolen car?'

'It could. Same model, but different number. He set off on the Dijon-Bourges road to Tours, but then he turned off and stopped in the square at Chanterrepie.'

'And?'

'And, lo and behold, soon afterwards a Citroën, colour yellow number 61 HR 17, appeared. Moissin got out and talked to the man who'd driven it in. They swapped papers, then called in a bar for a drink.'

'Any documents change hands? Registration documents, for instance.'

'Yes. They were both carrying the manufacturer's grey cards and they exchanged them. Then –' Aimedieu grinned '– instead of going back to their cars, Moissin got into the Citroën and headed back towards Dijon.'

'And the other type?'

'He got in the Renault and headed towards the Nantes road.'

'They swapped cars?'

Aimedieu frowned. 'They're changing the numbers, dodging up the registration documents and swapping them. Why?'

'We'll know before long,' Nosjean said. 'The type from Nantes. Who was he, do you know?'

'Marc Moissin called him Georges. We went into the same bar for a beer and did a bit of listening. They were noisy, cheerful and seemed very pleased with themselves. I think it was his brother.'

Nosjean smiled. 'I think so, too,' he said.

A report from Barribal, requested by Pel, arrived the following morning. It was short and to the point and was addressed to 'Chief Inspector Don Evaristo Clovio Desiderato Pel'. Pel promptly hid it under his blotter. Evariste Clovis Désiré were bad enough. Evaristo Clovio Desiderato were beyond the pale.

The message, to read which he waited until Claudie had disappeared, was short. 'Your friend, Marc Donck, alias Pierre Alaba, went round airlines in Mexico City claiming to be detective. By that means he learned that Jacqueline Hervé, alias Ramona Flores Guzmán, flew out of Mexico City on 17th, by jumbo to Paris, France. Have seen passenger list.'

Pel showed it to Darcy. 'It's obvious now, isn't it?' he said. 'He knew she came back to France and he knew why. Let's go and have a beer.'

As they reached the hall downstairs, the doors to the street crashed open and Bardolle, as big as a dray-horse and as usual just as noisy, appeared through them. He was hopping mad and Bardolle was big enough when he was hopping mad to make his presence felt. The noise was enough to shake the windows.

'That little creep, Fousse,' he was snorting. 'I thought he was up to something because he was always there. But I could never pin him down. Nothing had ever been pinched and no one had got inside. Now I've got him.'

Pel's eyebrows lifted. 'What happened, *mon brave*?'

'Talant,' Bardolle said. '*He* set up those alarms, *patron*. Deliberately. It was part of a plan. He found he could set them off with a wire, so he hatched a little plot. When the alarm went off, he bolted round the corner and only appeared after a police car turned up. He did it so often, in the end Traffic and Uniform began to get sick of investigating. But that was the idea. He noticed they took longer every time to arrive – naturally, because they always assumed it was going to be another false alarm. At Talant, it always was and they didn't rush. And that was what he was working up to, because last night it *wasn't* a false alarm. He forced a window at the back, but he knew he couldn't go inside without setting off the alarm. But he'd been timing our arrivals and he knew he had a good twenty minutes to do what he wanted. He got in and out again at the back, while the alarm went off and Traffic and Uniform were arguing at the front about whether to drag out the manager and what they were going to call him when he arrived. Traffic and Uniform are playing hell.'

'You're not doing badly yourself,' Pel said dryly. 'How did you find out?'

'Two kids kissing good-night under the trees saw him leave. The stupid con couldn't even make a good job of it.'

'Have you been to look him up?'

'He's disappeared, *patron*.'

Pet patted Bardolle's arm. It was like patting an iron girder. 'He'll be in the city somewhere,' he said. 'What's been taken?'

'Jewellery.'

Pel's eyebrows lifted. 'I thought they didn't carry anything worth while.'

'They don't,' Bardolle growled. 'But that's what he was after. His brother told me. Cheap jewellery. He wears it. He's crazy about it. You've seen him, *patron*. Ear-rings. Bracelets. Neck chains. He's spent all these hours and wasted all our time just for a handful of cheap jewellery.'

17

Pel rose early the following morning. Summer was on its way and the air was balmy. Madame Pel was in the garden, clipping the heads off a few dead flowers and quietly singing one of the obscure little songs she seemed to love:

Gais et contents,
Nous marchions triomphants,
En allant à Longchamp . . .

It was all very familiar and made Pel glad to be home. Pel's nesting instincts were stronger than he'd imagined, and long-distance telephone calls were never the same. Especially with Pel. If he tried to call an insurance company in Lyons he invariably found himself speaking to a brasserie in Pau.

Madame Routy served breakfast in the garden. Pel didn't like eating outside. In the evening, it made the onion soup congeal, and at breakfast time it made his coffee cold. However, he gave way as graciously as possible because Madame enjoyed it, and over the croissants she started asking him again about his trip.

'There are other things that are valuable, which could be considered treasure, apart from gold and silver,' she said.

'Such as what?'

'Skill, for a start. Could it be paintings? After all, Maximilian would undoubtedly have had a few valuable possessions of that sort.'

'Jacqueline Hervé would never have got old masters through the Customs,' Pel said. All the same, he decided, it was a thought worth investigating if nothing else turned up.

'Could it have been drugs?' his wife went on. 'After all, isn't

Mexico where marijuana comes from? Isn't that where it all started?'

Pel shook his head. 'What have drugs to do with the intervention in Mexico and the Emperor Maximilian?'

'It depends, I suppose, on what you consider valuable. An old man with no money probably considers his pipe valuable. My mother kept all the letters I wrote from school, all my drawings, every bit of needlework I did. Some of it was dreadful but she kept it and I've no doubt to her it had worth.'

When Pel left, Madame Routy opened the door for him – with an alacrity, he thought, that seemed to indicate she was glad to be rid of him. As he drove out of the gate, Yves Pasquier was in the road with the dog, Gyp. He was wearing a cowboy hat and was frightening the birds with a plastic tommy-gun which was emitting fiendish rattles. He appeared to be engaged in a running battle with bandits.

'They're there,' he pointed out. 'Behind the trees.'

'Who are?'

'The gangsters! They're after me.' Yves Pasquier paused. 'Did you find that cure for chewing-gum mixed up with string and marbles?'

'I'll have a word with the Forensic Laboratory,' Pel said. 'They might be able to come up with something.'

'Trying to get if off's the chief problem. *Maman* gets furious. She doesn't like chewing-gum. She says it's bad for the digestion.' He frowned. 'I suppose it is if you're delicate. *I'm* delicate.'

'You look as tough as an old sea-boot.'

'Oh, no. Listen.' Yves Pasquier coughed energetically. 'Lungs.'

'Continue wearing the hat,' Pel said. 'Keeping the head warm is good for the lungs.' He studied the plastic tommy-gun. 'Don't you use the Mexican gun I brought you?' Pel felt slightly hurt. 'I carried it a long way. It's a replica of the one carried by Pancho Villa, the bandit.'

The boy shook his head. 'Oh, no,' he said. 'That's different.'

'Is it?' To Pel it had seemed a very normal small boy's gun, not half as terrifying as the one Yves Pasquier was carrying at the moment.

'I keep it under my pillow. It's special, you see.'

Pel didn't argue. What Madame had said was right. Things had different values to different people. To Yves Pasquier a plastic gun, of no great value and bought without much effort, represented a treasure. All the same, Pel thought, he couldn't imagine Marc Donck committing murder for a plastic gun.

The day was too bright and too warm to be downcast for long, and he headed for the Hôtel de Police cheerfully. When he arrived, he was surprised to encounter Sergeant Bardolle just entering, as noisy as ever, pushing ahead of him a scared-looking Edouard Fousse, all gold ear-rings, necklaces and clanking bracelets. No wonder, Pel thought, he had plotted to rob the cheap jewellery stand at the supermarket. He obviously had great need of its wares.

As he drew nearer, he noticed that Fousse had a split lip, a bruised nose and a black eye. There was also a cut on Bardolle's head and blood on his collar, and he was carrying a piece of heavy old-fashioned metal conduit piping.

'I got the con, *patron*,' he said. 'He thought he could get away with it. But I found him. He was hiding in a shed at his mother's. Lacocq was with me. Lacocq took one side. I took the other. He was watching Lacocq and he didn't hear me.'

'You can move silently?'

'Yes, *patron*.'

'Old poaching habits, no doubt.'

Bardolle gave Pel a quick look, obviously wondering how he'd learned about his misspent youth, and hurried on, gesturing with the iron pipe. 'When he saw me, he took a swing at me with this. He got me, too. And he kept on swinging even when I tried to grab him. I had to let him have one to quieten him down.'

Pel glanced at Bardolle's huge fists. 'What are you charging him with?'

'Theft. Wasting police time. Assault on a police officer.'

Pel studied Bardolle's bulk and Fousse's black eye, split lip and bruised nose. 'I think,' he said dryly, 'that you ought to charge him with attempting to commit suicide.'

Nosjean was waiting in Pel's office, anxious to explain what he was up to. Pel sent out for beer and Nosjean sat in the window to describe what he'd been doing.

'Marc Moissin, *patron*,' he said. 'He has a brother, Georges Moissin, who works at Produits Métallurgiques de Nantes. We kept an eye on a certain Hilaire Baudon who claimed to have lost a green Renault, and found he turned up at work the following week in a red Citroën, remarkably like the one the Nantes police had said had been reported lost the following day by a certain Alain Tessler, who it seemed, was now driving a green Renault, without doubt the one Hilaire Baudon had reported losing.'

He outlined what Aimedieu had discovered. 'It looks remarkably simple, doesn't it, *patron*? Chanterrepie is just about halfway between Nantes and Dijon and a good place to swap cars.'

Nosjean had done his homework well and had looked up the list of those men who had reported their cars stolen and had claimed their value from their insurance companies. In this Aubineau had proved a great help.

It had also been necessary to check a few bank balances and it had come as no surprise to find that in almost every case the bank statement showed the unexpected appearance of a sum equivalent to the value of the lost car in the owner's account – clearly, the insurance company's money. But then, in every case, a proportion was removed a few weeks later – not sufficient to buy a new car, Nosjean noticed – but always a clear twenty-five per cent of the value of the car. And in some cases the money was paid to the Garage Moissin at Ferouelle. It was becoming clearer why Marc Moissin was able to flash 500-franc notes around.

'Keep watching them,' Nosjean had ordered and sure enough within days Aimedieu had appeared, grinning all over his face. 'Baudon's got a new car,' he had said. 'Brand-new Toyota Estate. Blue. Bought from a garage at Tubours near Lyons. Garage Poirons, Rue Clément-Marol. It's got the label stuck on the window. I went to Lyons and did a bit of checking. They've still got the red Citroën which they took in part exchange. I told them I wanted to buy one and got a look at the engine. The number's been changed. Cleverly. Hard to tell. But it *was* changed. I also got a look at the registration certificate. It's phoney. It looks good but it's got the new number on it, which makes it false and a criminal offence. One other thing. Garage Poirons at Tubours in Lyons is run by another Moissin – a cousin this time.'

It had taken only another forty-eight hours to discover that all the men from Métaux de Dijon who had lost cars and replaced them with fresh second-hand cars had all eventually changed them for brand-new cars bought from Garage Moissin at Ferouelle or, directed by Marc Moissin, from his cousin's garage at Tubours near Lyons. From there, it took no time at all to learn that the owners of cars stolen from Produits Métallurgiques at Nantes had done the same, directed in their case to the Garage Ribin at Bordeaux. A little more digging showed that the Garage Ribin was owned by the husband of the sister of the man who owned the garage at Nantes, which had done all the engine-number changes. Doubtless the Moissins drew a cut on every transaction. It was a carefully planned operation with perks coming from all directions.

'It's pretty clear what's happening,' Nosjean said. 'The Moissin brother at Métaux de Dijon persuades a workmate he needs a change of vehicle. The keys are handed over and the car's driven out at the end of the shift while the owner makes a point of letting himself be seen searching for it. At the same time a car of roughly the same value is stolen by the same method at the other side of the country. If the first one goes in Dijon, the other goes in Nantes, and vice versa. The engine numbers are changed and, with the aid of little brother Bruno in the Vehicle Registration Department, they also get a new registration certificate. All done at full speed. The cars are simply swapped.'

'But what do the owners gain?' Aimedieu sounded puzzled.

Nosjean gestured. 'They draw the insurance on the stolen car – a matter of around 33,000 to 40,000 francs – and they acquire a car to take its place at no extra cost. The owner of the exchanged car then sells his new second-hand car – the one he appears to have bought with the insurance he got to replace the one he's lost but hasn't – and buys a brand-new car, something everybody likes having, at the Garage Moissin or a garage recommended by them. So out of the deal they acquire a brand-new car and what's left of a sum of around 30 to 40,000 francs insurance, less twenty-five per cent to Marc Moissin. Doubtless, they also pay heavily for the numbers being changed, and the new registration certificate, but I reckon they're still around 20,000 francs or so to the good at the end. Moissin draws his twenty-five per cent and the cost of the numbers change, which is shared with brother

Claude who recruits the mugs. I bet the word of a complicated fiddle like this flew round Métaux de Dijon like a forest fire. Brother Georges and his brother-in-law in Nantes are doing the same and the brother in the Vehicle Registration Office gets *his* share for pinching the registration forms and seeing they're properly filled in – I expect, on another computer similar to the registration department's.' Nosjean smiled. 'There are going to be a lot of red faces at Métaux de Dijon and Produits Métallurgiques de Nantes.'

18

The Hôtel de Police was busy. Crowded into the hall were around 60 nervous-looking men, dressed in their best clothes and doing their utmost to look as innocent as schoolboys. They were the owners of the missing vehicles who were facing charges of falsely reporting cars stolen and fraudulently collecting the insurance, conspiracy, intent to defraud, wasting police time, and a few other associated things. Among them were the four Moissin brothers and a few odd brothers-in-law and assorted cousins. There were also a few lawyers, looking peevish because of the complications of the case; Judge Brisard and Judge Polverari, fretful and overworked; and Aimedieu, Brochard and Lacocq, who were the only ones there who were looking pleased with themselves. Nosjean was watching the milling crowed with an expression of bewilderment on his face.

'Why do they do it?' he asked. 'The car owners I can understand. They got a new car for nothing, plus a bit in the bank. But the Moissins didn't get such a fat lot – not sharing it among six or eight of them.'

Pel gestured. 'Perhaps it boosted sales,' he suggested.

When De Troq' appeared, he looked a little strained and tired. It wasn't entirely due to the reading he'd done, though he'd done plenty, but the night before he had been with Judge Polverari's secretary. It had been late when he'd left and, realizing he still had reading to do, he had continued without going to bed. He felt like something the cat had dragged in.

Assuming he'd been doing only a lot of hard work, Pel offered him a cigarette and asked Claudie Darel to produce coffee. De Troq' accepted both with gratitude.

'Well,' Pel said when he was settled, 'what had your venerable ancestor, the General, to tell us?'

'Not much we don't know already,' De Troq' admitted. 'He mentions the money lost at the Battle of San Jacinto and that Maximilian hid the rest of the war chest because he was beginning to realize he was going to be defeated and thought he could use it to bargain for his life. Already European diplomats were asking for his safe passage home and thought it could be bought. Unfortunately, it seems that, though the war chest was hidden, Maximilian could find no one he could trust to dig it up without also disappearing with it, and anyway, Juárez had no intention of freeing him and preferred to shoot him instead – *pour encourager les autres*.'

'So there *might* have been a treasure in the stables at Las Rosas and it *might not* have been dug up before 1920, as we were told?'

'Possibly, *patron*.' De Troq' frowned. 'But the General also mentions there was something else that Maximilian said might save his life.'

Pel pushed his spectacles up to his forehead and leaned across the desk. 'Inform me.'

'Maximilian didn't spell it out. I expect he was being cagey, but he mentioned the Hacienda de las Rosas again.' De Troq' paused. 'There's one other thing, too. After Maximilian was shot, his personal belongings were all sent back to Europe in a ship that had been waiting at Veracruz to carry him to Austria, and it seems the captain had been warned to receive, in the event of disaster, a large packet of letters and Maximilian's diary for 1867 – the last months of his life. These, he was told, were addressed to – among others – Maximilian's wife, Carlota, by then mad; his brother, the Emperor Franz Josef, of Austria; Napoleon III; Eugénie, Napoleon's wife; Marshal Bazaine, who'd been in command of the French forces in Mexico; the King of Italy; the King of the Belgians; the President of the United States; and Queen Victoria of England, to whom he was, of course, related. There were others to various other people, too. The General learned all this later from Felix zu Salm.'

'Whom we bumped into in Mexico,'

'Exactly. However –' De Troq' looked up '– I've done a bit of checking. In Austria. In Italy. In Belgium. There's no record of any letters ever arriving in Europe. They seem never to have left Mexico.'

Pel frowned. 'What was the content of these letters?'

'Impassioned appeals for help. Requests for money. For soldiers. For ships. Descriptions of how things were going. Pleas. Confessions. They must have told quite a story. Especially the diary.'

Pel was deep in thought. Without being aware of it, he lit a fresh cigarette from the stub of the old one. 'Would these letters have any value?' he asked.

'A letter by the composer, Lizst – not a composition, just a simple letter – fetched 15,000 dollars in New York last year, *patron*.'

'And how many of these letters were there by Maximilian?'

'I get the impression there were at least fifteen – probably more.'

Pel scratched a few figures on his blotter. 'That would mean a rough value altogether of around 225,000 dollars or say around 1,575,000 francs, not counting the diary. A rough estimate but near enough.'

'You think *they* were the treasure, *patron*?'

'You suggested it. Not me.'

'They're the sort of thing that would catch Martin's interest. It was his period. He was an expert on the nineteenth century. They're also the sort of thing that might catch Donck's eye. He was a scholar. Even if a scholar gone wrong. It would also explain Navarro's interest. He was a scholar too, and, what's more, a scholar with a Mexican background. He'd be able to assess their genuineness.'

'Do you know any more about these letters?'

'Yes, *patron*. I've made enquiries. If they didn't reach Europe, then they must have remained in Mexico. For some reason, they must have been kept there. Perhaps they were never passed on to whoever it was who was to carry them to Europe. And if they weren't, *patron*, Martin could have discovered that perhaps they hadn't been destroyed and still existed. Martin, more than anybody, would know their value to collectors.'

'So what happened to these letters?' Pel asked. 'If it's letters we're after.'

De Troq' opened his notebook, turned several pages and looked up. 'General de Troquereau,' he said, 'mentioned Agnes Salm-Salm.'

Pel sat bolt upright. 'Who?'

'Agnes Salm-Salm. Our missing friend, "ASS". The letters we couldn't understand. It was Agnes Salm-Salm, the American circus rider who married Felix zu Salm-Salm.'

'I thought his name was Felix Salm.'

'That's what people appear to have called him. The same way people call me De Troquereau or even De Troq', instead of my full name of De Troquereau Tournay-Turenne. These old names, *patron*. They can be quite a mouthful.' De Troq' gave a rueful smile but, he sounded quite proud of the fact, nevertheless.

'His full title was Prince Felix zu Salm-Salm. He was the son of one of the great families of Germany and he'd served as a cavalry officer, but mounting debts forced him to leave his regiment and take service with the Austrians. He was soon in debt again, though, so he went to America and fought with the Northerners in their Civil War and became a brigadier-general. While he was there, he met his wife, Agnes, the circus rider. They didn't appear to match much but, in fact, it seems to have been a good marriage. She was the more intelligent of the two and helped to further his career and followed him throughout the Civil War, working in hospitals. When the war ended, though, he had no job, but there was a full-scale war going on south of the border so they joined Maximilian. He was with Maximilian at Querétaro.'

De Troq' studied his notes again. 'The Siege of Querétaro started on 14 March 1867, and the Juáristas broke in on the night of 14–15 May, and Maximilian, Salm and many others were taken prisoner. Agnes Salm was allowed to visit her husband and the two of them plotted Maximilian's release. Given sufficient money, even the senior officers in charge of the prisoner could have been bribed, but Maximilian considered escape beneath his dignity and, anyway, the bribes were enormous and he had little money. In the end, Agnes Salm was ordered to leave, so she turned her attention instead to Juárez himself and, though he refused to pardon Maximilian, he did promise to save her husband. The emperor was shot but Salm was allowed to go free – though it didn't do him a lot of good. He was killed during the Franco-Prussian War three years later.'

'A brave woman.' Pel was impressed. He could see himself held prisoner and his brave wife struggling to free him. He shook his head to rid himself of the image.

'How did you get to know all this?'

'Her memoirs, *patron*. They were published. I looked them up.'

Pel frowned, deep in thought. 'During all this time,' he asked, 'did she stay in Querétaro?'

'No, *patron*. And this is the interesting part. She says she was lodged in the most comfortable hacienda in the neighbourhood.'

'Las Rosas?' Pel lit a cigarette at speed, again without even noticing. 'That's where Maximilian's treasure was supposed to have been hidden.'

'"Treasure" isn't a word that Agnes Salm ever uses,' De Troq' pointed out. 'She mentions being entrusted with documents and there are references to them in her unedited memoirs, though she cut them for the published edition. She says –' De Troq' glanced again at his notes '– that, while pleading for Prince Salm's life, she was entrusted with letters which, it seems, were smuggled from Maximilian to Salm who passed them to his wife at some point when she was allowed to talk to him. She took them away, intending to send them on, but, because it was dangerous to be found with them, she hid them – by the look of it, at the Hacienda de las Rosas. But after another visit to her husband, the Mexicans began to be suspicious and she was never allowed to go back to the hacienda. When Maximilian was shot, she assumed that the letters, which were largely appeals for help, had become worthless, so she left them where she'd hidden them, and by the time she produced her edited memoirs she seems to have decided they weren't worth mentioning.' De Troq' paused again. 'Perhaps they weren't worth anything then, *patron*. But they would be now. Perhaps *they* were the "treasure" Martin was after. They told us at the Hotel de las Rosas of hidden cupboards in walls and in beds and tables. We saw some. She must have hidden them there and Martin must have found them.' He juggled with his notes again. 'She published two lots of memoirs, both covering roughly the same period. But there was also another edition, unedited, produced in New York around 1900, probably after her death. In the copy I got hold of, she says she slept with Maximilian, Bazaine and Napoleon III.'

Pel looked startled. 'What was she? A *grande horizontale supérieure?*'

'No, *patron*. She seems to have been a very moral woman.'

'But Maximilian, Bazaine and Napoleon?'

'There are more, *patron*. She also mentions having the Emperor Franz Josef in bed with her, the King of the Belgians, the King of Italy, the President of the United States, the Prussian Minister in Mexico, the Austrian Minister, Garibaldi and the King of Prussia.'

'Good God!'

De Troq' was smiling. 'But she also mentions sleeping with the Empress Carlota, the Empress Eugénie, the Crown Princess of Prussia, who was Carlota's cousin, the Empress of Brazil, who nearly became Maximilian's mother-in-law, and Queen Victoria of England.'

Pel stared. 'Did she suffer from hallucinations?'

'A moment, *patron*.' De Troq' consulted his notebook. 'I copied one passage down. It goes, "I slept as usual with Maximilian, Napoleon, Marshal Bazaine, Vittorio Emanuele, Leopold of Belgium, Franz Josef, Eugénie, Carlota, and Queen Victoria."'

'All of them? At once?'

De Troq' paused. 'It puzzled me,' he admitted. 'I found the sentence in her unedited memoirs. It isn't in the earlier editions, which appeared in the States at the beginning of this century. Perhaps the American publishers, with a new century to please and freed from the moralities of the last century, thought the comment was salacious and would sell more copies. But I don't think she meant she actually *slept* with them, *patron*. I think she was speaking figuratively. I think it was a sort of code. She meant she was sleeping with the letters. She had them with her in bed. For safe keeping. That treasure we were looking for, the treasure Martin found and Donck and Jacqueline Hervé stole, wasn't gold coins. It was a bundle of letters.'

Pel remembered Yves Pasquier's habit of taking treasures to bed with him. Perhaps Agnes Salm-Salm felt the same way. And, after all, hadn't Yves Pasquier said he slept with his gun? Why shouldn't Princess Salm-Salm sleep with the letters with which she'd been entrusted?

De Troq' paused, allowing Pel to absorb the idea. 'This explains,' he went on, 'why Donck held up the bank. They had something of enormous value but couldn't raise money on it because who was going to give them money in exchange for letters? That sort of thing takes time. Proof has to be obtained. Handwriting compared. They'd need to be handled carefully, and they'd need to find a good buyer. It also explains why Jacqueline Hervé came back to Europe. She was intending to sell them here, where they would probably have most value. Perhaps, even, she was intending to approach the Austrian Government archivist. After all, their value would probably be greatest in Vienna.'

'I think you may be right,' Pel agreed. 'And, if you are, it would account for how Jacqueline Hervé got Martin's "treasure" to France. No Customs official's going to worry about a bundle of old letters. What would you rate their value at?'

'A letter from Napoleon I ordering a chicken for lunch would have value, of course, but one ordering the Grand Army to Moscow and saying why, would have more. It's the same with Maximilian's letters. A letter he wrote before he went to Mexico about nothing more exciting than the decorations for his home at Miramar, fetched 24,000 dollars in New York. But *these* letters are about a great tragedy and were written at a time of great stress, appealing to everyone he could think of, when he was facing defeat and finally death. They must be highly dramatic and would fetch more than that, perhaps 40,000 dollars each. And there are about fifteen, probably more. Ten would fetch around 400,000 dollars. Nearly half a million dollars, *patron*. Three and a half million francs. And there's still Maximilian's diary of the last months of his life. Agnes Salm calls it heart-breaking. It could be worth a fortune on its own as an antique, and a publisher would jump at the chance to publish it. That would double its value, because American publishers would pay a lot for it. Half a million dollars? That's not unreasonable these days for something like that. That's another three million francs. Perhaps more – four or five. Add to that publishers in Austria and Italy who would want to publish because, in addition to being an Austrian archduke, Maximilian was a popular provincial governor in Italy. French publishers. We're interested in the French intervention. British publishers. Probably others. Especially, if he has anything to say about his love-affair with the wife of one of his gardeners or about his wife's interest in the Belgian colonel. And magazine rights, *patron*. The diary alone could raise a fortune – probably twenty million francs on its own. Add to that the value of the letters. Say another three million. Twenty-three million francs, *patron*.'

Pel was inclined to be more cautious in his estimate of the sum involved but he felt the need to sit in reverent silence for a while, all the same.

'Martin would fancy it,' he agreed.

'So would Navarro. So would Donck.'

They sat back silently. Pel pushed across his cigarettes and they lit up.

'De Troq',' he said slowly, 'sometimes I'm very glad of the people I have on my team. They're intelligent. At least,' he added, thinking of Misset, 'most of them are. I think you're right and it was a brilliant bit of thinking. It will go in your file.'

'I may be wrong, *patron*.'

'It'll still go in your file because, even if you're wrong, it's the way a policeman *should* think. Now –' Pel leaned forward, deciding he had dealt out enough praise and had to avoid the possibility of De Troq' becoming swollen-headed '– let's check up. Send a cable to Barribal in Mexico City. We need to know a few things. Ask him if this Salm-Salm woman's name's in the visitors' book at Las Rosas for the appropriate time. And send him a picture of Martin and ask him to find out if *he* was the type they discovered unscrewing the knobs from the brass bedstead.'

Barribal's reply arrived five days later. It was simple and straightforward but Pel had no doubt that Barribal had enjoyed himself. He had probably even looked up his American girl-friend in San Miguel.

'Name Agnes, Princess zu Salm-Salm, found Las Rosas visitors' book. Stayed 15 May 1867 to 19 May. Again 12 June to 15 June. Given Blue Room, East Wing. Manager confirms Martin collector brass bed knobs.'

'So she *was* sleeping with Napoleon and Maximilian and all the others,' Pel said. 'She had the letters in bed with her. And she also must have left them there – hidden in the bedpost. She put them there for safety but couldn't recover them because she was told to leave. Martin worked it out and found them, but he couldn't reach them because, by that time perhaps, they'd slipped down. So he had the tweezers we found made and fished them out on his next visit. There were no attendants in the museum, so he'd have plenty of opportunity.' He paused. 'A hundred years is a long time for letters to be stuck in a bedpost.'

'Is it, *patron*?' De Troq' said. 'Bedposts were handy and often safer than drawers. In the last century when iron beds with brass knobs were fashionable it was very normal to use them to keep money or letters in. I've talked to Nosjean. That girl-friend of his who runs the antique shop says letters written by Garibaldi were found in a brass bedstead in 1948, a hundred years after he hid them during the 1848 rebellion. Letters of President Faure to his mistress, Madame Steinheil, were also found in a brass bedpost. The nineteenth century was a century of brass bedsteads.'

'And Martin guessed that was where they were. He even took off one of the brass balls the first time he went to Las Rosas and saw the letters. Because they'd slipped too far down to be reached, the next day he went to Mexico City to get the tweezers made. He didn't return immediately to Pilar Hernandez but went first to Las Rosas, removed the letters, then went to see Donck at Chapadores. He never came back.'

Pel paused, deep in thought, then he looked up. 'Where's Nosjean?' he asked.

De Troq' grinned. 'Right outside, *patron*.'

'He wants to see me?'

'No, *patron*. I said you'd want to see *him*.'

Nosjean came in cheerfully but looking tired. Pel managed a stiff smile.

'What about all your customers, Nosjean?'

'Everything's under way, *patron*. There was rather a lot of paper work. Sixty-nine different people, including twenty-three from Nantes and one or two from Bordeaux and Lyons.'

'Quite a case. I hope it's behind you now because I've got a job for you.'

Nosjean looked wary. Everybody looked wary when Pel mentioned jobs.

'That girl-friend of yours. The one in antiques.'

'Mijo Lehmann?'

'That's the one. Very pretty girl, if I remember right. Very intelligent, and very knowledgeable about the antiques trade.'

'That's right, *patron*.' Nosjean was sitting on the edge of his chair. He was fond of Mijo Lehmann but he was well aware that he didn't always play fair with her. Because she didn't live in the immediate vicinity, he was inclined to neglect her for more easily accessible girls.

'How is it with her?'

'All right, *patron*.'

'Good! You'll know by now what happened in Mexico?'

'I've learned something of it, *patron*.'

'Well, we've had no reports of Donck trying to flee the country and we've had all airports, even all minor airfields and airstrips, watched, so I think he's still here and that he still has the "treasure" that Jacqueline Hervé smuggled back from Mexico. We think now it consists of a bundle of letters and a diary – and we want it. We also want *him*. But he's lying low and we need to force him from his cover. We suspect the Hervé woman was hoping to sell the documents in Austria, but now Donck has the letters and he'll probably be willing to off-load at a lower rate and nearer to home, so long as he can raise cash quickly and get out of the country. I was wondering if we could get notices placed in magazines read by antique dealers, art dealers and dealers in historic documents. Nothing pretentious, because we don't want it to be too obvious, just something that would be noticed by someone like Donck who would be on the look-out for an outlet.'

'Would Donck read these magazines, *patron*?'

'Since, until she betrayed him, Jacqueline Hervé was his mistress, I'd be surprised if she hadn't discussed such things. Do you think your Mijo Lehmann would know how to set about such a project?'

19

Nosjean was back in Pel's office first thing the next day, accompanied by De Troq' and Darcy.

'I drove to Chagnay, *patron*,' he said. 'To see Mijo Lehmann.'

Pel smiled benignly. 'Was she pleased to see you?' he asked, because Nosjean blushed easily and it did Pel's cynical heart good to see someone of Nosjean's age who could still go pink when affairs of the heart were mentioned.

Sure enough, Nosjean obliged. 'She was very pleased,' he said, a trace defiantly. 'We had dinner. We were able to talk and I think we're in business. She agreed to see that an advertisement was put into the magazine, *Antiques et Beaux Arts*. As it happens, though, I think we've got a nibble before we've even started.'

Pel's eyebrows lifted. 'Inform me,' he said.

Nosjean looked at Darcy, who sat up, all smart suit, white teeth and smile, so that he looked like a replica of Plutarco Jacinto Barribal. 'Angélique Courtois, *patron*,' he said.

'The girl at the university?'

'That's right. She's secretary to Professor Fournier, of Arts et Métiers. She tells me there are vague queries floating around. Fournier told her about them first, but she also heard them from one of the lecturers in Beaux Arts.'

'And the substance of these queries?'

'Does anyone want to buy a packet of letters written by a royal personage?'

Nosjean joined in. 'Mijo Lehmann also says there've been rumours about a bundle of royal letters being available at a price.'

'Go on.'

'It started in Austria but now they've come closer to home.'

'It would make sense. Donck must have discussed their value

and where to offer them with the Hervé woman before she left him.'

'Mijo knew of Jacqueline Hervé,' Nosjean said.

'Would she know then if our friend has had a nibble at the advert?'

'She arranged with the editor of *Antiques et Beaux Arts* to be informed immediately anything cropped up, *patron*.' Nosjean looked worried. 'You don't think that Donck would try anything on with her, do you?'

'In what way?'

'If we organized money to be paid to Donck for these letters, she'd have to hand it over. But wouldn't he be wary about being seen or recognized? Wouldn't he arrange to see her somewhere quiet, after dark? And wouldn't that lead him to take the money and keep the letters?'

Pel frowned. Nosjean had hit on a point that had occurred to him, too.

'I think we shall have to take care of that one,' he said gently.

'*We'd* have to set the trap, but *she'd* have to spring it. I wouldn't want anything to happen to her.'

'Is it important, *mon brave*?'

'That sort of thing's always important.'

Pel looked at Nosjean with approval. Though he doubted if Mijo Lehmann was as important to Nosjean as she thought she was, it was entirely in Nosjean's nature to be concerned for her because he would have been concerned for any woman in a position of possible danger. Despite being an excellent policeman, Nosjean was still a left-over from the days of errant knights. The only thing he lacked was a favour to wear in his helmet, because he believed in honesty, kindness and courtesy, and lacked the harsh ruthlessness that Darcy had in plenty. While he was a good sergeant and would undoubtedly rise even higher, it would always prevent him reaching the very top.

'He's an educated type, *patron*,' De Troq' was saying. 'And he'd know – or, if he didn't, he'd soon find out – what magazines to read for news of antiquities being bought and sold. Doubtless, even, he'd talked a lot about it to Jacqueline Hervé before she bolted back to France. What they were going to do with the letters. How valuable they were. Who were the best people to approach. How to set about it.'

'As things stand at the moment,' Pel said. 'I'm hoping our friend, Donck, will notice the advertisement we've put out. After that, I hope he'll bite.'

'How can he, *patron*?' Nosjean asked. 'He must know we're after him for Hervé's murder.'

'He doesn't know we know about the letters, though. He'll try to get rid of them by some means that won't give away his identity. But we're not experts in the field of antiquities so we shall need someone always available to us for immediate advice.'

'Mijo Lehmann?' Nosjean asked.

'That was in my mind. Would she prepared to be always on hand so we can telephone her night or day, if we need help? Would she be prepared to combine this with her work at the gallery where she works?'

Nosjean smiled. 'I think she could do better than that, *patron*. She wants to leave Chagnay and move here. She's had a job offered at the Galéries Lafayette and she's due to start in a week's time. I think we could persuade her to wait for a while, providing we could arrange with the Galéries Lafayette to hang on for a month or so.'

'Could you undertake to arrange this?'

'I think so, *patron*. Mijo won't take any persuading. The Galéries Lafayette might. But I think they'll help.'

'Do it, *mon brave*.'

Nothing happened for some time, save for the fact that Edouard Fousse appeared before the magistrates, charged with theft, wasting police time, and with assaulting a police officer with an offensive weapon – to wit, an iron bar, produced as an exhibit. With his record, he didn't have much of a chance and went to Number 72, Rue d'Auxonne for a lengthy stretch.

Nosjean's case was more complicated because car owners who had been on holiday were finding themselves on their return being met by a police officer who explained the circumstances and requested their presence at the Hôtel de Police. It required a great deal of paperwork and kept everybody busy by the sheer weight of numbers. By this time, however, Marc Moissin, faced with the facts, had dropped the indignant denials he had first offered and had agreed to co-operate. It made things easier because he had kept meticulous records, which showed the name of every single car owner who had traded with him. It also earned him a black eye from his brother Georges from Nantes, who was in favour of denying everything in the hope they could manage to come up with a thumping great lie.

Then, twelve days after the advertisement had appeared in *Antiques et Beaux Arts*, Nosjean appeared in Pel's office.

'I think we've had a bite, *patron*,' he smiled. 'Mijo rang. The editor of *Antiques et Beaux Arts* contacted her. There's been a reply to the advert. In fact there've been three or four.'

'Get along there, Nosjean,' Pel rapped. 'Pick them up and arrange for anything further to be picked up the minute it appears.'

Nosjean was soon back, and they opened the letters cautiously. Three of them seemed to be genuine. Two were from established dealers in old manuscripts and books expressing interest in any letters from royalty of the last century, and one was from a collector in Paris – on headed notepaper which seemed to indicate his willingness to come into the open. The last one had no address and was typed and was wary in content.

It expressed interest in the advert, and the writer claimed to possess a packet of 'dramatic' letters from 'a royal personage' which had come into the writer's possession quite by chance.

'Chance!' Pel snorted.

'The letters are valuable,' the letter continued, 'and, for reasons of safety and security, I have no wish at this stage to disclose either my identity or my address or the whereabouts of the letters. However, I can assure you that the letters are genuine and were written in the second half of the last century by the royal personage to his relations at a time when he was in considerable difficulties and labouring under some stress. The letters are not concerned with trivial matters but with great and tragic events known to history. There is also a diary.'

'It *must* be Donck,' Pel said. 'Second half of the century. To his relations. Considerable difficulties. Under some stress. Not concerned with trivial matters but with tragic events known to history. There's nothing more tragic than dying. He also mentions a diary. This accords with everything we know.'

The letter concluded that any approach had to be made to the writer through a box number at the main post office in Dijon.

'So he's here,' Pel said. 'In this area, somewhere.'

'What do we do, *patron*?' Darcy asked. 'Get the post office to tip us the wink when he appears?'

'We get Nosjean's friend, Mijo Lehmann, to express an interest in what's to be offered, and to post her letter in Chagnay so that it will carry a Chagnay postmark. That ought to put him off guard a little. Then we wait until he picks it up.'

'What then? Do we grab him?'

'It wouldn't work. He'll not have the letters on him. They'll be safely hidden and, if we grab him, we'll never find them. He'll have them safe as an insurance. But we'll have the post office warn us when he turns up and we'll follow him. After that, we think again.'

Mijo Lehmann's letter was dispatched and three days later Nosjean and De Troq' were in the main post office in Dijon when the assistant dealing with poste restante boxes excused himself, took out a large red handkerchief and blew his nose loudly. Watching from the back of the hall, Nosjean quietly dropped the form he was occupied in filling and had been occupied in filling for some time. Standing by the bank of poste restante boxes let into the wall was Donck, quite recognizable despite the beard he had grown. He used his key to open one of the boxes, removed two or three letters and stood examining them as Nosjean headed for the door. Two minutes later Donck turned and headed for the car-park nearby where he had left his car. Nosjean followed him, while De Troq' moved slowly after him in an unmarked car.

Donck climbed into a cream Peugeot and shot away from the car-park. Waiting for De Troq' to appear, Nosjean was surprised when he didn't. Within a minute, it was too late and Donck had vanished. Red-faced with anger, Nosjean set off to find De Troq', who was just round the corner, the unmarked car jammed against the wall by a red Fiat which, apparently, had tried to climb inside it. De Troq' was bruised but not much hurt, though he was almost dancing with fury. Opposite him a youth sat on the pavement, weeping.

'Tu as bien foutu le bazar!' Nosjean snapped.

De Troq' glared at him and gestured at the weeping youth. *'Un type schlass!'* he stormed. 'The guy's stoned out of his mind. Why did he have to be *there? Then?'*

To their surprise, Pel didn't hit the roof. 'Inform me,' he said.

They explained what had happened, how De Troq', following Nosjean to pick up Donck, had been hit by an old banger driven by a student high on drugs. Pel listened quietly.

'It can't be helped,' he said. 'He doesn't know he was being followed and we still have plenty of time. Now he knows somebody's showing an interest, he'll want to move. We'll wait.'

But they waited another week and there was no further word from Donck. Was he suspicious? Had he been tipped off?

'It *was* Donck, wasn't it?' Pel asked, suddenly anxious.

'It was Donck,' De Troq' said.

Another week passed and they began to wonder if Donck had gone elsewhere, while Nosjean began to grow worried because he didn't want to be appearing in court just when – and if – Donck emerged from hiding. Having persuaded Mijo Lehmann to take a chance, it was in his nature to feel he ought to keep an eye on her.

They were just beginning to think something had gone wrong when they had a stroke of luck. The stories filed by Fiabon, Henriot and Sarrazin about Pel's trip to Mexico had appeared with the usual fanfare of headlines and they heard they had caught the attention of Pépé le Cornet. Everybody knew Pépé le Cornet. As they were all aware, he ran a highly efficient criminal organization in Paris, and they learned he had let it to be known that, in addition to his other activities, he was also a collector of antiques and was particularly interested in old documents. His name was sufficient to stir up more than a few alarms – as though Attila the Hun had expressed a close interest in the Roman Empire – and immediately they began to imagine what would happen to Donck's nervous system if Pépé appeared on his doorstep to persuade him it would be to his advantage to sell the letters to *him*.

'It would scare him silly,' Darcy said cheerfully. 'I bet he starts to think again.'

Sure enough, two days later another letter turned up at the office of *Antiques et Beaux Arts*, requesting a meeting.

'I am eager,' Donck said this time, 'to take up residence in the United States and am in need of money, because the United States has a strict law about having adequate means before granting a residence permit, so I wish to conclude the arrangements as quickly as possible.'

'He's bitten,' Darcy crowed.

'However,' the letter concluded, 'because of their enormous value, I have no wish to sell the letters and the diary on the open market and am prepared to let them go for a quick sale for five million francs.'

'He's come down,' Pel said. 'I think he's got the wind up. Tell him we'll buy. And this time, when he picks up the letter we'll make sure we follow him. We'll have cars all round the area.'

'This time,' Darcy warned, glancing at Donck's letter, 'it won't be as easy as that. It's occurred to him by this time that he could be followed and he says he'll telephone for the reply. He says we've to put a telephone number in *Antiques et Beaux Arts*.'

'Think he's on to us, *patron*?' Nosjean asked.

Pel frowned. 'He's probably more afraid of Pépé le Cornet than he is of us,' he said. 'But we'll put the telephone number in. It had better be a special one. Arrange it with Telecommunications. It must be in the directory because he's bound to check up where it is and if he finds it doesn't have an address to go with it, he'll be suspicious. I think we need to find someone who could well be acting as an agent for a wealthy buyer. He's got to be involved in antique manuscripts and prepared to allow us to use his house. It's also got to be someone who knows something about the subject so that when Donck telephones he'll be able to discuss the subject with conviction, because Donck's bound to try him out first to make sure he's not a cop. What about your lady friend at the university, Daniel? Would she know someone of that nature? Preferable as little like a cop as possible.'

Darcy nodded. 'I'm sure she will.'

Two days later, he appeared in Pel's office with a small square man with a beard. He was no longer young but, though he didn't look like a cop, he looked quite capable of looking after himself.

'Jean-Pierre Delahaye,' Darcy introduced. 'Lecturer in Fine Arts and Antiquities. Played scrum-half for Perpignan for three years.'

A faint smile appeared on Pel's face. 'I think he'll do,' he said. 'Get a tape recorder attached to his telephone.'

Jean-Pierre Delahaye was more than willing to help. He himself had had manuscripts stolen and he felt helping the police might give him a little satisfaction.

On Pel's instructions, he acquired leave of absence from his job and sat down at home to wait, always with De Troq' or Nosjean available to listen in with him. The advert duly appeared and within twenty-four hours the telephone rang.

Delahaye gave his name and the voice on the wire, cautious and wary, spoke. 'This is Box Number 21,' it said. 'Are you the type who's interested in my letters?'

Nosjean leaned closer.

'I'm that man,' Delahaye said. 'In fact, I'm acting as agent for the buyer who lives in Paris.'

'It was a woman before. Name of Marie-Joséphine Lehmann.'

'She put me on to you. That's all. She's a dealer and she merely keeps an eye open for me.'

'Who're you? What do you do?'

'As a matter of fact, I'm a lecturer at the university in Antiquities and Beaux Arts. I do this as a side line.'

There was a laugh that indicated that Donck considered that Delahaye's activities were probably as dubious as his own.

'All right. What are you offering?'

'The sum you named. Five million francs.'

'They're cheap at the price.'

'They are if they're what my client wants.'

'He'll be glad to have them.'

'Who wrote them?'

'The Archduke Maximilian, Emperor of Mexico. While he was a prisoner of the Mexicans after they'd captured him. He wrote them asking for help just before he was taken out and shot by a firing squad. There's also a diary; believe me, it's good reading.'

'I'd like to see them.'

'Not before the money's delivered.'

'I'm not prepared to buy something unseen for my client. I must be able to identify them. My client will pay the sum requested, I'm sure, providing the letters are genuine, because he feels they'd be an asset to his collection. If not, providing they're genuine, he feels he could recoup his loss by reselling them.

However, first, he requires photocopies of them to indicate they *are* genuine, and he'll require something in the nature of provenance – proof that they're genuine and not forgeries. He'll require dates, times and places of acquisition, and a period of a week to get proof of the genuineness.'

'I'll send you photocopies and contact you again.'

'You'll want my address.'

Donck's reply showed he was one step ahead of them. 'I have your address,' he said.

It was tense as they waited for the photocopies to arrive.

'We're wasting time,' Darcy grumbled.

'No,' Pel insisted. 'You might say we're playing spider to his fly. He's got to come out into the open before long if he wants the money. He knows nobody's going to turn over several million francs until he has his hand on the letters.'

This time the reply came more quickly. It was in the form of a thick envelope, postmarked 'Dijon.'

'He's not taking any chances on us discovering where he's hiding out,' Darcy said.

Pel opened the envelope and took out the first of the photocopies. It was addressed to 'The Emperor Napoleon III' and the first words he saw inside were 'Sire, my brother –.' He studied the letter for a while, then glanced at the other photocopies. They simply showed the names of the addressees and the beginning of the letter, and were directed to the Empress Carlota, the Emperor Franz Josef, and Queen Victoria. According to the nationality of the recipients they were written in their own language.

'I don't think there's much doubt,' he said. '*These* are the letters. When he telephones, tell him the money will be ready and will be handed over in return for the letters and that he's to name a rendezvous.'

The tension was growing. It was a little like a game of chess with an experienced player. It was difficult to concentrate on anything else and Nosjean had been taken off the Moissin case so he could concentrate on the letters.

Pel's temper shortened and at breakfast time when, as she brought in the croissants, Madame Routy opened her mouth to make an observation on some comment of his, Madame Pel caught her eye and by the faintest movement of her head, forbade her to utter a word. Fortunately Madame Routy caught the signal and her mouth closed like a gin trap. Click.

Heading with Darcy for Delahaye's home by a roundabout route and entering through the back door from the garden of the adjoining house, Pel was waiting with Nosjean and De Troq' when the telephone went and the tape recorder clicked. They leaned forward as the voice came, reproduced for them all to hear on an amplifier.

'Well?' There was only one word.

Delahaye drew a deep breath, aware of Pel's eyes on him. 'I think the letters are genuine,' he said. 'At least the one that's reproduced in full is.'

'You'll pay my price?'

'My client is not prepared to argue. You can have your cheque –'

'No cheques! I want no cheques.'

Delahaye paused and looked at Pel who nodded. 'I didn't really think you would,' he said. 'Very well. How do you want it?'

'In cash. Notes of a hundred francs and less. No big ones that will be difficult to dispose of.'

'I have a feeling that this isn't very honest.'

There was a laugh. 'That's what I was thinking. What's a lecturer at the university doing buying antique letters for some client in Paris. Is he American?'

Delahaye looked at Pel who nodded. 'Yes, he's an American.'

'Pity I didn't ask for more. I expect he can afford it. Americans normally can. How much is he paying you for getting into this?'

'That's my business.'

'You can't touch pitch without being defiled, you know. Does he know that?'

'I think he's quite happy with the situation,' Delahaye said brusquely. 'Can we get down to business? I can have your money ready within a day or two. What about the letters?'

'They'll be ready. I'll have them in a small blue holdall.'

'How will I know I'm getting the genuine articles?'

'You can have a look at them. Bring the money in a holdall of the same sort and same colour. You can buy them at Nouvelles Galéries for about 100 francs. Then all we have to do is exchange bags.'

'As soon as I've convinced myself the letters are what my client wants.'

'And as soon as *I've* satisfied myself that the money's genuine.'

'Very well. When and where?'

'Friday, the 19th. Midnight. Crossroads south of Chassellis St Pierre. Where the N413 crosses the road to Auxerre. Got it?'

'Friday, the 19th. Midnight. Crossroads south of Chasselis St Pierre. Where the N413 crosses the road to Auxerre.'

The telephone clicked and went dead.

'Do you know the place, Daniel?' Pel asked.

'I know it, *patron*. He's picked a good spot. There's a small wood to one side but the other side's open country.'

'Houses? Could he be watching from a house?'

'No houses, *patron*, apart from the village, which is across the fields.'

'Right.' Pel looked at Delahaye. 'Will you be prepared to make the exchange?'

'Is it dangerous?'

Pel paused. Police work was always untidy, often inconclusive, and sometimes *very* dangerous.

'It might be,' he admitted. 'And I think we should go through a few drills with you because you'll need to signal us somehow as soon as you know the letters are genuine, so we can move in.'

'And in case,' Darcy said grimly, 'once he gets his hands on the dough, he snatches the letters back so he can sell them again somewhere else.'

Pet lit a cigarette from the one he'd just finished, realized what he'd done, was about to stub it out, remembered the cost of cigarettes, and changed his mind. It gave him an idea.

'It had better be a cigarette,' he said. 'We'll fix something else as well but a cigarette will do. You can hardly use a torch.' He pushed the packet across to Delahaye and watched him light it. 'So a cigarette would be best. Donck won't be alarmed at seeing you light up and it's the obvious thing for someone to do when they're a little nervous.'

'Which I shall be.' Delahaye gave a grim smile.

Pel nodded. 'In the meantime, we'd better survey that road, Daniel.'

'How're we going to do it without him seeing us? Assuming, of course, that he's watching.'

'There are plenty of unmarked cars around the Hôtel de Police. Use them all. Go backwards and forwards, every time in a different car. And don't stop. Nothing more than a long pause before crossing the junction. Keep your eyes open for somewhere we can post men. We'll need photographs so we can work something out, and they'll need to be taken with a long-distance lens in case he *is* watching. Pick your best men. Young men. Not Lagé. He's too old. And not Misset. He'll bungle it. They've got to be planted within easy reach, so it's up to you to find somewhere. We'll also need a searchlight ready to shine on the crossroads, and night-glasses so we can see what's going on. We'll also need cars on every one of the four roads, but well back and well hidden so they can't be seen. In the meantime, we'll set about providing the money.'

Darcy looked surprised. 'Are we going to *give* him the money?' he asked. It didn't sound like Pel.

'No.' Pel almost snapped the word. 'We have a stock of small counterfeit notes from Lyons' Jean-Paul Leroy case, as you know. That's what he's going to get. It'll be dark –' he glanced at the window – 'and probably raining and he'll be in no position at the Chasselis crossroads to spend any time examining them. So long as the ones on top are genuine, and the ones underneath will pass in a cursory inspection as genuine, that will do.'

'Let's hope he doesn't notice,' Darcy said. He paused. 'There's still just one small problem.'

Pel's eyebrows lifted and he went on quickly. 'When we get the letters back – as I'm sure we shall – whom do they belong to? France? The Mexicans? Or Vienna?'

Pel considered for a moment. 'That's not something for us to worry about,' he said. 'The Chief can sort that one out. But I'd say myself that finders are keepers.'

20

The next twenty-four hours saw a great deal of activity around the Chasselis crossroads. Among the traffic that passed and repassed were cars from the Hôtel de Police. None of them ever stopped but they all paused before crossing over, while their drivers, apparently cautious and checking the road was clear, took a good look round them.

A long-distance camera was situated in the spire of the church at Chasselis from which a series of photographs were taken. A lone walker complete with back pack and stick, came up from the direction of Auxerre, paused on the crossroads to check his map – and have a good look round as he was doing it – then continued at a leisurely pace towards Chasselis. On the other road which crossed it, a man with a shot-gun and a dog halted to adjust his shoe laces, fill and light a pipe and pat his dog before continuing. During the afternoon a tractor came across the field, driven by Brochard – who had been brought up on tractors because his father was a farmer – with Darcy riding on the trailer behind. They both wore yellow rubber boots, dungarees and caps and they spent some time clearing a ditch near the crossroads, shovelling the mud they extracted into the trailer before disappearing towards Chasselis.

By evening they had a pretty shrewd picture of the locality.

'There's a hollow twenty yards away,' Darcy said. 'Part of a ditch. And a wall that could conceal another man, running almost to the crossroads. We could also have a couple of men among the trees, one of them with a radio. As soon as it's obvious something's happening he could contact the cars waiting to pick up Donck if he tries to bolt.'

'We've got to know the letters are genuine before we move,' Pel said. 'Delahaye's got to give us some signal. If Donck's offering photocopies or something like that, Delahaye's got to identify them as such. It's no good moving in on him if he hasn't got them with him.'

'We've also got to be able to hear what's said,' Darcy pointed out. He turned to Delahaye. 'Would you be willing to wear a microphone? One that'll pick up any conversation.'

Delahaye shrugged. 'No problem. What happens if the bag doesn't contain the letters?'

'Say so. Simply say "I'm not satisfied" or "These aren't the letters." We'll hear.'

'What happens then, *patron*?' Darcy asked. 'If that's the case, Donck's going to snatch the money and run. We'll have to pick him up and chance losing the letters. We're taking risks all the time. If we guess wrong, our reputation's in tatters.'

Pel shrugged. 'I expect we'll learn to live with it,' he said.

The 19th was a grey day with a lot of cloud and a drizzle of rain, and it suddenly occurred to Darcy that it was also the dark of the moon. Donck had picked a good time. It would be a very black night and impossible to see a thing.

Plain cars, their crews complete with sandwiches and Thermos flasks, took up their places as soon as it was dark – four of them, each covering one of the four roads that made up the crossroads. In the same way, men on foot and all armed, were waiting to take up their positions after dark and settle down for a long wet miserable bone-aching wait. A radio van had been driven into the wood in the dark of the previous night and hidden among the undergrowth, Brochard and Lacocq doing watch until Pel and Darcy took over. Aimedieu, Bardolle, Debray and Morell were also around, while Lagé was watching the radio back at the Hôtel de Police with Claudie Darel. Misset, not trusted with anything important, was answering the telephone.

During the afternoon, the Chief appeared in Pel's office. He was clearly worried. 'Is it going to work?' he asked.

'It had better,' Pel said darkly.

'He's killed three times so he'll stop at nothing. Oughtn't we to have a policeman to do the job? To say he's Delahaye.'

'We've no one who knows enough about antique manuscripts to be able to talk intelligently if Donck decides to ask questions.'

'What about De Troq'? He knows about antiques.'

'De Troq's not an expert.'

'He helped crack the château thefts.'

'That was furniture, porcelain, and paintings. He also knows enough to answer a casual query or two because of his great-great-grandfather being in Mexico at the time the letters were written. But Donck's been called an educated thief. He'd soon spot that De Troq' doesn't know enough to be a lecturer at the university, because he went to university himself. Besides, Delahaye doesn't look like a cop and I think it's best that way. Donck can't suspect him of being a plant.'

'Suppose Donck pulls a gun?'

That was something that had been worrying Pel. 'We think he might not have one,' he said. 'He obviously had to get rid of the gun he acquired in Mexico because he'd never get it aboard the plane.'

'He'd know where to get another.'

Pel said nothing. He was hoping he hadn't.

Evening came early. The drizzle hadn't let up for a minute all day and it had turned out to be one of the most miserable spring days they'd had for years. As a result, darkness came grey, wet and clinging, and the home-going crowds, huddled together as they waited for buses, thankfully scrambled aboard out of the wet when they arrived. Drivers collecting their parked cars thought nostalgically of home and more than a few considered the possibility of a quick one on the way. Slowly the city emptied as the queues of vehicles, windscreen wipers going, glass reflecting the dazzling kaleidoscope of the red, green, blue and yellow of neon lights that had been turned on early, wheels throwing up a mist of water from the streaming road, headed out to the suburbs.

At Chasselis, cars arrived singly to drop a man or two men in the square then headed off into the darkness while their passengers, heads bent, shoulders bowed, disappeared among the houses as if on their way home. In fact, they were skirting back gardens to begin a long muddy trek over the fields in the darkness to their places of vantage.

Pel and Darcy, who were the last to leave the Hôtel de Police, were just considering a quick rum to help keep them warm when the telephone went.

'That'll be Nosjean to say he's got Delahaye and the money and is on his way.'

It was Nosjean all right, but, while he had the money, he didn't have Delahaye.

'*Patron* –' there was a note of panic in his voice '– Delahaye!'

'What's wrong with Delahaye?' Pel snapped. 'Don't tell me he's been run over.'

He was being sarcastic but that was exactly what had happened. Delahaye had been struck by a car and was on his way to the hospital.

'Broken leg, *patron*,' Nosjean said.

Pel didn't know whether to throw in his hand or dance with rage. 'You're sure?' he demanded, not because he doubted Nosjean's sanity but simply because he just couldn't believe what he heard.

'Quite sure, *patron*. I've just seen his wife, as I arrived to pick him up. She's just been told. She's on her way now to the hospital.'

There was a long silence as Pel considered what to do. He looked at his watch, certain that it was impossible to replace Delahaye in the time at their disposal.

'*Patron* –'

Pel felt like climbing into the telephone and starting a fight with Nosjean. He knew it wasn't Nosjean's fault because Nosjean had given Delahaye strict instructions not to move from his house. And, in fact, Delahaye had obeyed the spirit of the order if not the letter of it, because he hadn't been looking forward to a cold night any more than anyone else and had only been crossing the road to the *épicerie* opposite his home for a bottle of brandy to fill a small flask. But it had been quite enough.

'Well?' Pel snapped, chiefly because just then he couldn't think of anything else to say.

Nosjean's voice came back, faintly apologetic. 'I've got Mijo here, *patron*.'

Pel was on the point of demanding why. If Nosjean had been going about his business he should have had no time to be with Mijo Lehmann. Then he paused. Nosjean wasn't a man to neglect his duty or go against orders. There must be some reason.

'So?'

'She'll do it, *patron*?'

'What?'

'She knows everything that's been going on. We brought her into it and she knows the moves we've made. She said she'd do it.'

At first Pel was inclined to say no but then he realized that Mijo Lehmann might even be better than Delahaye. She wasn't a thickset ex-rugby player, just a pretty girl with a crush on Nosjean. But she obviously wasn't short of courage and he knew she wasn't short of intelligence and certainly knew the antiques business inside out.

'Bring her in,' he said.

Mijo Lehmann looked excited when she appeared, though whether that was because of what she was about to do or because it was Nosjean who had suggested it, Pel couldn't tell.

'Could you do it?' he asked.

'I think so.'

'He's expecting a man,' Pel said. 'Delahaye. Suppose he asks questions?'

'I'll tell him the truth. Or almost the truth. That Delahaye was knocked down by a car and asked me to take over for him. I'll tell him I was the person who first contacted him after he answered the advert in *Antiques et Beaux Arts* and that Delahaye, knowing I knew what was going on, asked me from the hospital to stand in for him.'

'Think he'll accept it?'

'Why not? If he's in any doubt I'll tell him to telephone the hospital. They'd confirm that Delahaye's there. That ought to settle any doubts, surely. And surely he won't consider *me* a menace. I'm not as tough-looking as Delahaye and he'll not expect me to bring him down with a flying tackle.' Mijo Lehmann smiled. 'In fact, I'd suggest I'm a better bet for the role.'

Pel glanced at Darcy and then at Nosjean who was suddenly beginning to look worried, as though only now had he seen the possible dangers.

'You sure you can do it?'

'I'll need to know everything there is to know about the letters. I know most of it already, but it'll be as well to know the lot. I know the period. I know the history. I can talk to him, if that's what he wants.'

Pel glanced again at Nosjean and Darcy then he gestured.

'You'd have to drive out there and be at the crossroads at midnight. He'll be there waiting. If not, he'll arrive shortly afterwards. He'll want to see the money.'

'Do I give it to him?'

'No. Insist on seeing the letters first and get a good grip on them before the money's handed over. Once you can identify them – you'll have to use the car headlights for it, as he will to identify the money – light a cigarette. That's the signal for us to move in.'

Mijo Lehmann looked at Nosjean and there was a sudden alarm in her eyes. 'I don't smoke,' she said.

For a moment there was consternation. Pel stared at her, and was just on the point of saying he wished *he* didn't when he controlled it. 'Never?' he asked.

'Well, I have done but I gave it up when all the fuss started about lung cancer.'

'Do you think you could manage to light one?'

'I don't want to. I'm afraid I'll start again.'

'It's too late now to change the signal. Everybody up there's in position. We'll be in touch with you. You'll be wearing a microphone so we can hear everything that's said. Unfortunately, while we can hear you, you won't be able to contact us. A cigarette's the only way you can signal us without him being suspicious. You could offer him one, in fact. If he takes it and lights it, perhaps you needn't.'

She managed a nervous smile. 'I think I could manage *one*,' she said.

'Right.' Pel rose. 'Brief her, Nosjean. Brief her well. Tell her everything we know. Then get her out to the crossroads with the car by a quarter to midnight. What are *your* arrangements?'

'De Troq's waiting for me in a farmyard a couple of hundred metres from the crossroads. Delahaye was supposed to drop me there and De Troq' was to drive me to Chasselis St Pierre from where we were to walk across the fields to the radio van. Brochard and Lacocq are waiting there until we arrive. When we arrive, they'll take their places where they can see the crossroads.'

Pel stared at the streaming window. 'I doubt if anybody at all will see the crossroads tonight,' he said. A thought occurred to him and he looked at the girl, knowing how ham-fisted some girls were with cigarettes. 'There's just one point,' he said. 'Can you light a cigarette in a wind?'

She smiled, a little nervously. 'I've done it often. I was a proper chimney-pot.'

Pel looked at Nosjean. '*Bon*. We'll be on our way. Give her a good briefing, Nosjean, then get her out there to where De Troq's waiting.' He paused. 'And don't forget to make sure she has a cigarette and matches on her.'

The rain hadn't stopped and the night was as dark as a cow's inside.

Mijo Lehmann's car drew to a stop and in the dim glow from its sidelight Nosjean could see De Troq's car waiting for him.

He turned to the girl. 'You have everything?' he asked. 'Cigarettes? Matches? The money?'

She patted the deep pockets of the mackintosh she wore and reached behind her to feel the bag containing the money. 'Yes,' she said.

'What about the microphone? Comfortable?'

She touched the open collar of the mackintosh where the microphone was concealed, and nodded.

'Good,' Nosjean said. 'I'll be off then. It's now 11.45. Don't move up to the crossroads until midnight. In fact, make it five minutes past. Then perhaps he'll be in position first. That'll give me time to be in position. I shall be listening to everything you say.'

She threw him a nervous glance. 'You won't miss anything?'

'Afraid?'

'A little.'

'Don't worry. We've done this before.' So they had, Nosjean thought, but there had been occasions when their ambushes hadn't come off.

He touched her hand and immediately her fingers grasped his and squeezed them. He wasn't sure if it was because she was afraid, but he liked to think it was more than that. Abruptly, he leaned over and kissed her cheek. It felt icy, and he knew her fears had hold of her. But he also knew she had courage and wouldn't let them down.

She looked at him but in the poor light from the dashboard he couldn't see her expression. He touched her hand again and, climbing from the car, closed the door softly. She hadn't stopped the engine because there was no wind to drown noises and an engine starting might be heard at the crossroads and could well make a nervous Donck suspicious. Why had the car started? Were there police around? He might well have guessed the police would be involved, and they could only hope that all the manoeuvrings between himself and Delahaye would seem to have been on behalf of some dubious buyer who, for his own sake, would want no contact with the police.

As he walked to De Troq's car, he looked back and saw Mijo Lehmann sitting still in the car, staring forwards. Climbing in alongside De Troq', he closed the door quietly and De Troq' let in the clutch, allowing the slope to carry the car forward. Turning on to the road, he continued to allow the car to run forward under its own momentum until eventually he felt it safe to put the car in gear. The engine caught and De Troq' gently applied the accelerator. Eventually, he swung off the main road and turned towards Chasselis. Ten minutes later, he and Nosjean were reporting to Pel and Darcy in the back of the radio van. Considering them the two most intelligent and active members of this group, Pel was using them as his flying squad, ready to leap forward and grab their quarry.

He looked up as they appeared. 'Bardolle's just reported in,' he said. 'He's on the Auxerre road and he thinks Donck's waiting in a car a bit ahead of him.'

As they waited outside the van, their collars up against the drizzle, every minute or two Nosjean glanced at his watch. At a minute after midnight, the radio came to life. It was Bardolle's voice.

'Car's started, *patron*,' he said. 'He's moving. He has only sidelights. Do I move forward?'

'As near as you can get,' Pel said. 'But don't let him see you.'

Faintly through the drizzle, they saw two dim lights appear by the crossroads.

'He's there!'

Another four minutes passed then they saw the beam of headlights appear, lifting through the drizzle as a car came up the hill. They couldn't see the car, only the headlights' beam, and eventually the twin red spots of the tail-lights.

'That's the girl,' Pel said.

'I'm moving forward, *patron,*' Nosjean said.

'Wait!'

'I'm moving forward,' Nosjean insisted.

Pel glanced at him, aware that in his knightly way, he considered himself responsible for Mijo Lehmann's safety. It was Nosjean who had brought her into the scheme in the first place and Nosjean who had involved her in that night's work. So he said nothing, and Nosjean vanished out of the glow from the open door at the back of the van.

Pel was still staring into the darkness after him when the radio caught his attention. It was a harsh male voice that was unfamiliar, and they knew it was Donck.

'What do you want?'

'I think you're the man I've come to meet.' The voice was Mijo Lehmann's.

'What in God's name do you mean? Who are you?'

'My name's Marie-Joséphine Lehmann. I'm the dealer who first wrote to you about the letters.'

'I was expecting a man.' Donck's voice was harsh and angry. 'A lecturer from the university.'

'He was knocked down by a car this afternoon outside his house. He contacted me and asked me to take his place.'

'How do I know?'

'You could ring the hospital.' The girl's voice had been nervous but it was growing stronger and more confident with every exchange.

'How in God's name do I ring the hospital from here?' Donck was demanding.

'You could try from the bar at Chasselis.'

'It'll be closed.'

'Tell them it's an emergency. They'll open up. Tell them you're a relative.'

Pel listened with fascination as the girl handled what was clearly an irritated, angry and suspicious Donck.

'In any case, you're late,' he snapped.

Mijo Lehmann's voice came back coolly. 'Only a minute or two.'

'Six, to be exact. When I said midnight, I meant midnight.'

'What does it matter? I have the money. You have the letters. What's the difference?'

There was a silence then Donck's voice came again. 'I didn't expect anybody else to be involved.'

'Delahaye didn't expect to be knocked down and break a leg. I've been involved from the start. I knew what he was up to because he happens to be my fiancé.'

Darcy looked at Pel and grinned. 'This one ought to be a cop, *patron*,' he murmured.

There was a further silence then Donck's voice once more. 'Get the money.'

'When I've seen the letters.'

Another silence was followed by Donck's voice again. 'Here they are!'

Again there was no sound for a while and they assumed Mijo Lehmann was examining the packet.

'Fifteen, I was told,' she said. 'And a diary.'

'They're all there. Give me the money, and let's get away from here. I don't like this place.'

There was a long wait then they heard a car door slam. 'She's giving him the money,' Darcy murmured.

There was another silence as they waited for the lighting of a distant cigarette. But it didn't come and Pel began to wonder if Mijo Lehmann had been unable to manage it in the drizzle and the breeze. Or had something gone wrong? Had Donck offered forged letters? Had he produced a gun?

His fingers began to tap and he had just decided they couldn't wait any longer when they heard Mijo Lehmann's voice. 'These look good,' she said.

Pel glanced at Darcy and he was just about to call the cars when the voice came again, this time louder and agitated.

'Come back!'

'He's snatched the letters back!' Pel said. 'Let's have the light!'

With startling suddenness, the powerful searchlight illuminated the crossroads. For a moment, they saw the two figures frozen and silvered in its glare, the girl, slim and small in her wet mackintosh, struggling with Donck, a strong, thickset shape alongside her, clutching a blue holdall.

'It's a trick!' His voice came in a snarl.

'Go, De Troq',' Pel said and De Troq' started forward.

As he vanished into the darkness, they saw Nosjean appear, heading towards Mijo Lehmann. Donck had released the girl and begun to run. Seeing Nosjean, however, he turned back and, grabbing the girl's hand, wrenched her arm behind her and held her in front of him.

'Stop!' he yelled. 'Or I'll shoot her!'

She was leaning against him and they could see the terror on her face. The blue holdall containing the money was on the ground by Donck's feet with the holdall that had contained the letters, and they could see the glint of metal by her head. Nosjean had come to a standstill.

'Hold everything, everybody,' Pel said. The Chief's fear had been sound. Donck *had* a gun.

Nobody moved and only Nosjean was visible. De Troq' had sunk out of sight and the image was frozen again, with Donck holding the girl, clearly wondering what to do, how to handle the money and the girl and still make his escape.

'Drop the gun!' Darcy's voice came over the loud hailer. 'You're covered from half-a-dozen angles.'

Donck's head turned. He looked desperate, uncertain how to use the few facts that were to his advantage. Then he looked down at the holdall containing the money, clearly wondering if he could still get away with the loot. The letters had disappeared into an inside pocket.

Then, suddenly, they saw a movement beyond him. It was Bardolle. Despite his size, Bardolle's days of poaching had taught him to move silently and to take advantage of every shadow. Then abruptly, another shape emerged beyond Donck and Pel recognized it as Aimedieu. Like Bardolle he had managed to move close. But he hadn't been as skilful as Bardolle and Donck saw him. As his head turned, Nosjean leapt forward and, reaching out, snatched the girl away. Donck yelled, the gun went off harmlessly, then he grabbed the holdall and started running.

The gun went off again, this time in Aimedieu's direction, but Aimedieu was running, too, now. Donck was close to his car. If he reached it there was a chance he might escape.

'Cars,' Pel snapped into the microphone. 'Stand by!'

Seeing Aimedieu closing up in front of him, Donck had swerved and was running in a curve to his left. As he did so, however, a burly figure rose up abruptly in front of him and they saw a heavy fist swing. Donck stopped dead in full flight and with the blue holdall flying from his hand, seemed to perform what looked like a perfect backwards somersault to land on his face. They even saw the splashes from the wet grass in the glare of the searchlight as he fell.

By the time they reached the crossroads, Bardolle was rubbing his knuckles, Aimedieu was staring down at the unconscious Donck in amazement, and Nosjean was holding the shuddering Mijo Lehmann tightly in his arms.

Bending down alongside Donck, Pel felt into the wide pocket of the windcheater he wore.

'Torch,' he said.

Aimedieu produced a light. By this time, the headlights of cars were visible on every one of the four roads to the crossing, and men were moving swiftly forward across the grass and from the woods towards them.

'What did you hit him with, Bardolle?' Darcy said. 'An iron bar?'

Bardolle looked down at his great fist and said nothing.

Pel had the packet open now and was bending by the headlights of one of the cars, flicking through the contents. At once, he saw the words 'Napoleon III' and he opened the old stiff paper. 'Sire, my brother,' he read. *'Il m'est impossible de vous dire comme j'ai souffert et comme je souffre encore. Je vous écris de Querétaro où nous sommes assiègés . . .'*

'It is impossible to tell you how I have suffered and am still suffering. I write to you from Querétaro where we are besieged . . .'

He nodded and pushed the letter back into the packet, then he checked the remaining documents one after the other and made sure the diary was there, too, before putting the packet into his pocket. By this time Donck was beginning to regain consciousness and Bardolle reached down to his collar and hoisted him to his feet in one vast bone-cracking heave that lifted his shoes from the ground. Pel glanced round him at the men in wet coats, the angles and planes of their faces, damp from the drizzle, catching the glow from the car headlights. Nosjean still had his arms round Mijo Lehmann and she was clinging to him as if he were her last support on earth. It seemed to call for a pronouncement of some importance. He did his best to supply it.

'After a hundred years,' he said, 'Maximilian's appeals for help have finally reached Europe. Let's go.'